UNBRIDLED MONTANA PASSION

BEAR GRASS SPRINGS, BOOK SEVEN

RAMONA FLIGHTNER

GRIZZLY DAMSEL PUBLISHING

To the Babcocks:
Your generosity inspired my creativity,
and half of this novel was written during
the days I spent in your beautiful cabin.
Thank you.

CHAPTER 1

Bear Grass Springs, Montana Territory, August 1887

It was an improbable day to turn a man's world upside down. A soft wind blew, cooling the hot August heat to a more tolerable level. Warren Clark, Bear Grass Springs' resident lawyer, stood on Bears's doorstep and paused a moment before raising his hand to knock. He stared at the letter in his hand and shook his head, before letting his knuckles fall onto the worn wood.

"Lawyer," Bears said as he opened the door with a frown. His raven hair hung freely to his waist, and he wore simple tan pants and a navy-blue shirt with a few buttons open at the collar. "You seem to be lost. The party is at the café tonight."

Warren smiled and motioned for an invite into Bears's simple one-room home. "No. I've just received something I think you'd like to read."

The wood door closed with a *thunk* behind Warren, and Bears pointed to a chair at the table. Warren mumbled his thanks, as he sat and accepted a glass of water from Bears, his discreet gaze taking in small changes to the living area. The patchwork-quilt-covered bed could be separated from the room by a curtain installed by Fidelia

Evans and her sister, Annabelle MacKinnon, although it was not closed off now. A rocking chair sat near the foot of the bed, while the table with two chairs was near the stove and tiny kitchen area. A lace doily covered the table, while a framed picture of Bears's father hung on the wall. An eagle feather rested atop it. A gentle breeze blew in through the open windows.

"I heard you had a challenging day," Warren said with a twitch of his lips, unable to hide his amusement.

Bears glared at Warren and then shrugged. "That beast should be put down. He's untamable. Untrainable." He rubbed at his shoulder, while Warren lost his battle and burst out laughing. For months Bears had been working with Brutus, Harold Tompkins's horse, in an attempt to ease it of its wilder tendencies. Today, even Bears seemed to have had enough.

"I never thought to hear the tale that you'd had your pantaloons and shirt ripped open by Brutus," Warren gasped through tears of laughter.

Bears shook his head. "He was angry because I denied him a carrot, which he thought he was due. He's too smart for his own good."

"Did he get the carrot?"

"He ate the whole damn bucketful when I dropped it, after I was virtually stripped naked by him." Bears relented and smiled as Warren swiped at his eyes. "I'll have to think of another way to train him."

"Find another treat. Something that isn't a reward," Warren suggested. After a moment, he sobered. "As you know, talking about your adventures with Brutus is not why I came by today." He saw Bears stiffen and nodded. "I have a letter for you."

Bears shook his head. "There's no reason for you to receive a letter addressed to me."

Warren set the envelope on the table, tapping the paper with a finger a few times. "It's from Sara Parker." He watched as Bears jolted, as though struck by lightning. Warren nodded in understanding. "It's not as though you receive a letter every day from the dead woman you'd once considered your wife."

"She's been dead for some time," Bears rasped, his throat thickening. He cleared it, and his mask of impassivity once again fell in place. "I don't understand why it took so long to be sent to me." His jaw tightened. "If it is really from her."

The lawyer nodded. "I understand your hesitation. However, I believe it to be authentic, although I have not read it." He raised an eyebrow to soothe Bears's sense of propriety. "I am somewhat known in Helena, and the judge there realized that I might know you and could discretely deliver this letter. They found it when they were investigating Bertrand, and they did read it. Judge Hammond advised me that the contents of Sara's letter helped aid in Bertrand March's murder conviction. The judge broke with propriety in this instance, as the original should have been kept in the official record of materials for this trial. Instead, the judge had a copy made for the court record and sent the original to you."

"Why?"

"He feared that you would believe it all a lie, if you did not read the letter in her own hand." Warren raised his fingers from the envelope and waited for Bears to react.

Bears's intense gaze bore into Warren's for a long moment before he reached for the letter. The ripping of the outer envelope from the judge sounded, and then Bears slipped the pages free. His eyes moved rapidly over the written lines, and his hands shook as he finished the letter.

Warren frowned, reaching for his friend. fearing Bears would faint. "Bears? What did she tell you?"

"I have a daughter," he whispered. "All these years, I've had a daughter."

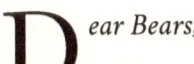

D*ear Bears,*

June 27, 1883

3

It has been seven years since I last saw you, when I left for my adventure with Bertrand March.

I will not lie to you and say that it has all been wonderful. I will not lie and say that I have not yearned for you. I will not lie and say that I did not quickly understand what I lost when I left your home. However, I made my decision, and I had to live with it. I believed you would never want me back.

I have come to understand that Bertrand made me feel unworthy of you and of your love. And that he made me feel as though he were the only one who would ever care for me. However, I've also come to realize that love does not come from the back of a man's hand. Nor is it expressed by cruel words. You showed me, in your quiet way—that I was too young and too stupid to understand—exactly what love was.

I'm sorry, Bears. I'm sorry for how I treated you. I'm sorry for denying you what you had always dreamed of—a family. I would never write you now and rip open old wounds, except that I know I will die soon. Bertrand has a way of making those he no longer finds useful disappear, and few in this town will listen to a woman who isn't legally married to a man. When I am gone and, if you receive this letter, please come to Helena.

Please find Mildred Renfrew March.

For she is your daughter. I've always thought her real name should be Bright Fawn.

Your,

Sara

~

Warren set down the letter and gaped at his friend, who looked as though he had been poleaxed. A fine tremor ran through Bears, and he seemed to control a deep emotion through sheer force of will. "Bears," Warren whispered, "what do you want to do?"

"Will you go to Helena with me? Travel with me to see this judge friend of yours and to find my daughter?" Bears's brown eyes were black with their intensity. "I must find her. She's all alone in that city, now that they're both dead."

"Of course," Warren murmured. "Will you tell the family?" he asked, referring to the large MacKinnon family who considered Bears part of their clan. His small house was near the home of Cailean MacKinnon, the eldest of the four MacKinnon siblings.

Bears gave an immediate shake of his head. "No. Not until I return with her. I … I can barely reconcile that I have a daughter. I can't handle their hopes and fears any more than I can my own."

Warren grunted and shook his head. "They consider you family, Bears. They would want to support you in any way they can, and you deny them that right by not speaking with them."

Bears nodded.

"What about Fidelia?" Warren's gaze was knowing, as Bears's shoulders tightened at the mention of the woman who had fascinated Bears for years.

"I will advise her that I was called away. She'll learn what she needs to when I return." His mutinous gaze clashed with Warren's disappointed stare.

"You will find more harmony in your life if you are more forthright with those you care about. Fidelia may be more skittish around you than Brutus, but she cares for you. She will want to know the reason you are making a sudden trip to Helena. She has earned that right."

Bears stared into space a moment before absently nodding. "I will consider what you say, lawyer."

Warren patted him on his arm. "I know you far prefer to dole out your wisdom than to receive any. Would you like to depart tomorrow?" He smiled at the relief in his friend's gaze. "The MacKinnons and Irene and Harold will ensure my wife is safe during my absence. Helen will understand, although I promise I will not divulge my reason for accompanying you to Helena." He shared a long look with Bears. "As we all know, her brother, Walter, will return. And, when he does, he will bring strife."

Bears nodded, and his eyes clouded with anger for a moment as he thought about something other than his search for his daughter. "When he does, he'll discover how unwelcome he is."

5

Warren nodded and rose. "You know everyone will be curious tonight, if you are absent from Sorcha's party."

Bears closed his eyes. "I will speak with Sorcha and Frederick." His gaze was wild and filled with worry as he looked at Warren. "I'm not fit company for a party."

Warren shrugged. "A party might be just what you need to keep your mind from overthinking. And Hortence will miss you." His smile broadened as Bears lost his momentary worry as he thought about Leticia and Alistair MacKinnon's eldest daughter. "If you decide to brood, I'll keep your secret."

"Thank you, Warren," Bears whispered. "I expect a difficult time in Helena. Having a reputable lawyer with me will make it much easier."

Warren nodded and rose. "Think about what I said about Fidelia." He slipped out the door, leaving Bears deep in thought.

Early the next morning, John Runs from Bears Renfrew—who preferred to be called Bears—entered the livery. He was a one-third owner of it, along with Cailean and Alistair MacKinnon. Although Bears often maintained a reserved presence and preferred the company of horses, he was considered an integral part of the MacKinnon clan. He didn't expect to be disturbed by any of the MacKinnons, as they had been up late into the night celebrating Sorcha's marriage to Frederick Tompkins and the news of her impending motherhood. Bears had had a few moments alone with her and Frederick before the festivities began to wish them well but had remained away from the family.

Bears approached the stall to his favorite horse, Lightning. He had a streak of white down one haunch but was otherwise pitch-black. Rather than the ornery Brutus, Lightning nickered softly at Bears's arrival and butted his head against Bears's soft caress, so Bears would scratch behind his ears.

"You like that, don't you, my fine fellow?" he murmured. "I wonder what life would be like if it were as uncomplicated as yours." He closed his eyes as he fought hope and fear in equal measure for what he would find in Helena.

At the soft touch to his arm, he jerked and spun. He relaxed instantly as he saw Fidelia watching him with wide eyes. Her chestnut-brown hair was tied back in a loose braid, and she held a shawl over her simple mint-green day dress. "What are you doing here?"

"I never thought to be able to surprise you," she whispered, her brows furrowed. "What bothers you, Bears?"

He shook his head and then frowned as she took a step away. "No, don't go." He grabbed her arm, his fingers stroking up and down her wrist to ease the gentle trembling provoked by his touch. "I'm out of sorts."

Her eyes widened farther at that admission. "I never thought to hear you say that."

"I'm a man, Fidelia." He spoke in a soft voice. "I promise to never be like the ones you've known, but I'm still a man." He sighed and closed his eyes.

She took a step forward and smoothed a hand over his cheek.

His eyes opened as he stared at Fidelia, leaning his head into her palm.

"We missed you last night at Sorcha's party. But you know that." She took a deep breath, her gaze looked deeply into his, as though remembering their conversation from the previous night. When she'd snuck into the barn to see him. When she'd run away from any intimacy with him. "I'm so tired of being afraid."

Her whispered admission caused a spark to flare in his gaze a moment before it was hidden. "You have no idea what those words mean to me." He stared at her with blatant frustration. "I have to leave Bear Grass Springs for a while." He held his breath and then relaxed when she didn't run away. "I have to travel to Helena."

She shook her head in confusion. "Why? What could you possibly have to do there?"

He raised a hand slowly, testing to see if she would jerk away from him, and, when she remained still, he rested it on her shoulder. He gave her shoulder a gentle squeeze and then said, "I received a letter yesterday. From the woman I once loved." He saw pain flash in Fidelia's eyes and squeezed her shoulder again. "I haven't seen her in eleven years, and she's dead now. One of the casualties of that cousin of Helen's. Of Bertrand March's."

Fidelia's jaw tightened at the mention of Bertrand, the man who had attempted to force her friend and the town's midwife, Helen Clark, to marry him. The previous year Fidelia had confronted the man with little more than a pair of knitting needles in an attempt to keep Helen safe. "I should feel remorse, but I will never react with anything but joy that he was hanged."

Bears nodded. "I agree."

She waited for him to say more and then shook her head. "How long ago did she die? What more did she write to upset you?"

His thumb stroked Fidelia's shoulder, as though soothing himself as much as her. "Her letter was four years old. I never received it until yesterday. She wrote to tell me that she thought she'd be dead soon." His intense stare bore into Fidelia's. "And that I have a daughter. To beg me to come and to find her and to care for her."

Fidelia jolted in his arms, as though slapped. Any color in her cheeks faded away, like she had been gutted, and his hold on her tightened for fear she'd faint dead away. "I must go," she whispered as she attempted to free herself from his hold.

He shook his head and leaned toward her. "No, Fidelia. Why would discovering that I have a child affect you so?" When she remained quiet, he growled in frustration. "You know I will do what I must to bring her here with me. That I will be her father." When she still refused to speak, he released her, watching with confusion and disappointment as she stumbled away. She grabbed onto a stall door to keep herself from tumbling to the ground.

"You don't understand," she whispered as a tear rolled down her cheek.

"No, I don't. And you don't either. I'll tell you this until you finally understand. I'm not like those other men who've disappointed you, Stitch. I'm a man of my word. I honor those I love. I will not walk away from my child. I will not walk away from you."

She flushed as he stared at her. She watched him with wide, unfathomable blue eyes.

"I'm not afraid of you," she whispered. "I fear I will disappoint you. And I can't bear to do that." She turned on her heel to race from the livery, stopping once to look at him over her shoulder. "I wish you luck, Bears. Your daughter will be the most fortunate of girls to have you as her father."

She turned again and eased open the livery door to return to the main house.

Bears kicked at the stall door. He gave a final pat to the waiting Lightning and then sat on a stool as he puzzled through Fidelia's actions. It was the first time in his acquaintance with her that she had not shied away from physical contact with him. He closed his eyes at the memory of her soft touch to his cheek. "A man could live off such a memory for months," he whispered to himself.

"What memory?" Alistair asked, wandering down the livery's central aisle. He was the second eldest MacKinnon sibling and a one-third owner of the livery. Alistair had married Leticia Browne two years ago, and together they had a beautiful baby boy, Angus, with another babe on the way. Alistair considered Hortence, Leticia's daughter from her first marriage, to be his own.

"Dammit," Bears muttered. "That's the second time today I've been caught unaware." He saw the surprise in his friend's gaze and motioned for him to sit. "We are busier than we've ever been, and Ewan will hopefully start the expansion of the livery in a few weeks. But I have to go away."

Alistair nodded. "Aye, Warren told us last night. 'Twould have been better for ye to inform yer partners yerself." He sat facing Bears. His brown-black hair had a sprinkling of gray in it, and his brown eyes were filled with concern as he stared at his friend. "Ye ken we consider ye family."

Bears nodded. "I know. And I'm very thankful for that now, since I don't know how long I will be away."

Alistair studied his usually composed friend, who always knew his purpose and who loved to dole out wisdom in a few sentences.

Instead, this Bears fidgeted, stared into space with unseeing eyes, and seemed at a loss for words. "What happened to ye, man?"

"Do you remember the first woman you ever loved?"

Alistair nodded. "Aye, a man doesna forget her." He waited for Bears to say more, but, when he remained silent, Alistair said, "Greer McGregor. She kent about life on a croft, was the bonniest lass I'd ever seen, and could kiss like a dream." He sighed. "But then our fathers found out, and she was sent to live with an aunt in Portree, and I dinna see her again. I thought my heart would break." He smiled at Bears. "I dinna feel that way again until I met Leticia."

When Bears remained quiet, Alistair frowned. "Dinna tell me that ye've been playin' Fidelia false all these months an' that ye've a woman in Helena? 'Tis no' like ye, Bears."

Bears's eyes widened in horror and shock at the suggestion. "Of course not. No." He pulled out two sheets of paper and handed them to Alistair. "Warren gave me this yesterday before the party. It's the reason I didn't come. I … I would have been useless at a party."

Alistair studied him a moment and then focused on the letter. After reading the last few lines, he canted forward, his brows furrowed as he stared at the missive. "Ye dinna ken?" At Bears's shake of his head, Alistair growled. "Do ye want one of us to go with ye?"

"Warren is coming with me. I will need a lawyer. No one will listen to a half-breed."

Alistair growled at Bears's description of himself. "Cail an' I could get help in. One of us could go with ye."

Bears stared into his friend's gaze, as though contemplating the offer. After a long moment, he shook his head. "I couldn't deny your families your presence. It wouldn't be fair."

"Ye are as a brother to us, Bears. Ye ken we want to do this for ye." Alistair rose and paced, kicking at a stall door with nearly as much force as Brutus. "I canna believe ye dinna ken until now. No wonder ye're flummoxed."

"Who's flummoxed?" Cailean asked as he entered the livery, frowning at the tension he sensed in the room. He looked around, as though in search of an adversary, and, when he saw none, he focused on his brother and Bears. When Alistair thrust the papers at him, he grabbed them and read the letter. His impatience faded to incredulity and then anger. "This is why you're going to Helena?"

Bears nodded. "I have to find her. She has to know I want her." He tucked the letter back into his breast pocket.

Cailean nodded. "Aye. And she should know that all of us here will love and want her too."

Bears's eyes widened at that proclamation, and he gave a sigh of relief and gratitude. "I won't be much of a partner for a while."

Cailean waved away any of his concerns. "You've worked hard here for a long time. You ensured we remained open when Belle was sick and when, after Leticia had her baby, Alistair wanted time at home. You've earned this time off." He shook his head in frustration. "Besides, you're family. You must go. For however long it takes."

Alistair nodded and shared a long look with his brother. "Aye. I asked him if he wanted one of us to go with him. He doesna want to take one of us away from our wives."

Cailean shook his head. "Belle and Leticia love you, Bears. They will want you supported and safe. If you want either of us there, just say so."

Bears nodded, deep in thought. "No, for now, I'll go with Warren. If I have further need, I'll telegram." He saw their reluctant agreement. "Don't give Brutus too many carrots. I need to find another way to train him."

Alistair chuckled. "If you think I'm denyin' that beast anythin' when I need to move him to a new stall, ye're mad. If he wants a carrot, he'll have a carrot."

Bears stood, and they all shook hands. Cailean pulled him close into a tight hug and slapped him on the back a few times.

"Bring her home," Cailean whispered.

Bears tightened his jaw and nodded. "I will—or die trying."

Fidelia slipped into the bakery that morning. Her sister, Annabelle, was elbow deep in kneading bread. Annabelle's partner, Leena Johansen, was home with her newborn baby girl, Mette, and they did not know when Leena planned to return to the bakery. Fidelia pulled on an apron and moved to the sink to wash the bowls and other cooking instruments that had already accumulated, relishing the quiet of the bakery until Leticia arrived to work the front of the store. Leticia's baby was due near Christmas, and she planned to work as long as possible.

"You're later than usual today," her sister murmured. She ran Annabelle's Sweet Shop with a kind efficiency. After she had partnered with Leena, Annabelle had expanded the space, so that the kitchen was larger and so that the front room was bigger to sell their baked goods. It also afforded space to highlight Fidelia's fine needlework and lacework and Sorcha's beautiful homespun yarns. The small bedroom off the kitchen was now mainly used as a nursery.

Fidelia froze at her sister's comment. After a moment, she scrubbed a baking tin with fierce intensity. "I'm sorry to be behind in my work."

Her younger sister frowned at her, running a hand over her forehead, streaking it with flour as she always did. "You know you don't have a fixed schedule here, Dee. You work here as much or as little as you want, and I'm thankful for your help. Your goods are selling more rapidly than you can create them, so I understand if you want time at home to sew or to tat lace."

Fidelia's shoulders stooped, and she rinsed and dried her hands before she faced her sister. "It has nothing to do with my work. It's Bears."

"Bears? Are you upset he's going to Helena? I know the trip is mysterious, but he'll return." Annabelle's black hair was pulled back in a tight bun, and her light-brown eyes flashed with concern.

"He will return, and, when he does, everything will be different." She moved to a stool and sat in dejected silence.

"Now you're talking in riddles," Annabelle murmured. "I've always

12

thought there was something between you and Bears, but I'd hate to think he led you on. Or that you had to rebuff his advances because you never cared for him as anything more than a friend."

Fidelia stared at her sister in wonder. "Have you never thought I'm unworthy of his regard? Of any man's regard?"

Annabelle immediately shook her head. "No. I can't imagine what horrible circumstances brought you to the Boudoir. A despair beyond anything I want to envision. But I do not believe you should live your life as a persecuted woman for the rest of your life. You are not Charity any longer."

Fidelia flinched at the use of her old Boudoir name. "No, I'm not. And, if I'm honest, I never really had charity for any of those men. I did what I did to survive. As any woman in that situation does." She wrapped an arm around her middle, warding off memories of her time working as a prostitute at Betty's Boudoir, Bear Grass Springs' house of ill repute.

Her sister stared at her. "Then why must you continue to believe that we will judge you and treat you poorly? For you must know that I won't. The MacKinnons won't." She sighed in frustration. "There will always be those in town who are narrow-minded and unforgiving, but they aren't worth your energy."

"I find I can't forgive myself."

Annabelle let out a huff of breath and stood in contemplative silence, while she gave the bread dough a few pats. "Until you do, you won't believe any man should want anything to do with you. Not even a man as wonderful as Bears." Her gaze softened, and she added, "If you won't speak of those demons with me, at least talk to Helen or Irene. You mustn't keep your fears bottled up inside." After a long pause, as she waited for a response from her sister but received none, Annabelle whispered, "Why is he going to Helena?"

Fidelia raised a tormented gaze to meet her sister's inquisitive one. "He received a letter last night that he has a daughter. That the woman he loved, the woman that Bertrand March murdered, had born him a daughter."

13

Annabelle pulled out a stool and sat with a *thud*. "All this time he's been denied knowing her?"

"Yes. And he's racing to Helena to find her. He fears for her well-being." Fidelia fought tears as she sniffled. "That is the man you'd have me ensnare."

Annabelle gave a growl of displeasure that matched any noise her Scottish husband, Cailean MacKinnon, could make. "You stop right there, Dee. You are a remarkable woman, who has overcome things I can't even begin to imagine. You do yourself and Bears a discredit by denying yourselves the joy you could find together." She paused as her eyes clouded with concern, while she watched Fidelia fidget. "Is it that you fear having any man touch you again?"

Fidelia shook her head. "Until recently that was one of my excuses." She flushed. "It's not as though we've kissed. But he touched me today. And I him. And all I felt was joy." She lowered her head. "I fear that means I'm shameless."

Annabelle reached forward and gripped her sister's hand. "No, it means you're human. You should know the joy of being with a man who cares for you. Not because he paid a few coins and had no concern for your well-being." She bit her lip. "You should again have something like you had with Aaron."

Fidelia's expression blanked, as it always did whenever the man she had run away from Maine with was mentioned. "I have work I must complete."

"Dee, someday you'll have to tell me what happened with Aaron. I cared for him too."

Her sister shook her head. "No. Some things deserve to remain buried."

CHAPTER 2

Helena teemed with life. Wagons, carts, and horse-drawn carriages maneuvered through clogged streets with frequent swearing and shouting when parked wagons impeded easy movement. Boardwalks lined either side of the streets, with peddlers and merchants eager to sell their wares. Well-to-do women wore fancy clothes with tight corsets and protruding bustles, causing them to walk slowly and to waddle.

"Why would that be considered fashionable?" Bears asked Warren as they paused before crossing the street.

Warren followed Bears's gaze and smiled at Bears frowning at well-dressed women. "I wouldn't look so fierce if I were you. You'll frighten them."

"And you never know what that might cause their ignorant menfolk to do," Bears said, lowering his gaze and shaking his head.

Warren gave a grunt of agreement. "Even though they live in the wilds of Montana Territory, many women yearn to be fashionable. Even if it is last year's fashion." He grinned at Bears as he gaped at his friend for knowing about women's fashions.

They continued their walk from the train station to a well-appointed hotel, passing solidly constructed brick buildings. The brick gave a sense of permanence to the city and also helped prevent the spread of any fires.

"Come," Warren said as they entered the stylish hotel. The large reception area had freshly painted white wainscoting, and royal-blue carpets covered the pine floors. The pine reception desk gleamed from a recent polish with key boxes behind it on the wall.

"Mr. Clark," the man at the reception desk said with an obsequious smile. "I was delighted to receive your telegram, informing me to reserve two hotel rooms." His smile dimmed as he looked at Bears.

Warren met his gaze with an implacable calm. "I'm uncertain if you've had the pleasure of meeting my colleague, John Renfrew. His father, Jack Renfrew, was a trapper of some renown."

The man looked from Warren to Bears and then back to Warren again. "I'm certain I did not have that pleasure." He cleared his throat. "This would be highly irregular for us, Mr. Clark."

Warren raised an eyebrow. "To rent a room to my associate for the duration of our stay? I thought that is what one did in a hotel."

The young man leaned forward and whispered in a carrying voice, "We don't generally rent rooms to his kind. Our patrons believe such people belong on reservations."

Bears rolled his eyes. "My father was a white man, and my mother's people are peaceful. I have no reason to live on a reservation, far from my ancestral homes."

The clerk shook his head, studying Bears—with his brown skin, black hair, and distinctive features—and shrugged. "Too many would be uncomfortable at the sight of you. You might claim to be peaceful, but why should we believe you?"

"Because I've never acted in a violent manner in my entire life." Bears's brown-black eyes kindled with anger, and his lips formed a straight line, meeting the young man's contemptuous stare. "I'd think you'd concern yourself about whether or not you'd be paid. Nothing more."

Warren nodded. "You can't imagine an associate of mine would harm a guest at your fine establishment?"

The clerk tilted up his jaw. "I've heard you never know what his kind might do if provoked." He shook his head. "I'm sorry. I must speak with the manager."

"Do," Warren said, his voice tinged with rage. "And be advised. If John doesn't stay here, I will never stay at your hotel again. I will also advise all my associates to avoid your hotel and restaurant."

The clerk paled and scurried off.

Bears waved away Warren's attempt at an excuse or apology and wandered the well-appointed room. "I knew I was correct in insisting you travel with me," Bears muttered.

After nearly half an hour, the manager appeared, grim faced, as though about to attend a public hanging. "Mr. Clark. Always a pleasure to see you."

Warren failed to match his greeting and stared at the short man until he flushed. "Well?"

"I'm afraid it is as my colleague said. We have no available rooms for your ... associate."

"I see," Warren said. "I refuse to bid you a good day." He turned on his heel and walked outside to the boardwalk, where Bears stood beside him, watching the townsfolk bustle by. "Come. Let's find lodging."

Three hours later, they had found a room in a ramshackle boarding house near the red light district. Warren stared at the dank, dark room. stinking of the previous occupants, and sighed. "It's better than nothing."

"Is it?" Bears asked. "I think I'd prefer to sleep in a hay pile in a stable. But then I'm sure they'd suspect I'd rob them of their horses in the middle of the night too."

Warren set down his bag. "I knew there was prejudice, Bears. Forgive me for not understanding how severe it is."

Bears shrugged. "In Bear Grass Springs, it's rare that I notice. But I have my own home and a job."

"And you prefer the company of horses over that of men. After today, I can't say I blame you." Warren scratched as though already battling bedbugs. "Come. Let's find dinner. Tomorrow we visit the judge, and our search for your daughter begins."

～

Warren glanced at Bears and smoothed down his waistcoat and jacket. Stained-glass panels on either side of the door glinted in the midafternoon sunlight, and Warren reached for the polished brass knocker. After giving it a few resounding taps, he waited. He shook his head subtly as the door opened, slipping a card from his waistcoat pocket to give to the man who answered the door. "Mr. Clark and an associate to see the judge."

He followed the servant into the entryway, ignoring the fine mahogany paneling, the plush red of the cushions on the chairs—meant to soften the long wait times when visiting a man of importance—and the ornate carpet covering part of the floor. Warren watched as Bears wandered the space, his boot heels *click*ing on the exposed wooden floor. "I've been told that's an original," Warren murmured.

Bears studied a painting on the wall opposite the stairway and shrugged. "It's pretty enough." He frowned at the romantic rendering of a sunset over the mountains.

Warren chuckled. "Well, I'd compliment the artist, since the judge's daughter painted that."

A throat cleared, and they faced the impassive servant, who motioned for them to follow him. They entered a large office space off the front hall. The judge sat behind a huge desk with books and papers in front of him. Sunlight streamed in from the window behind him, and similar paintings hung on the office walls as in the front hall. He rose and moved around the desk to grip Warren's hand. Although not as tall as Warren, he had a commanding presence, and his sharp gaze missed little.

"Warren, it's good to have you in Helena again. I continue to hope you'll see sense and leave that backwater town to join my firm here in Helena." Judge Hammond looked to Bears. "I'm Judge Hammond. It's a pleasure to meet a colleague of Mr. Clark's."

Warren smiled. "This is Bears Renfrew. Jack's son. He's a close friend of mine."

Bears shook the judge's hand and met his curious gaze. Warren and Bears took the seats facing the judge's desk. Soon the judge had settled in his comfortable leather chair that creaked with his movements, and he watched them with blatant curiosity. "I never thought that letter would cause such a precipitous arrival."

Bears frowned. "I was told you had read the contents of that letter." His frown deepened as the judge nodded. "I was informed I have a daughter."

The judge nodded once more. "Yes, and we have no reason to believe her mother lied. Her letter, along with the testimony of women who did not die at Bertrand's hand, helped to convict him. However, are you certain you wish to burden yourself in such a way?"

Bears looked from the judge to Warren in confusion. He then tilted his head at the amateur paintings on the wall. "Do you consider your daughter a burden? Do you wish you had been spared knowing her?" He saw the judge flush with indignation. "I have only ever wanted a family. I will know my daughter. I will never consider caring for her a burden."

Judge Hammond nodded and steepled his fingers as he met Bears's hard stare; his countenance softened as he smiled with satisfaction. "I suspected you would travel to Helena. Many men wouldn't. But I knew your father." He met Bears's surprised gaze.

Warren smiled incredulously. "How would you know Bears's father?"

"In part of my misspent youth, I thought to rebel against my father and his plans for me to be a lawyer and, hopefully, a judge," he said to Warren, but then the judge faced Bears. "I ran away to the wilds of Montana and met your father, Jack." He shrugged. "I thought myself tough until I spent a few days in the backcountry with him. After a week, I realized I never wanted to go without the modern conveniences again. After a month, I dreamed about returning home to Chicago and fulfilling my father's wishes."

Bears smiled. "Father always talked about the young hothead from the east who he brought on the worst trapping trip possible to scare you into returning to where you came from." Bears's smile deepened at the shock on the judge's face. "And to ensure none of your friends were inclined to follow in your footsteps."

The judge let out a booming laugh. "If that doesn't sound like your father. The rascal." He shook his head. "When I was sent to Montana Territory as a judge, I thought it was fate's way of punishing me for my youthful mischief."

"Do you still feel that way?" Warren asked.

"No. I like living in Helena. With any luck, it will become the capital, and then it will be more than a boom-and-bust town." He looked at Bears. "Because of my association with your father, I was inclined to send you that letter, Mr. Renfrew."

Bears nodded. "I appreciate it. Now I must find her."

The judge shook his head. "No, she's already been found. She's at the small orphanage on the edge of town run by Mrs. Marday."

"What does that mean?" Bears asked. "The *small* orphanage?"

"It's the poorer of the two orphanages and always struggles to receive adequate funding. I regret to say that our town needs two such establishments." The judge grimaced. After a long pause, he asked, "What would you like?"

Bears shared a confused look with Warren. "I beg your pardon, sir?"

"Do you want to see her? Ensure that she is well?"

Bears shook his head in immediate denial. "No. I want her to return to Bear Grass Springs with me. To live with me as my daughter. To consider herself my daughter."

The judge nodded. "It's highly irregular for a female orphan to live with an unmarried man."

"She's not an orphan," Bears ground out. "I'm her father. I will care for her."

The judge smiled, a gleam in his eyes. "I agree. As I said, it is irregular but not unheard of. I will ensure everything is acceptable with Mrs. Marday. However, a generous donation to her orphanage will go a long way to soothing that woman's concern."

Warren studied the judge shrewdly. "Her concern or her tongue?"

The judge shrugged. "Both. I fear she has a tendency to gossip, and it is not restricted to those who visit the orphanage."

Bears shook his head. "I am not a rich man, sir. I work with my friends at a livery and earn a comfortable living. I will not promise to pay that woman money I don't have."

The judge waited a long moment before nodding. "I understand. But be forewarned. That woman, when scorned, will find a way to tarnish what you hold most dear."

~

Fidelia slipped out the back door of the bakery and gasped as she bumped into someone. "I beg your pardon," she said, giving deferential head bob.

She froze as a hand gripped her arm, and she looked into the eyes of a smiling man she did not recognize. Her gaze roved over him from head to foot, and she shrugged her arm free.

"Don't want you fallin', miss," he said with a broad grin. "Couldn't have the prettiest woman in Bear Grass Springs gettin' injured afore the next dance. Then who'd we have to dance with?" He stood tall at nearly six feet, long and limber. His brown hair was dampened, as though he had just visited the barber, and his beard was trimmed.

Fidelia flushed. "I thank you for your kindness, sir." She moved to walk around him, pausing when he didn't step out of the way. "I'm expected at home."

"I'm Asa Schuman. I work in the mines and do well for myself. Perhaps you'd let me call on you sometime."

She shook her head and backed up a step. "I … No. … I'm flattered, of course, but, no, sir. I don't walk out with gentlemen." She raised a fleeting glance to his and saw the confusion and frustration in his gaze.

"There ain't enough town dances to get to know you, miss. And you stand behind a wall of family, as though you need protectin'. Dancin' ain't ever hurt no one."

"I'm not the dancing type. If you will excuse me, I am expected." She pushed past him, stilling when he grabbed her hand.

"It's just your sister you run to, ain't it? You ain't got no man you're runnin' to?"

Fidelia pulled her hand free and half-walked, half-ran home. When she entered the kitchen, she attempted to force a bright smile but couldn't still her shaking.

Annabelle set down the drying cloth and moved toward her. "What happened, Dee? Why are you as white as a sheet?"

Fidelia shook her head. "I'm being silly. I … A miner flirted with me as I left the bakery. He did nothing improper."

Her sister urged her to sit at one of the comfortable chairs at the dining room table and joined her. "Are you sure? You've dealt with a lot of flirtatious men since you began working at the bakery, and I've never seen you this upset."

Fidelia closed her eyes and took a deep breath, then met her sister's worried gaze. "There were a few moments where I felt over-whelmed and powerless. I hate feeling like that." She shared a long look with her sister. "I never want to feel that way again."

Annabelle nodded and gripped Fidelia's hand. "Nor do I. Will he cause trouble?"

"I don't know. I hope not." She flushed and hid her gaze. "Every time a man looks at me, I wonder if he knows what I was. If he thinks I am an easy mark because of it."

Annabelle sighed. "You'll never know for sure. And I'm certain some men feel that way. But not all. And not the honorable ones." After a few moments, where the sounds of rattling carriages rolling through town and of Alistair calling out to Cailean could be heard, Annabelle murmured, "I want more for you, Dee. I want you to live life to the fullest. Not hidden away at the back of the bakery or even hidden here, taking care of Skye or tatting lace. If you want more from life, I hope you're brave enough to seek it out."

Fidelia let out a stuttering breath. "It's so hard to dare to dream of more when I already have so much now." She looked at her sister with gratitude. "If I hadn't left the Boudoir when I did, if you hadn't helped free me from the laudanum, I'd be dead by now." Her eyes filled. "And I never would have known Skye. I never would have known how much more my life could be."

Annabelle smiled. "And yet your life can still be so much more, Dee. Never stop dreaming. Even if those dreams don't come true, the dream is worth having."

Fidelia leaned forward and hugged her sister. "Thank you, Anna."

Mildred stood in a corner of the playground at the orphanage, making drawings in the dirt. She ignored the fancy carriage coming up the drive; the men and women inside them never desired a half-grown half-breed. Or so said Mrs. Marday. Mildred sighed as she pushed down any yearnings and her memories of her mother, then made a picture of a river with the sun high above it.

She yowled in protest as one of the older girls grabbed her stick and broke it in half. "You had no right!" Mildred screamed as she jumped on the larger girl. Mildred had surprise on her side, as Becky never expected anyone to question her actions. Becky was the unofficial leader of the orphans, and anyone who didn't agree with her self-proclaimed role suffered. Mildred was used to the mistreatment, and her thighs and arms were covered in bruises from their vicious pinches.

As they tumbled to the ground in a heap of skirts, petticoats, and flying braids, Mildred realized she had had enough of being picked on. "I may be a half-breed, but I'm still worthy!" she screamed as Becky kicked out and hit her in her stomach.

Mildred gave another howl of protest when she was picked up from the ground and held away from Becky. Belatedly Mildred noted two well-dressed gentlemen watching their fight, and she flushed in embarrassment. She closed her eyes in defeat, and her shoulders slumped. Meanwhile Becky simpered and cried at her mistreatment from "the half-breed who shouldn't even be allowed to live in a place with her betters."

As Mrs. Marday turned to Mildred with fire in her gaze, Mildred stiffened, expecting a slap, knowing two days without food were in her future. However, a soft, penetrating voice stilled Mrs. Marday's actions.

"I'd ask the other girl what occurred. Seems to me you only got one view."

Mildred shivered at the deep, melodious voice but kept her gaze down.

"Well, girl, what happened?"

"I was drawing, and she took my stick and broke it. I'm tired of her picking on me," Mildred whispered in a quavering voice.

"That's not true!" Becky screeched.

"Seems to me that one's a liar, and one isn't," the stranger said again, while Mrs. Marday dithered.

Finally Mrs. Marday faced Mildred and asked, "What proof do you have that she picks on you?"

Mildred took a deep breath and then rolled up one long sleeve of her dress, exposing the rows of bruises on her skin. She heard a deep inhalation of breath from the man who had spoken earlier. The other man with him swore.

"That's it. She will not remain here another minute," said the man with the deep voice.

Mildred looked up and met the irate gaze of the man with the hypnotizing voice. Her brown eyes widened as she looked into a gaze that resembled hers. He had long silky black hair, like hers, and his brown skin was a shade darker than hers. She shook her head in confusion. "I don't understand," she whispered.

"This man would like to adopt you," Mrs. Marday said. "It is most irregular, as he is a bachelor, and I don't approve of such things."

The other man, dressed in an impeccable black suit with a cranberry waistcoat and a white shirt, interrupted Mrs. Marday. "As you are well aware, Miss Marday, this is *not* a usual situation." His stare silenced the woman, who gave a huff of displeasure.

"Well, come along then, girl," Mrs. Marday snapped, marching toward the orphanage building.

Mildred stood still, staring at the two men.

"Will you come with us, Mildred?" asked the man who looked like her. "Will you let us explain?"

She nodded and took a step toward him. When he held out a hand to her, she shook her head in refusal. Instead, she ran her hands over her skirts, dusting off the dirt gathered there. "I don't like practical jokes."

The man chuckled. "Nor do I." He tilted his head toward the imposing granite building and walked beside her. The other man walked a few paces in front of them.

When they reached Mrs. Marday's office, they took their seats.

"Now, dear, you may find this hard to believe, but someone would like to adopt you."

"Stop your prattling this instance," snapped the man with the deep voice. "Please grant us a few moments of time alone with Mildred. You may wait outside the door, if you wish to listen, but I do not want you in here interfering." He stared at Mrs. Marday, until she rose in a quivering mass of affronted femininity and slammed the door behind her.

When she had left, the man turned and stared at Mildred a long moment. "Do you know who your father was, Mildred?" He frowned when she hung her head, as though in shame.

"A murderer," she whispered. "He killed my mother and other women too. They hanged him."

"Did you look anything like him?"

She frowned at his question. "No. He always said I was his greatest disappointment. That he should have known better than to take the crumbs of another man's affections." She continued to frown as she shook her head. "I don't know what he meant."

The man smiled as he looked at her, his gaze filled with tenderness. "It means that you weren't really his daughter. You're mine." He waited a long moment as her gaze filled with shock. "I know you've realized how much we look alike."

"You're a half-breed too," she whispered.

His jaw ticked with anger. "I am half-Indian, yes. I come from a proud people. As do you. I also had a wonderful father, who was white. He would have adored you." They shared a long look, and he smiled. "Your mother was right. Your name should be Bright Fawn."

She shook her head in confusion. "My name's Mildred."

"Yes, but you can have more than one name. In fact, I recommend it." He waited a moment and then said in a soft voice, "My name is John Runs from Bears Renfrew. I prefer to be called Bears."

"Bears," she whispered. "Where do you live?"

"In a small town called Bear Grass Springs. We'll take a train to get there. I work in a livery with friends, and I have a small home."

"You'll have to see if Ewan can build you another room," murmured the man in the fancy suit.

Bears nodded and then focused on his daughter. "I promise you that, if you decide to leave this orphanage and to come home with me, you will always have food. You will always have a home. And you will always know love."

Her eyes filled, and she shook her head, her black braid falling over one shoulder. "I know you lie. No one can love me."

He reached forward to hold one of her hands. "I promise you that's not true. It will take time for you to get to know me. For you to trust me." Regret filled his gaze. "I did not know I had a daughter until a few days ago. I would have found you long ago had I any idea."

"You want me?" she whispered, her eyes now on the verge of over-flowing.

"Yes."

A tear spilled onto her cheek, and she sniffled. "No one's wanted me since my mother died."

"Well, I do. And I fear you will be overwhelmed with others who want you too, once you reach Bear Grass Springs. For the men I work with are like family. And they are eager to meet you."

She bit her lip and stared at him. "I will go with you. But I will disappear if I don't like how you treat me."

He smiled and nodded. "I consider that a fair warning." His gaze flitted to his friend's. "Can you deal with that woman? I don't have the patience."

He chuckled and nodded. "I'm Warren Clark, Mildred. I'm a lawyer. I'm also an honorary member of the MacKinnon clan, which Bears belongs to, and I already consider myself your uncle. I'll get this straightened out, and we'll be on our way to Bear Grass Springs soon."

~

Bears smiled at Mildred as they were left alone. He sat on a chair near her and frowned as he looked at her patched and faded navy-blue dress.

Mildred tugged at the sleeve of her dress in an attempt to make the ill-fitting garment more presentable. As Bears continued to study her, she flushed and ducked her head.

"The other girls appear to be wearing newer clothes," Bears said.

She nodded and kept her gaze on the floor.

"Why is that?"

Mildred played with the frayed sleeve. "Mrs. Marday said that money is tight and that those with benefactors or with greater prospects of adoption would receive new clothes."

Bears made a noise of disgust. "When is the last time you received a new dress?"

She shrugged. "Never." When the silence stretched out between them, she peeked at him and froze. He had flushed red, and his eyes sparked with rage. "I didn't deserve one."

Bears reached forward, slowing his movement when he saw her tense. "You *always* deserved a new dress. You were *always* worthy." He smiled as she relaxed when he clasped her small hand. "I have a friend who has a fine hand at sewing. I'll see if she can make you new dresses."

"Oh, no, that's not necessary. I have all I need. I don't want to be a burden and …" Her words faded as Bears watched her with patient understanding.

After a moment's silence, he took a deep breath. "I need you to understand a few things, Mildred. I am not a rich man, but I will provide for you. A few dresses will not beggar me. They will not make me think you are a bother or a burden or that my life would be better without you."

He watched as her gaze filled with disbelief and doubt. "I will never raise my hand to you." His eyes clouded at the thought. "Not ever." He took a deep breath and calmed. "That doesn't mean we won't argue or disagree. If you're anything like me, I know we will." He smiled tenderly at her. "The worst I'll do is raise my voice."

He paused, but she remained quiet. "You have no reason to have any faith in what I say. With time, you'll learn that what I tell you is the truth." He glared at the door as Warren entered.

Warren looked from Mildred to Bears and shrugged apologetically. "I tried to soothe Mrs. Marday with my eastern charms, but she's having none of it. She insists she must speak with you, Bears."

Bears nodded. "Will you wait here with Mildred?" He slipped past Warren and walked down the dark hallway devoid of decoration or rug to the open doorway at the opposite end. He paused and then knocked on the doorjamb.

At the sullen "Enter," he took a few steps into the opulent room. He stopped to stare at the fine furnishings, the Oriental rug on the floor, the stained glass in one window, the green velvet on one settee. He clenched his fists and took a deep breath, while Mrs. Marday watched him from a comfortable lady's chair near a dormant fireplace.

"I can see your friend has all the charm," Mrs. Marday said, waving him to a wooden high-backed chair. When Bears sat, it tilted to the front, and he adjusted how he sat so as not to tumble to the floor.

"You wished to see me, Mrs. Marday?" Bears asked in as deferential a manner as possible.

"Yes," she said as she smoothed a hand over her rust-colored wool skirt. "I am most uncomfortable with you snatching away one of my girls. She is treasured here."

Bears bit back a snort. "I find that hard to believe. Mildred tells me that she's never had a new dress. I assume that ill-fitting excuse for a garment is a hand-me-down from an older girl?"

When Mrs. Marday glared at him and remained silent, Bears

shook his head. "I know your game. You understand I wish to claim her as my daughter, and you want to bleed as much money from me as you can." He looked around her extravagant room. "How many of your benefactors have seen this room as you pronounce your poverty and line up your girls in their worst dresses?"

She glared at him. "If you hadn't thrown me out of my office, you never would have been invited into my private sanctum." She watched him shrewdly. "I have no desire to allow Mildred to suffer living with you."

Bears watched her with a deep loathing in his gaze. "No, you prefer that she continue suffering living with you. To continue believing your lies that she is not worthy of any caring, love, or kindness." He took a deep breath. "She has suffered enough because she has heard your lies so often that it will take time for her to believe she is worthy of love and a dedicated family." His voice lowered with his rage. "But she will *never* suffer for being my daughter."

"I refuse to allow you to adopt her without a $500 donation."

Bears blanched. "That's ridiculous."

"She is precious to too many of us here."

"Only as an outlet for your venom and your prejudicial judgments," he snapped.

"Judge Carlisle will never allow you to adopt her," she said with a sly smile. "Not without my approval."

Bears shook his head. "Does he get half of what you bleed from the donors? Is that your agreement?" He reached into his pocket and extracted a sheet of paper. "It is your misfortune that Mr. Clark and I visited Judge Hammond. He is a friend and ally and has already approved Mildred's adoption. Even though I know she is *my* daughter, too many believe Bertrand March was her father. Thus, I opted for a formal adoption to prevent any future problems." When Mrs. Marday gaped at him, he smiled. "This is an official decree, signed by Judge Hammond. He feared Judge Carlisle would be too … busy to address the matter in a timely fashion."

"You snake! You had no right to go behind my back!" She screeched and reached for the paper.

"If you tear it up, it does not matter. Warren has a copy, as do I. And the judge would make another one for me. I'm certain he'd enjoy a visit with you in your private sitting room while he discusses his desire for a more active role in your orphanage."

"How dare you imply any wrongdoing? How dare you come here and steal a child from my care?" She tossed the decree at Bears. Her cheeks had reddened with her anger, and her breaths emerged as pants.

"Considering Mildred has known very little care since she's been here, I would think you'd be relieved she is leaving with me immediately. Good day, Mrs. Marday." He stood, tucking the official adoption paper into his pocket, and marched from the room, ignoring her shouting at him.

He returned to the office where Mildred and Warren waited for him. They were playing a game of naming every animal they could think of that started with the letter *E*. "Elephant," Bears said as he entered the room.

Mildred rolled her eyes. "I already said that!"

He smiled at her and met Warren's inquisitive gaze.

"I gather Mrs. Marday wasn't pleased with the judge's order?" Warren said with a wink to Mildred, who giggled.

Bears shook his head and held out his hand for Mildred. Some of the tension in his shoulders eased as she gripped his hand. "Thankfully the judge didn't stand on protocol in this case."

Warren shrugged. "There was no need. You're her father. There's no reason for her to remain in an orphanage." He looked at Mildred, who stared at him with wide brown eyes. "For Mildred is *not* an orphan."

Bears nodded. "Come. Let's collect whatever items you wish to bring with you and depart." Mildred tugged on his hand, and he crouched at her eye level. "What is it, little one?" he asked as he swiped a hand over her head.

"I have nothing." A tear trickled out. "Everything that was Mother's was taken away."

Bears looked into her grief-filled gaze and shook his head. "No, everything that was your mother's was not taken away. For she lives on inside you. Her wisdom. Her love. It is there, Mildred, and no one can take that from you."

Another tear cascaded down her cheek, and she nodded.

Bears rose and held onto her hand. "Come, Mildred. Let's find dinner, and then tomorrow we'll head home to Bear Grass Springs."

F idelia exited Jessamine's print shop and paused, staring at the bank next door. She nearly gave in to her curiosity to determine if her sister had truly set aside money for her. She halted after taking a step toward the bank. When Annabelle had first arrived in Bear Grass Springs, she had told Fidelia that half of their father's estate had been set aside for Fidelia's own use. At the time, Fidelia had lived at the Boudoir and had no reason to discover if Annabelle had told her the truth. "Besides, I'm sure Annabelle and Cailean have had need of it by now," she whispered to herself. After a moment, she shook her head at her foolishness and turned toward the bakery.

"Well, look and see who we have here."

Fidelia froze. It was a voice from her past. From her nightmares. One she hadn't heard in months. Twenty-one months.

"I wonder why you've been so lax in visiting us, Charity."

Fidelia glared at the woman, dressed in an emerald-green gown that enhanced her bosom and waist. "I'm surprised they allow you to walk on the boardwalk, when it's not the whore's shopping time."

The Madam laughed, her hand looped through the arm of the large man beside her.

Fidelia barely spared a glance for Ezekial, the Madam's henchman. Fidelia knew the Madam was her true adversary.

"I am not one of the girls."

"Nor am I," Fidelia said. "And my name is Fidelia."

The Madam held out a manicured hand to pat Fidelia on the arm, as though consoling her. "Oh, you poor girl. How you must suffer,

31

being forced to live the life you do with such boring people. You must admit. We were more fun." The Madam gave her a sly smile.

Shaking her head, Fidelia brushed the Madam's hand from her arm. "No, you weren't. If I had truly believed that, you wouldn't have had to drug me to keep me docile."

"No other girl has complained about the laudanum. They seem to enjoy it." She shared a perplexed stare with Ezekial.

"Because they are out of their minds and have no idea they deserve better!" Fidelia snapped. "One day, Madam, one day you will pay for what you've done to those who were in your charge."

The Madam gripped Fidelia's arm with an iron strength, provoking a gasp of pain. "No, my dear. One day you will realize that I saved you. I saved you from being a two-bit whore, selling your wares from darkened alleys, before you froze and starved to death. Before you died from some dreadful disease. I saved you, and you will thank me."

"I will never thank you."

They glared at each other for long moments as the Madam's hold on Fidelia's arm tightened.

"What's this?" Ewan MacKinnon, the youngest MacKinnon brother, called out as he walked toward them from the Stumble-Out Saloon across the street. "I dinna ken ye were to have a reunion today, Fidelia." He stood beside her, reaching forward, as though to shake Ezekial's hand, instead severing the Madam's hold on Fidelia's arm in the process.

"It's not a reunion," Fidelia hissed.

"Aye, looks more like a pair of rattlesnakes gettin' ready to strike." He shook his head at Ezekial. "If they killed each other, would ye bother to do anythin', or would ye watch an' then walk away?"

Ezekial stared impassively at Ewan.

"He knows who butters his bread," the Madam snapped.

"Or something," Fidelia muttered, provoking a cough of laughter from Ewan. She turned to Ewan and walked away from the pair without a goodbye. "Come. I'm certain there's something special at the bakery for you."

"Oh, 'twould make my day. I'm to meet Bears an' Warren when the train comes in." He looked over his shoulder to see the Madam glaring at Fidelia. "She doesna like ye much, ye ken?"

"She's hated me since the day I left the Boudoir." She smiled. "You're not her favorite either, seeing as you're the one who won me in a card match."

"She was the daft woman who made a bet she couldna pay any other way. I'll no' be havin' any sympathy for her." He gently squeezed Fidelia's arm. "An' it got ye free, aye?"

Her smiled broadened. "Yes, it got me free."

CHAPTER 3

Bears held Mildred's hand as they disembarked the train in Bear Grass Springs. He knew gossip would spread faster than a wildfire about his arrival with a girl who was his spitting image. Mildred leaned into his side, and he regretted her fear and uncertainty. "Come," he murmured.

As they exited the station, Ewan waited for them with a wagon. "There ye are!" he called out with a broad smile. Ewan worked as the town carpenter and ran a successful business, while his wife, Jessamine, was the town reporter. "I kent from Alistair ye were to return today and thought ye might like a ride to the livery."

Bears gave him a grateful look. "Thank you, Ewan." He paused as he rested a hand on Mildred's shoulder. "Mildred, this is Ewan. He's one of my best friends and a MacKinnon." He smiled at her reassuringly. "Ewan, this is my daughter, Mildred."

She frowned. "So are you an uncle too?"

Ewan laughed and nodded. "Aye, I'm yer uncle, ye wee imp." He tousled her hair and helped her onto the wagon's seat.

Warren waved at them as he was waylaid by a townsperson wanting free legal advice.

"Ye'll have plenty more vyin' for the honor of bein' yer uncle. But never forget that I'm yer favorite, aye?" He winked at her.

"You talk funny," she said and then gasped, as though she had said something wrong. When Ewan laughed and agreed, she relaxed between her father and Ewan on the wagon seat.

"Aye, 'tis because we MacKinnons are from Skye. 'Tis an island off Scotland. Only Cailean, the eldest, worked to lose his accent. Thought it made him sound more professional." Ewan shrugged. "I dinna ken if he's more successful for it, but, if ye make him mad, it reappears. Sometimes I give him a hard time to hear him sound like the brother from my youth."

Mildred giggled, and Bears gave a sigh of relief at Ewan's ability to ease his daughter's tension. Wagons and carts rattled down the street, while pedestrians walked nimbly to avoid them and the horse droppings. Townsfolk stopped to discuss the weather, the preacher's latest sermon, and the fear of another harsh winter like the previous year's. The sound of hammers hitting wood, the blacksmith striking his anvil, and the traffic in the road added a gentle cacophony to their conversation.

The entire ride to the livery, Ewan gave a running commentary. "Now ye are no' to enter that building. 'Tis the house of ill repute, called Betty's Boudoir. The bank is next door, an' we finally have an honest banker. Over there"—he nodded across the street—"is one of the town stores, an' then another fine establishment ye are no' to enter, the Stumble-Out Saloon." He pointed out his wife's newspaper office, then Annabelle's Sweet Shop, the café, and the Odd Fellows Hall before pulling up next to the livery.

"Ye'll have no need for the fine hotel we passed. The school and church are over there." He nodded across the road. "An' this is our livery. Yer father is partner with my brothers, an' they run a fine business."

Ewan set the brake, hopped down, and lifted Mildred to the ground. After he saw Bears grab their belongings, Ewan gave them a nod. "Was a pleasure to meet ye, Mildred. I'll see ye tonight."

"Tonight?" Bears asked.

UNBRIDLED MONTANA PASSION

"Aye, the family is plannin' a welcome party for our newest family member. Even Sorcha and Frederick are comin' in from the ranch, and the Tompkins are closin' the café. 'Twill be quite a party." He tipped his hat at Mildred. "Welcome to Bear Grass Springs, Mildred."

She watched him openmouthed as he entered the livery and then stared at Bears. "Why do all these people want to meet me?"

"They are my friends. They are like family to me." He looked deeply into her eyes. "They already consider you family."

She shook her head. "But I might not even be here that long."

He frowned and took a step closer to her. "You are my daughter, Mildred. From the moment I saw you, I knew." He took a deep breath. "One day I hope you will accept me as your father and will forgive me for not finding you until now." He motioned for her to follow him. "Come. I have a simple home, but I will find a way to make it comfortable for you."

He led her past Cailean MacKinnon's large home to a small house that resembled a cabin behind the paddock. "I used to live in the tack room, but Ewan thought I should have a better home, especially during a Montana winter." He pushed open the door and stopped short at what he saw.

Rather than the tiny home he was used to, this was a two-room house. Ewan had managed to build onto the back of it during the short time Bears had been away in Helena. However, the change had not been visible from the front, and thus the surprise had not been ruined.

In the front room was the small table with a vase of wildflowers on a lace doily. The black potbellied stove stood on bricks and, on the other side of the room, was a bed and a rocking chair. On the bedside table beside the lamp was a sharp knife with a piece of wood half whittled next to it. A beaver hide covered a chest at the foot of the bed. In the center of the opposite wall, a new doorway covered by a sheet led to another small room. Inside, the freshly painted cream-colored walls gleamed in the afternoon sun streaming through the small back window, looking out at the hills in the distance. The single bed had a multicolored patchwork quilt thrown over it, the predomi-

37

nant color being red, and a small lamp sat on a bedside table with a lace doily covering the scarred wood.

"In the summer, you'd most likely prefer the back room. In the winter, I fear it will be cold."

Mildred stood there and looked around. "This is a wonderful home." She shook her head. "I'll be happy on a pallet by the fire."

He gave a grunt of displeasure. "No, Bright Fawn. I want you to have a place that is yours. All growing girls need such a place." He flushed. "Or I imagine they do. I needed one as a growing boy." He saw her inch toward the small room. "If you prefer the small room, it's yours."

"You don't mind?" she asked.

His breath caught at the hope and fear mingled in her gaze. "No, daughter, I don't." He clenched his hands to keep from stroking her head as he desired.

She moved into the room and fingered the multicolored quilt. "This is beautiful."

"Sorcha Tompkins would have made that for you. She was Sorcha MacKinnon, the youngest MacKinnon sibling. She now lives on a ranch a little ways from town." He nodded as his daughter continued to trace the finely sewn pattern of the quilt. "She would want you to feel welcome. They all will."

"But they don't even know me."

He shrugged. "That's how they are. Some don't need a reason to love." He paused. "Do you want to see the livery? It's where I spend most of my time."

She flushed and looked down.

"What is it, Bright Fawn?"

"Why do you call me that?" she whispered. "I've only ever been called Mildred at the orphanage."

"Do you like that name?"

She shook her head. "I hate it. Mother used to call me Millie. I liked that better."

"You're already used to more than one name." He smiled at her. "I call you Bright Fawn for a few reasons. One is that your mother wrote me that she thought you should always have been called that. After I first met you, I realized she was right. However, an Indian name is never looked upon with much favor. And a white woman would not have referred to you in that way." He stared at her. "I'm proud of my mother's people. Your grandmother's people. I have not seen them for many years, but I honor them by giving my daughter a true name."

He waited, but she remained with her gaze downcast. "Do you wish for me to only call you Mildred or Millie?"

"No," she whispered. "I like you calling me Bright Fawn."

He nodded. "Why do you want to avoid the livery?"

"I'm afraid of horses," she blurted out.

His brows rose in surprise. "Do you want to come and meet my favorite horse? He'll snuffle all over your hand and let you tickle his ears. He's quite friendly." She watched him with wide brown eyes, and he yearned to banish the doubt and fear from her gaze.

"Horses bite and stomp and hurt you."

He shook his head. "Only if the master is a mean man who treats his horses badly. Or if the wild in a horse cannot be tamed. Generally horses are much nicer than humans." He smiled at her. "They have bad days and moods, like we do. You just have to learn to read how they feel, and then you know how to avoid getting hurt."

She bit her lip and stared at him. "Will you teach me?"

His smile spread, and he motioned for her to follow him. "Of course." He led her from the cabin around the paddock and to the barn. "Never enter the paddock unless one of us is with you. Promise me."

She nodded. When he waited for her words, she said, "I promise."

He led her through the wide door, into the livery from the direction of the paddock, and paused as she gasped and stood still. Horses dozed in stalls, while a few shifted from hoof to hoof. Some poked their heads over the stall door as though sensing his presence. "Hello, beauties," he murmured, moving toward them to give them scratches along their muzzles.

"This one is Sugar," he said. "She's generally very docile, but she did throw Sorcha last fall when she was spooked. Sorcha broke her leg and had to spend months at Fredrick's ranch."

"Is that why they married? Because of scandal?"

He frowned. "I fear you know too much about the seedy aspects of life and not enough about the good parts." He shook his head. "No, they fell in love. I think they'd already been in love but had been circling around each other for a while. When she had time at his ranch, they finally were forced to face their feelings."

"Only a fool marries for love," Mildred said.

He turned and looked at her. "That's not true. You'll see many couples tonight who have married for love. They are happy, as I hope you will be one day." He paused and then spoke in a very soft voice. "I hope you will cease parroting whatever Mrs. Marday and others may have said. Especially any nonsense from that man who pretended to be your father. Ignore his lies. For he knew very little about what makes a life worth living."

"Did you know him?"

Bears nodded. "Yes. And our short association was much too long." He motioned for her to follow him to another stall. "This is Lightning." He smiled as Lightning nudged at his shoulder. "Hello, boy. I've missed you too." He scratched at his forelock and then behind his ears. "Do you want to meet my daughter?"

Lightning seemed to nod in agreement, and Bears waited to see if Bright Fawn would reach for his horse. When she lifted a shaking hand, Lightning lowered his head, so she could brush her fingertips over his muzzle.

"It's like velvet," she whispered in awe.

"Yes, it is. Come," he said with a groan, as he hefted her up, so she could scratch behind Lightning's ears.

She giggled as Lightning closed his eyes and gave a snuffle. "I think he likes that."

"He loves it," Bears said, then set her down. "I'll show you the tack room." As they walked down the aisle, a horse made a whinnying noise and kicked the side of a stall. Bright Fawn jumped to stand on Bears's other side.

"That's Brutus. He lives up to his name, and I want you to always avoid his stall. He's a mean horse, and he would hurt you." He waited until she nodded. "Come," he murmured as he showed her the tack room.

The room was well organized with bridles, harnesses, bits, saddles —everything they needed to work with the horses in one place. On the wall was a wooden box of cubbyholes with assorted hardware, while the larger items, like harnesses, hung from pegs on the wall.

"You know how to use everything here?" she asked in wonder.

"I do," he said with a smile. "It's not that hard, once you've been trained. However, it's not the things you need. More than anything you need an understanding of the animal. An appreciation that each one is different and special in its own way. Much like people. Only people are harder to understand."

After she had spent time tracing her fingers over the tack, he asked, "What is it that you like to do?"

She flushed and shook her head. "I'm not gifted in anything."

He waited with his arms crossed over his chest and shook his head. "Somehow I don't believe you. Is it drawing?"

Her head jerked up at the question.

"You were drawing in the dirt the day we met."

"I was bored."

He frowned. "Seems to me you wouldn't care that your stick got destroyed if you didn't care much about drawing."

"It'll never amount to much, so why does it matter?" she whispered.

He rested his hand on her shoulder. "It's important to you, so it matters."

Cailean called out, "She's here!"

Bears dropped his hand from his daughter's shoulder and faced the doorway. "Hi, Cailean," Bears said, stepping outside the tack room. "Mildred is getting settled in."

"I'd rest if I were you, Mildred, for there will be a grand celebration tonight," Cailean said with a broad smile as he stared at the girl who hid herself halfway behind Bears. "I'm Cailean. The eldest and wisest MacKinnon." At Bears's snort at the proclamation, Cailean gave Bears a belt on his chest. "The women baked extra today, so come hungry. At around six." He entered the small office, and his whistling could be heard.

"What does he do in there?" she asked as she peered into the cluttered room.

"Paperwork. How the man can whistle while doing paperwork is beyond me." Bears smiled as she giggled, and hope again bloomed in his chest that she would soon accept him as her father.

M ildred tugged on her ill-fitting dress as she walked beside her father to the large house beside the livery. Loud voices and laughter could be heard inside, and delicious aromas wafted from the open windows. She followed him up the steps and hid behind him as he opened the door.

"She's here!" someone proclaimed, and the chattering momentarily ceased as the focus shifted to the kitchen door.

A plump elderly woman with a broad smile and kind eyes approached. "Oh, if you aren't the spitting image of your father, dear. I'm Irene, and I run the café with my rascal of a husband, Harold. Any day you need a chat or a treat, you come to my café. You'll always be welcome." She looked over her shoulder to the wiry man behind her. "This is my husband, Harold. He'll try to sweet-talk you into thinking he's your favorite grandparent. Never forget. *I* am." She winked at Mildred as she and Harold gave way to the wave of MacKinnons.

Mildred smiled at Ewan and Cailean, who she had met earlier in the day, and eased out from behind her father.

Cailean had an arm around an attractive woman with black hair. "This is my wife, Annabelle." He nodded across the room. "And that's our daughter, Skye, being spoiled by her aunt Jessamine, Ewan's wife."

Mildred nodded and then stared at Alistair with wide eyes as he swooped down to give her a hug.

"Aye, ye're very welcome here, an' I ken my Hortence is lookin' forward to havin' an older cousin to play with." He had a hand on the shoulder of a red-haired girl who looked to be a little younger than Mildred and who eyed Mildred with blatant curiosity. "This is my wife, your aunt Leticia, and another cousin, Angus." He winked at Mildred and backed away.

The front door burst open with a clatter, and a plump woman with red-brown hair burst inside. Although barely five feet tall, Sorcha Tompkins had a commanding presence and pushed her way through her brothers. "Oh, look at ye! Are ye no' beautiful?" Sorcha said as she ignored Mildred's reticence and tugged her into her arms. After a moment, she held her at arm's length again. "'Twas as I feared. There are always dismal clothes at an orphanage."

Mildred blushed and ducked her head as she fought tears.

"Sorcha," Bears rasped in a warning voice.

Sorcha ignored Bears. "I've made ye a few dresses, wee Mildred. Will ye come with me to try them on?" She smiled at Mildred and then at Bears. Meanwhile the girl stared at Sorcha with wonder. As they walked out of the kitchen, Sorcha said, "That man who is as kind as he is handsome is my husband, Frederick." She beamed at the tall cowboy standing in one corner, talking to Ewan. His eyes sparkled as he watched his wife.

Mildred frowned.

"Dinna fash. Ye'll ken who we are soon enough." She led Mildred upstairs to a vacant bedroom, where three dresses were laid out on a bed. One was light-blue calico, another green, and the third pink. "Frederick placed these here when I made a scene to meet ye." She paused and studied the dresses and then Mildred. "I dinna ken yer measurements, so I guessed off of Hortence. They will no' fit ye perfectly, but they will be a better fit than what ye are wearing."

When Mildred frowned again, Sorcha said, "Ye dinna ken her yet, but Hortence is now yer cousin, an' she'll be a great friend. She's Alistair's girl by marriage, but he could no' love her any more were he her real father, ye ken?" She chattered as she helped Mildred strip off her old dress and pull on a new one. "Aye, much better."

Sorcha held up a mirror, and Mildred gasped. "I look like a

princess." Mildred fingered the soft fabric and shook her head in wonder.

"Aye, an' ye do. I can make adjustments, but it should do for tonight."

Mildred spun and giggled with joy. "Thank you, Aunt Sorcha!" She threw herself into Sorcha's arms and froze.

Sorcha held her close, until Mildred relaxed in her embrace. "Aye, ye wee precious girl. Ye will ken hugs. Ye will ken love. An' ye'll ken strife too because we MacKinnons enjoy a good argument, aye?" She met Mildred's wide eyes. "But an argument doesna mean ye dinna love a person. Remember that. Sometimes ye need to bellyache."

"My belly aches sometimes," Mildred said.

Sorcha laughed. "Aye, so does mine. But I meant that sometimes ye need to complain an' blather on about it for a while." She saw when Mildred understood. "Come. Enjoy the party in this dress, and I'll visit tomorrow to make any needed adjustments."

"Are you a seamstress?" Mildred asked as she walked with Sorcha downstairs.

"I sew only for my friends, ye ken? An' I sew well, but I love to spin yarn and knit. Working with wool is my great joy." She stepped back, so Mildred entered the kitchen alone.

"Look at ye!" Ewan proclaimed with a broad smile.

Mildred blushed, and her gaze met her father's. He smiled with pride, although he remained silent. "Aunt Sorcha made me three dresses," Mildred said.

"How is she already an aunt, an' she's kent ye less than I have?" Ewan teased.

Mildred giggled and shrugged.

Soon Warren arrived with his wife, Helen, the town's midwife. Mildred ran to him and twirled in her new dress. "It's beautiful," Warren said. "But you didn't need new clothes to shine, Mildred."

Helen nodded her agreement. "I couldn't have said that any better. I'm so happy to meet you, Mildred."

Mildred stood near Helen and Warren, watching as platters of food were placed on the table and counters.

44

Annabelle looked to Helen and frowned. "You look tired, Helen. Have you had difficult cases recently?"

Helen shook her head. After a moment, the other conversations in the room quieted. "I'm tired because I was attending Leena." She met their concerned gazes. "She caught a fever after the birth of Mette. Leena is weak, but I think she will be fine."

"Oh, how terrible," Annabelle said as she reached out a hand for Cailean. "We must visit them soon." She snuggled into her husband's embrace a moment, and Mildred watched as each couple did the same.

"Karl must have been out of his mind with worry," Cailean said, holding Annabelle close. "Why didn't he ask us for help?"

Helen shook her head. "He thought she was tired from the birth. It was fortunate I had planned a visit to check on her and the baby. If I hadn't ..." She looked at Sorcha, who cradled her belly and leaned into Frederick.

"We all ken there's risk with any childbirth," Sorcha murmured. "But, aye, we must visit them soon and make sure they have plenty of food."

After a few moments, the conversation shifted, and Mildred looked to her father. Rather than watching her, he tracked the reactions and movements of an attractive chestnut-haired woman as she worked in the kitchen. "Who's that?" Mildred whispered to Helen.

"Fidelia. Annabelle's sister. I'm surprised she didn't make you a dress, for she's the expert seamstress in this town," Helen said.

Mildred looked in Fidelia's direction, but Fidelia never looked toward her. "I think she doesn't like me or my father."

Helen shared a look with Warren. "She's shy, Mildred. Even after all her time among us, she's shy. I think you'll like her, once you get to know her."

Mildred shrugged and focused on the food on the table. "Who eats all this?"

Helen laughed. "We do. And what we don't eat now, we save for tomorrow in our iceboxes."

"Can I ..." She bit her lip and took a deep breath. "Do you think I could have a little of it?"

Helen froze and then dropped to her knees, so she could better meet Mildred's gaze. "You can eat until your belly aches. And then eat some more tomorrow. No one will ever keep you from eating if you're hungry, Mildred."

Mildred glared at Helen. "Don't lie to me."

Helen sent a frantic gaze in Bears's direction and waved at him to join them. When Bears stood next to her, she murmured, "Mildred believes she has no right to eat any of this food. That it is here to torment her."

Bears pulled out a chair and sat. He waited until Mildred met his gaze and then waited until she eased closer to him. When she stood near his knee, he held out his hand, waiting for her to grip his. When she did after many long minutes, he nodded. "Have I lied to you, Mildred?" She shook her head. "Have I treated you like Mrs. Marday?" Another shake of her head. "Are the MacKinnons and our friends mean?" She shook her head, and a tear coursed down her cheek. "Then why would you think we'd deny you supper?"

She took a gulping gasp of air and blurted out, "I always had to eat last. Me and the other girls who were mixed blood. There was never enough food, so we always went hungry." She lowered her head in shame.

Bears tugged her close, so she stood between his legs as he hugged her. "You'll never be denied food, little one. I promised to care for you, and I will."

"I ... They will think me a baby for crying," she whispered as she clung to him.

"No, they understand you suffered at that orphanage, as no child should." He eased her away. "Come. The food is cooling, and fried chicken should always be eaten when warm."

"Wee Mildred, the first plate's for ye, as ye are the guest of honor!" Ewan called out with a bright smile and another wink for her. He stood near the counter with a plate and motioned for her. "Ye tell me what ye want, an' I'll fill up yer plate, so ye dinna have to fash about droppin' it."

She rubbed at her cheeks and looked to Bears, who gave her an encouraging smile. "Thank you," she whispered to him and then scampered away to join Ewan.

~

Mildred escaped to the back porch after dessert. She took a deep breath and stared at the stars, as she listened to the adults chatter. She rubbed at her belly and wondered if she could sneak inside and get another piece of cake or if she would have her hand slapped. She hoped she wouldn't, but some fears were hard to let go of. When the door opened, she tried to hide in the corner but gave a huff of frustration as the other young girl in attendance appeared.

"I'm so glad you've joined our family," Hortence said with a wide smile. "I have young cousins, and Bears is wonderful, but now I have a cousin my own age!" She gave a little jump for joy. "We'll be best friends, and school will be so much fun."

Mildred watched her in fascination. "Do you like school?"

Hortence shrugged. "It's all right. I like learning, and my favorite class is reading. Or writing. Or history." She shrugged. "I guess I like all of it. But the teacher never controls the students, and the boys are always misbehaving. Last year they filled the girls' outhouse with toads."

Mildred raised her eyebrows in horror. "What did you do?"

"I ran to Uncle Cailean's house and used his outhouse. But the other girls cried and didn't know what to do. Fathers had to be called from work, and we had special dispensation"—she smiled widely at saying such a large word—"to use the church's outhouse. It took over a week to rid the school's outhouse of all the toads."

"Why?"

"I think the boys snuck in each morning with a new supply," Hortence said. "I saw one of them with reddened knuckles one day, and it wasn't from the schoolteacher, and the appearance of the toads ceased."

Mildred giggled. "I never had a friend at school."

Hortence frowned. "Why not? I know you'll be so much fun! And you'll probably tell the best stories, like your father."

Mildred shook her head. "I don't tell stories. I've always known I'm supposed to be quiet and to not be noticed."

Her new friend frowned even harder. "That makes no sense. And I'd have no luck with that." She fingered her red hair. "How am I supposed to be invisible with hair that looks like this?"

"It's beautiful," Mildred breathed. "I wish I had hair that wasn't black and straight as a pin."

Hortence reached out and touched a strand of Mildred's loose hair. "No, this is beautiful. My mother always said how it's funny the way we want what the other person has. We have to learn to be thankful for what we do have." She gave a nonchalant shrug.

"What are you thankful for?"

"My family. My mother and I lived a long time alone, and now I have a father and a brother and my uncles and aunts. It's more than I ever hoped we'd have, way back when we sat in church, listening to the pastor go on and on about not wishing for too much." She shrugged again. "If I have to live with the devil's mark, I will."

"The devil's mark?" Mildred asked in outrage. When Hortence fingered her hair, Mildred shook her head. "Well, I don't believe that red hair has anything to do with the devil, and I'll be proud to be your friend."

Hortence gave a small *whoop*. "And you have Bears as your father. You have so much to be thankful for."

Mildred shrugged. "For as long as he wants me. I doubt I'll be here that long."

Her new friend frowned. "Bears will always want you. You're his daughter. He'd never cast you aside."

Mildred shrugged again and then asked, "Do you think we could sneak another piece of cake?"

Hortence smiled widely. "If you ask, we will. You're the reason we're having a party, and they shouldn't deny you what you want. Not tonight. Be sure to insist that your best friend have a piece too."

Mildred laughed, and they reentered the house, their friendship solidified over a huge slab of cake.

~

In early September, nearly a week after the welcoming party, Fidelia knocked on the door to Bears's simple home and waited. After a long moment, she turned to leave.

"Wait!" Mildred called out. "I wasn't sure if I should answer, but I know you're friends with the MacKinnons."

Fidelia nodded. "Yes, I am. I'm also friends with your father. A few nights ago, everyone was busy giving you welcoming gifts. I wanted to wait a few days before giving you mine." She held up the basket in her arms and flushed. "I'm Fidelia."

"I'm Mildred. Helen told me that you're Annabelle's sister. Hortence is my best friend." She spoke with the assurance of a girl who knew her place in the world. However, when Fidelia looked deeply into the girl's eyes, the old insecurities and doubts remained.

"You are very fortunate. Hortence is a wonderful girl. And her mother is too." Fidelia looked at the door. "Might I come inside?"

Mildred nodded, and Fidelia followed her into the simple cabin. She smiled as she saw the addition to the back. "Ewan is always generous."

"That's my room." Mildred's exuberance faded. "For now."

Fidelia frowned. "Do you have any reason to believe you are going somewhere? You just arrived."

Mildred shrugged. "What if he gets tired of me?" Her gaze filled with dread. "What if he dies, like my mother? I'd have to go back."

Fidelia set her basket on the floor and knelt before Mildred. "None of us would allow that, Mildred. You're one of us now."

"I keep thinking this is a dream," she whispered.

"That means it's real and it's good. I've felt like I've been in a dream for a while now too." She smiled at Mildred. "But I can't explain why."

"Will you call me Millie? I hate Mildred."

Fidelia nodded. "I will, if you help me with my latest project." She extracted two samples of fabric. One in green velvet and the other in a plusher red velvet.

"Oh," Mildred sighed, her fingers caressing the fabric.

"I can't decide which is prettier, Millie."

Mildred scrunched up her face and then pointed to her choice. "The red. It has a hidden pattern in it, and it's softer."

Fidelia smiled. "Excellent. I'll order enough for a dress for you. Every girl should have a special dress for the holidays, and Christmas will be here before you know it."

Mildred gaped at her. "For me? You want to make me a dress?"

Fidelia nodded. "Of course. If there's one thing I do well, it's make clothes. Or tat lace." She smiled. "I'd be honored to make you a dress."

"But I've never celebrated Christmas. Why would I need a dress?"

Fidelia sobered as she stared at Bears's daughter. "You'll celebrate this year. The MacKinnons find every reason they can to celebrate, and Christmas is the largest party of the year."

"Even bigger than the party they threw me?"

Fidelia laughed. "Oh, heavens, yes. At Christmas, everyone gets presents. And there's even more food. And special drinks. And mistletoe and stories and blessings. It's … magical." She smiled at Mildred. "It might seem overwhelming, but, after only two Christmases with them, I can't imagine missing one."

"I don't need a fancy dress," Mildred protested.

Fidelia shook her head. "Say 'thank you,'" she teased. After Mildred parroted her, Fidelia said, "It may be hard to believe you deserve all this, when you've had so little. But you do. Never doubt it."

Fidelia rose. "Come. I must get your measurements, so I know how much to order." She winked mischievously at Mildred. "Hortence will have the green dress this year."

CHAPTER 4

The following Sunday in mid-September, Hortence raced to Mildred's home and knocked on the door, soon answered by Bears. She jumped up and down with excitement as she stared at Bears. "Can she come? Please, can she come?" She beamed at her new friend, peering at her from behind her father.

"Where are you going?" Bears asked with a fond smile, as he watched Hortence's red pigtails fly around with her exuberance.

"Ewan and the ladies of the family are going to visit Leena and Karl. Mildred should come too." Hortence gave a firm nod as though her logic were faultless.

Bears raised a brow and turned to look at his daughter. "Well, Bright Fawn, what would you like?" When she bit her lip and shrugged, he said, "Do you want to spend time in the livery, helping me clean out stalls and rub down horses, or do you want to visit Leena and eat cookies and cake and play all day?" He smiled as she brightened at the second alternative but waited for her to respond.

"I want to eat cookies and cakes and play," she said. She giggled as Hortence let out a *whoop* of delight and pulled her into a hug.

"You girls be careful. And, Bright Fawn," he said, grabbing her hand before she raced away with Hortence, "mind your aunts and your uncle Ewan."

She beamed at him and ran off, hand in hand with Hortence.

The two girls raced to the livery, where Alistair corralled them before they tried to run across the busy main street. "Come here, girls," he said, while he hitched a horse to a large wagon. "Come greet Butter." He squeezed Hortence's shoulder as she scampered to him and held her hand out to the horse. After a moment, she patted its snout.

Alistair held his hand out to Mildred. "Come, Mildred. She's a docile creature and likes to ken ye'll appreciate the work she'll do today." He waited as Mildred sidled up to the horse and held out her hand, mimicking her friend and cousin. After Mildred gave the horse a few pats, Butter grunted with agreement.

"Aye, she'll be contented to drive ye wherever ye want to go now," Alistair said with a wink.

Cailean emerged from the livery. "She'll be contented because she knows there are extra oats for her at the end, don't you, Butter?" he asked in a soft voice as he scratched behind her ears. Cailean looked to the nearby house and smiled at the girls. "Come. Let's help your aunts Annabelle and Fidelia with the treats they've prepared for Leena and Karl."

He led the girls to his house, where Annabelle and Fidelia placed packages of goodies in a few boxes. "What can we do to help?" Cailean asked as he kissed Annabelle on her cheek.

"Oh, love, thank you," she said, leaning into his embrace. "Carry out the heavy box, and perhaps the girls could carry the smaller ones?" She smiled at them. "I never thought to be so lucky to have so many helpers!"

Hortence and Mildred raced to their small boxes, poking their heads over the sides to see what they carried. "Cookies," Hortence whispered as she breathed deeply of the sweet fragrance.

"Bread," Mildred said in a reverent voice with her eyes closed. "I love bread."

"Come along, girls. Let's load the wagon, and then we'll settle everyone in for the short ride to Leena and Karl's," Cailean said.

Soon the wagon was ready and was loaded with MacKinnon women. A pregnant Leticia sat next to Ewan and Jessamine in front, while Annabelle and Fidelia sat in the back with Hortence and Mildred. Skye crawled around the floor, giggling as the swaying motion of the wagon foiled her every attempt at walking.

A gentle sun warmed them, and a soothing breeze blew as they left the livery. Wagons surrounded the church after the morning service. Children ran around the school playground after the long Sunday service. Their mothers chatted as they called out to prevent squabbles, while their husbands stood in small groups discussing farming, mining, or the hope that Montana would soon be a state. Many other parishioners ventured into town to make weekly purchases at the two town mercantiles or to stop into the café for a meal and a gossip session with Harold Tompkins.

Soon the MacKinnon party was away from town. Birds called to each other from willows lining the nearby creek. Little snow remained on the distant mountain peaks, the granite gleaming in the bright sunlight. The fields were a burnished gold in the bright sunlight.

Mildred and Hortence were quiet as they listened to the adults visit during the short journey. Soon they passed a well-constructed home and a cabin near the sawmill. Ewan pulled the horses to a halt in front of a newly constructed two-story home a short distance away from the mill. The creek ran nearby, and a cleared space behind the home was set aside to be a kitchen garden. A small chicken coop stood near a lean-to barn.

Karl stood on the front porch with a wide grin. "You are most welcome!" he called out. He jogged down the front steps to hitch the horses to the post and to help Leticia and then Jessamine down.

"Where is Leena?" Annabelle called out, waiting for Ewan to unlatch the back of the wagon before she hopped from the wagon. She held her arms out for Skye, who made a small sound of glee before jumping into her mother's arms. "We are so worried about her."

"Leena is inside with Mette and is anxious to see all of you," Karl said. He grinned at Ewan as his friend slapped him on his back. "She is much better, thanks to Helen."

"Congratulations, Karl," Ewan said. "I canna wait to see how yer wee bairn grows."

Karl nodded. "*Ja,* she's almost two months old. She grows every day. You won't recognize her." His eyes held a look of wonder and pride as he talked about his daughter.

"Ye ken ye only have to ask, an' we'll help ye in any way we can?" When Karl nodded, Ewan moved to help cart the boxes of goodies inside.

"Oh, this is a beautiful home," Jessamine said as she looked at the large living area and kitchen. Stairs led to the bedrooms upstairs.

"No reason to sound surprised, love," Ewan teased his wife with a wink. "My men an' I built it."

She gripped his arm. "I know. It amazes me how talented you are." She wrapped an arm around his waist to pull him close a moment.

Hortence and Mildred stood to the back of the crowd of adults, as Leena emerged from the shadows at the back of the room with baby Mette in her arms.

"Leena!" Annabelle exclaimed as she rushed toward her friend and bakery partner. "Oh, look at your beautiful daughter." She stroked Mette's head and hugged Leena. "I'm so happy for you."

"*Ja,*" Leena said with a tired smile. "I have never been so full of joy. Or so tired." She flushed as the truthful words slipped out.

"Mette keeps us up much of the night," Karl said, his arm slung around his wife's shoulder to pull her closer.

"Well, you don't have to worry about dinner for a while," Fidelia said. "We've brought plenty of food to fill your icebox."

"Thank you," Leena said as she fought tears and handed Mette to Karl.

Leticia pulled Leena into her arms. "We know what it's like to have a new little one and to have all your focus on him or her."

Fidelia was in the kitchen, putting on a kettle for tea, and Jessamine helped to put away much of what they had brought. "We will celebrate your Mette with a cake," Jessamine said. "Although you should always be thankful Annabelle baked it and not me." Jessamine winked at Hortence, Mildred, and Ewan.

Leena sat at the table, exhausted yet smiling at the two young girls. "Who's your friend, Hortence?"

Hortence gripped Mildred's hand and smiled at Leena. "This is Mildred. She's Bears's daughter."

Leena's smile broadened. "Sorcha wrote me about meeting you," she said. "I'm so glad you could join us and meet Mette."

"And eat cake!" Hortence said. The adults laughed.

Soon Mette was in her cradle, and Nathanial, Leena's brother, had joined them.

Mildred stared at him with wonder. He was one of the tallest men she'd ever seen.

He saw her interest, and he bowed down, so he was at her eye level.

She backed away, bumping into a wall. "I'm sorry," she whispered.

"I'm Nathanial, Mette's uncle," he said with pride. "You must be Bears's daughter, *ja*? He told me all about you, when I visited him at the livery last week." He smiled as her hands reached out to play with his thick blond hair.

"It's a different color than yours," he said, standing to his full height again. "Come. There's cake, and it's never a good idea to miss out on Annabelle's cake."

Mildred followed him to the kitchen area and joined Hortence in handing out pieces of vanilla cake.

"How are things at the bakery?" Leena asked.

"Busy," Annabelle said with a smile. "I close the bakery two days a week now."

Leena cast a furtive glance in the direction of Mette, sleeping peacefully in her crib. "I don't know when I'll return."

Annabelle gripped her friend's fisted hand. "Or if you want to return. I understand. Take as much time as you want. I'll figure some-thing out."

The doorway burst open with an *oof*, heralding Sorcha's arrival. She held a box in her arms and had tripped over the threshold. "I'm no' that big. Why do I have such terrible balance?" she asked the room as she smiled a hello to everyone. Ewan grabbed the box from her and kissed her cheek, and she ran to Leena to pull her into a hug. "Oh, I'm so happy to see ye well! I was terrified when Helen told us how ye'd been taken ill." She looked at her friend and nodded at seeing no sign of illness. "Now, where's the wee bairn?"

"She was sleeping before you barreled into the room," Jessamine said. She giggled along with Hortence and Mildred.

Sorcha laughed. "I've lost any grace I had with this pregnancy." She looked to the door at her husband, as he entered carrying a larger box. "I'm thankful Frederick doesna mind."

He shook his head and muttered, "Never."

Soon the men had wandered outside to help Karl with chores, like chopping wood and mucking out the barn. Nathanial smiled his appreciation, since he'd been doing all the chores and running the sawmill while Karl spent time with Mette and Leena.

"How are ye, Karl?" Ewan asked, when they were out of earshot.

"Better," Karl said, although his hands trembled. He set aside the ax, his hands too unsteady to chop wood. "My ignorance almost cost me my Leena."

Frederick shook his head. "No, you would have run for Helen or the doc the instant you knew she was sick. You would never have allowed her to worsen."

Karl ran a hand through his blond hair and sighed. "You don't know what it's like to be helpless as you watch the woman you love struggle." He cringed. "Hearing her cries when she birthed Mette was terrible enough." His terrified gaze met theirs. "What's a man to do?"

Ewan gripped his shoulder. "What ye are already doin', man. Ye support her an' show her how much ye love her."

Frederick took the ax from Karl and slammed it down in quick succession as he split wood.

"Frederick?" Ewan asked, studying his brother-in-law.

Frederick panted, pausing in his exertion. "Sorcha won't listen to me, but I don't want her giving birth on the ranch. I want her in town."

Karl nodded. "*Ja*, I understand. You still have time to convince her."

Ewan snorted. "Tryin' to convince Sorcha of anythin' is no' easy." He looked at his brother-in-law. "Would your brothers remain here for the winter and run the ranch?"

Frederick rolled his eyes and shook his head, rubbing at the sweat on his brow. "No, they desire the adventure. If they can bring one more herd north from Texas next spring, they don't want to miss that opportunity."

Karl looked at Frederick. "I would have lost my business if I hadn't had Nathanial. Who would run the ranch? Your grandfather?"

Frederick shook his head, a small smile spreading as he thought about his grandfather, Harold Tompkins. "No, but Slims could easily run the ranch, especially in the winter."

Ewan gave a grunt of agreement. "Aye, an' he loves yer horses as much as ye do."

Karl looked relieved. "Convince your wife, Frederick. Hopefully she'll want to soothe your concerns as you do hers."

Fidelia looked out the window, watching as Hortence and Mildred raced to play in the road. They drew in the dirt and then hopped around.

Leena peered out the window and smiled. "You are coming to care for her," Leena said as she watched her friend.

Fidelia blushed. "She's a good girl, and she suffered at the orphanage." She looked up to see all the women watching her. "We all want her safe."

Jessamine nodded. "Yes, but we don't imagine her our daughter."

Fidelia became beet red, and she bowed her head. "I will never be a mother."

Jessamine frowned, while Sorcha gave a grunt of disapproval. "*Never*'s a long time, aye?" She sat with a *thud* as she held a hand to her burgeoning belly. "An' ye ken we'd all be delighted for ye." She looked at Leticia and frowned. Leticia was due earlier than Sorcha was but maintained more grace with her pregnancy.

Fidelia shook her head and focused on Leena. "How are you, Leena?"

Leena shrugged. "Weaker than I'd like to be but getting stronger each day." She looked at her friends. "Thank you for all the food. Karl has tried to cook but …" She bit her lip before saying anything more.

"I can't tell you how delighted I am to see you doing well. To see how happy you and Karl are together," Annabelle said. "This sort of illness takes time to recover from. I know."

The women sobered as they remembered the two times Annabelle had almost died when she had miscarried.

After a long moment of silence, Jessamine pasted on a smile. "Now tell us how you decided to name her Mette."

Leena brightened. "My mother is Mette. We wanted to honor her." She looked at her friends. "She always treated Karl well and loved him like a son. She never thought of him as lacking because he is an orphan."

"Oh my," Fidelia breathed. "How fortunate he was to meet your family."

Leena beamed at them. "How fortunate was it that our neighbors adopted him, you mean. I can't imagine my life without him."

Annabelle hugged Leena. "I know you had trouble in your marriage last year, and I'm delighted you're past it."

Leena's smile broadened. "We are. We are happier than I ever knew we could be." Her eyes filled. "I've never seen him so desperate as when he thought I might die from my fever." She swiped at her cheek. "I realized I don't want to imagine living without him."

Sorcha stared at her as though dumbstruck. "Aye, ye'd do for him what he did for ye," she whispered.

Leena stared at her in confusion.

"Sorcha?" Fidelia asked. "What bothers you?"

Sorcha rubbed at her stomach. "I ken I have months until I have my bairn, but I'm already terrified. Of the pain. Of the chance I might not survive."

Leticia shared a look with her, running a hand over her pregnant belly.

Sorcha smiled as they remained silent and didn't attempt to soothe her concerns with the usual platitudes. "I realized I was bein' unfair to Frederick."

"How?" Annabelle asked as she squeezed Sorcha's shoulder.

"He wants me to move into town afore winter arrives. To birth the baby near Helen or the doc. Near family." Sorcha rubbed at her belly.

"Why don't you want the same?" Leticia asked in a soft voice. "I can't imagine not having the family nearby and Helen so far away." Her gaze became distant, as though remembering Angus's birth or envisioning this next baby's birth.

"I love the ranch, aye? The thought of bein' in town for weeks or months is almost more than I can bear." Sorcha closed her eyes. "The gossiping and curiosity about things that are no' anyone else's business."

Annabelle held Sorcha's hand. "I fear you may have to accept that, Sorcha. Allow Frederick to care for you in this way. He can do so little as you give birth. Grant him some sense that he has done everything possible to protect you and your baby."

Fidelia met Sorcha's uncertain gaze. "If something happened on the ranch, Frederick would live with that guilt forever."

Sorcha nodded. "Aye, I ken ye're right. I already kent I'd have to move into town, but I'd hoped ye'd have reasons I could stay on the ranch." She shook her head. "Remainin' on the ranch would be selfish, an' I canna deny Frederick what he needs." She nodded to her friends. "Livin' in town will bring him a sense of peace."

Annabelle winked at her. "Yes, and you'll have all of us to cook for you. It could be worse."

The women laughed and began to tidy the kitchen, before leaving to return to town.

~

The following week, Harold Tompkins wandered over to the livery. He shared the running of the Sunflower Café with his wife, Irene, and he enjoyed the few moments he could escape the gossiping and the dishes. Well, the dishes. He thrived on the gossip and in being in the know about the goings-on in town. As he entered the livery, he saw Bears exiting the paddock with his horse, Brutus.

Brutus walked placidly beside Bears, until he caught sight of Harold. When the horse saw Harold, he reared, pawing at the air with his hooves. Bears motioned for Harold to back away, and he moved to a corner of the barn that was deep in shadows. Bears gave a few harsh commands, yanked on the bridle, and calmed Brutus enough to ease him into a stall. Once inside, Brutus gave a good kick to the stall door and then whinnied, before calming to eat his oats.

"Damn horse. Don't know why I don't send him east to be made into glue," Harold muttered.

"It's because Brutus knows he has such a future at your hands that he reacts as he does when he sees you," Bears said. He swiped at his forehead. "I've been working with him for over a year. I'm making little headway. I don't know what you want me to do. You're spending a fortune in boarding fees and for me to continue in my attempts to train him."

Harold frowned. "He hasn't attacked you again, has he?"

Bears shook his head. "No, and he's accustoming himself to fewer carrots. Although he's not happy." He nodded to the stall. "Ewan worked on that stall to reinforce the door and walls so he can kick out and not bust through."

"Damn horse. Don't know why we bother with it." Harold rubbed at his head. "Well, give him another few months. He might have some redeeming quality."

Bears laughed. "If we haven't found it yet, I doubt we will." He motioned for Harold to follow him to the paddock and the water pump. Bears shucked his shirt and dunked his head under the water. "Ah, heaven on such a hot day." A towel always hung on the peg by the pump, and he dried off quickly before donning his shirt again and hanging the towel to dry. "What brings you by?"

"Well, I wanted to see how you got on with Brutus. And I saw your daughter today with young Hortence. They seem as thick as thieves."

Bears smiled as he thought about his daughter. "They are. I should have realized they'd become such good friends, but I hadn't allowed myself to hope that Hortence was as generous in spirit as her parents."

Harold gave a grunt of displeasure. "You've lived with the notion that you must live alone for too long. First because your father was a trapper and never came to town. Then because that woman didn't have the sense that God gave a goose and left with Bertrand. However, now you have the chance for a family. With more than just Mildred." He stared at him pointedly.

Bears shook his head. "I ... How would I court a woman now? All of my waking energy is for my daughter or my work."

Harold shook his head again. "You find a way. You show that woman of yours that you still want her just as much now as you did before you realized you had a daughter. Otherwise, you make her feel like all you were interested in was a brood mare or for her to be Mildred's caretaker."

Bears shook his head. "Of course not!"

Harold gave a quick nod. "You and I know that, but some women get odd notions in their heads. Just as your daughter does." He saw Bears frown and said, "Now I shouldn't eavesdrop. But how else would I learn what I want?" He shrugged in an unrepentant manner. "I listened in to some of the conversations those young'uns were having when they were decidin' if they would be friends or not the night of Mildred's welcoming party."

"You mean Bright Fawn and Hortence?" Bears flushed as he'd never used his name for Mildred with Harold before.

"*Bright Fawn*," Harold mused. "Yes, that's a good name for her. I shudder to think what you'd name me." He waved his hand and continued. "When they were on the back porch, forging their friend-ship, your daughter made it known that she didn't think you'd want her here very long."

Bears frowned. "She says that frequently. I don't know what to do to reassure her."

"You keep doin' what you're doin'," Harold said. "Be steady and constant in your love—somethin' you've never had trouble with—and she'll see that you'll always be there for her."

Bears kicked at a dry piece of horse dung. "I hate that she doubts. That she still has fears."

"She's been here a few weeks. She'll have fears and doubts for some time. But they'll lessen as she learns that her place in this world isn't quite as tenuous as she's always believed." Harold paused. "Now don't forget about the other woman in your life. She's as skittish as your daughter, and I'd hate to think you're still circling around each other when you're eighty." He slapped Bears on his back and then sauntered away.

Fidelia punched at her pillow, sleep eluding her again. She stared longingly at the bedside table, before glaring at it as she remembered that laudanum and other sleeping tonics had been forbidden. Her sister, Annabelle, did not want Fidelia addicted to them. The quiet sounds of the night were interrupted by a soft giggle and then the stifled sounds of lovemaking. Fidelia curled onto her side and attempted to ignore the muffled noises coming from her sister's room kitty-corner to hers. More than that, she attempted to battle the envy snaking through her.

She pulled a pillow over her head, admitting to herself how ridiculous she was being, considering she had been one of the most sought-after whores at the town's whorehouse, called Betty's Boudoir. However, the difference between the sounds of lovemaking and a business transaction evoked memories Fidelia had tried to bury. After a moment, she threw back the covers, tugged on a dress, and pulled on a pair of boots.

She tiptoed down the stairs, missing the two creaky steps, and grabbed her long coat from a peg by the front door. She slipped out the rear kitchen door, shivering at the cool evening air, and rushed to the livery. The barn door slid open soundlessly, and she was welcomed by warm, humid air and the sounds of horses snuffling. She moved to a stall, where the friendliest horse stood, and held out her hand.

"There you are," she murmured. "I should have stolen a carrot for you. Instead, how about I steal you away and we escape? Wouldn't you like that?" She smiled as the horse chuffed out a breath, while Fidelia scratched behind one ear, leaning into her caress.

"I doubt Annabelle or Alistair would be happy. No man wants his horse stolen from him."

She jolted at the deep raspy voice and spun to face the man standing in the shadows. He was naked from the waist up, and his long black hair hung loose around his shoulders.

"Bears," she stammered. "I didn't know you'd be here."

He took a step toward her. When he saw her tense at his approach, he stilled his motions. "I had trouble sleeping tonight. My daughter is spending the night at Hortence's, and my house was too empty. Thought I'd work in the tack room to clear my thoughts and then decided to sleep on the cot here. When I heard the door open in the middle of the night, I got up." He moved into a shaft of light, coming from the lamp in the tack room. His brown eyes appeared black now.

"I'll leave you to your sleep," she whispered.

"Stay. Brindle likes company."

"What about you?" she whispered. When he raised an eyebrow, she asked, "Do you like company?"

He stilled and watched her intently. "What bothers you, Stitch?"

She sniffled. "Is that all I am to you? The woman who sews clothes for your daughter?" When she saw his confusion, she shook her head. "Didn't Mildred tell you that I'm making her a holiday dress in red velvet?"

He shook his head. "We don't talk as much as I'd like."

Fidelia stroked a hand down his arm. She flushed when she realized what she'd instinctively done and moved to back away from him.

"No, don't go," he murmured as he reached out to hold on to her hand. "Stay with me a while."

"It's scandalous. I should know better." Her gaze met his.

"Who's to know? The horses won't tell." He smiled. "Besides, when was talking with a man scandalous?"

"When you're me." She flushed at the bitterness in her voice.

He nodded but didn't let go of her hand. "Thank you for being good to my daughter."

"I wanted her to have a welcome gift. I never expected Sorcha to have made her three dresses and the quilt."

Bears shrugged. "Frederick says she's nervous about the baby and needs something to occupy her time."

"And her mind," Fidelia said. "Be patient with Millie. She's fearful and uncertain of her place, no matter how confident she acts."

Bears nodded and took a deep breath. "I will be." He paused and studied Fidelia a long minute. "Why are you filled with desperate energy, Stitch?" He shook his head. "And, no, that's not all you are to me."

She tugged on her hand and backed up a step. "I'm sorry. I shouldn't have come out here tonight. Intruded ..."

He watched her with patient tenderness. "I'll always hope you visit. You never intrude." He waited until she met his gaze. "You are always welcome. But I will not be coerced into acting like the men you've known. I will not have what we have"—he waved at the space between them—"spoiled because of an impetuous, emotion-filled action that you'll regret."

He frowned as her eyes filled. "Never doubt how I want you, Fidelia." He met her startled gaze. "But I will not act until you want me as much as I want you."

"Be patient," she whispered. When he nodded, she leaned forward to kiss his cheek and then raced from the barn.

The next afternoon, Fidelia exited the rear door of the bakery and stopped short to see the Madam waiting for her. Fidelia straightened her shoulders and stood tall as she met the Madam's mocking stare.

"Look at you. In clothes barely fit for a rag woman," the Madam chided. "When I think of the fine clothes, the satins and silks you wore …" She sighed and shook her head. "Such a waste so see a beautiful woman lowered to such a level."

Fidelia glared at her and took a step forward. The Madam matched her movement, and there was no way past her unless Fidelia pushed by or thrust the Madam to the ground. "And what level is that? That of a decent woman, working to earn her living?"

The Madam scoffed. "No matter how many times you tell yourself that tale, you aren't a decent woman, and you never will be." She watched Fidelia with a cunning understanding in her gaze. "Do you think the half-breed wants you for anything other than a mother to his daughter? That he will treat you any better than the men at the Boudoir?" She smiled as she detected a flicker of doubt in Fidelia's gaze. "Why is he intent on you now, when he's kept his distance for so long?" She leaned forward. "Why would you ever think that he'd be different from any other man?"

"How do you know anything about my private life?" Fidelia demanded in a raspy voice.

The Madam glared at her. "Since you were stolen from me, I've made it my business to know what goes on in your life."

Fidelia flushed, and her hands clenched into fists. "I wasn't stolen. I'm not an object that is owned."

The Madam snorted. "That's where you're wrong. I owned you, Charity. From the minute you accepted your first meal from me in Albany, you were mine." Her gaze blazed with anger. "And you're a fool if you don't understand any man you're with will own you too. Women are simply pawns in this world."

Fidelia shook her head. "In your world, Madam. In your world they are pawns. Not in mine. Not anymore." She took a deep breath and pushed past the Madam, wrenching her arm free as the Madam attempted to hold on to her.

Rather than return home and face her sister's inquisitiveness, she turned and walked up the back steps to the café. "Irene?" she called out.

Irene sat at the kitchen table, resting between the lunch and dinner rush. "Why, Fidelia, I didn't expect to see you when you're not delivering a basket of treats." Her gaze sharpened as she noted the tension thrumming through the younger woman. "Sit. There's nothing a good chat and a cup of coffee won't fix."

After they were both seated with mugs of coffee before them, Irene sat in silence. She had already shooed Harold out of the kitchen. The wall clock ticked the passing minutes, but Irene remained patient.

"I saw the Madam today," Fidelia blurted out. She flushed as Irene raised an eyebrow.

"I imagine that was … unexpected." Irene frowned as Fidelia fidgeted. "What bothers you about seeing her, Fidelia?" When Fidelia shrugged, Irene murmured, "Surely you don't miss your old life?"

"Never!" Fidelia exclaimed. "I never want to work there again." She met Irene's gaze. "I give thanks, every day, that Ewan won that poker match. That Annabelle still wanted me as a sister. That she was stubborn enough to help free me from laudanum." Her eyes filled. "I'd be dead now if I were still there."

"Or wishing you were," Irene murmured. After a moment, she asked, "Then what is it? For you can't believe any of the lies the Madam tells you. She's in financial difficulties again and dreams of your return to ease them."

"No. I won't go back." She shuddered. "I don't care if I die starving on the streets this time. I won't do that ever again." She flushed as Irene looked at her with compassion and understanding. "I try not to listen to what she says, but it's difficult."

Irene sat back in quiet contemplation a moment. "If I were the Madam, I'd try to convince you the man interested in you is no better than the men who frequent the Boudoir."

Fidelia gaped at her. "How did you know?"

"Always attack the soft underbelly, when you want to win in a ruthless manner. Never when it's someone you truly love. For then, that can be disastrous to your relationship." Irene took Fidelia's clenched hand and squeezed it. "It's no secret you're as skittish as a virgin on her wedding night around men who aren't related to you. The Madam knows you well. She'll use whatever weapon she has to try to control you."

"The Madam said women are pawns in this world."

Irene gave a *humph* and shrugged. "What did you say?"

"I told her that was true in her world. Not mine." Fidelia let out a deep breath and forced herself to relax. "I hope not in mine."

Irene pointed at herself. "Am I Harold's pawn? Is Annabelle Cailean's? Look to your family, and you will see that the world is not as the Madam would have you believe." Irene frowned. "She wants you to see the world as it was when you were powerless, friendless, and poor. You are not that woman now. For the Madam is not a pawn, and she's a woman."

Fidelia nodded. She closed her eyes and whispered, "I have trouble believing I deserve such a life."

Irene gripped her hand and squeezed it. "Until you believe it, you won't have that life, Fidelia." She smiled tenderly as Fidelia's eyes filled. "But never doubt that I believe you do." She pulled Fidelia close as the young woman sobbed on her shoulder.

Bears sat at his small kitchen table set for two and watched the meal he had prepared for dinner cool and then congeal. He sighed in aggravation that his daughter was as stubborn as he was. Although he'd asked her to be home for dinner, she had disobeyed that request. Again. This was the third night out of five that she had not come home for dinner.

The other evenings, he had waited for her to return home and had spoken to her about his disappointment that he hadn't shared a meal with her. That they had no time to discuss their day's adventures together. Tonight he would find her and drag her home, if he had to. "I've had enough," he muttered. He left the plates on the table and walked out of his cabin past the paddock and into town.

He had a good idea that she was at Alistair MacKinnon's home. Bright Fawn had been spending all her free time with Hortence, and, although Bears was pleased that his daughter had made such a good friend so quickly, he wanted time with her too. He paused as he walked across the main thoroughfare through town, realizing he was storming to Alistair's house in a fit of near rage. He took a calming breath and belatedly remembered what Harold had told him days ago. That Bright Fawn was waiting for the day she'd be sent away.

He shook his head at his own folly. He had been so focused on being a good father and on ensuring Bright Fawn was safe and well fed that he had not realized her small acts of defiance were attempts to see how far she could push him. To see when he would have enough and would send her back to the orphanage.

He took another calming breath and approached Alistair's house with a greater sense of equanimity. He knocked on the door and battled envy when he heard laughter and joy inside. Sounds he'd yet to hear in his own home with his daughter. Alistair opened the door and nodded.

"I kent ye'd come by one of these nights. It did no' seem right ye never wanted to have dinner with yer daughter." He slapped Bears on the shoulder and let him in.

Bears nodded to Leticia, who sat with Angus on her lap, and then he focused on Bright Fawn. Before she realized he was there, her young face was filled with joy and youthful deviltry.

When she saw her father, she paled, and any happiness leeched away.

He frowned. "I had hoped to have dinner with you tonight, Mildred." He hated using her other name, but it was what she preferred with her friend.

"I don't know why it's so important. It's just a meal," she said with a roll of her eyes. She shared a glance with her friend Hortence and then frowned as Hortence seemed taken aback at her comment.

68

Leticia looked at them both. "Would you care to join us, Bears?"

He shook his head. "No, thank you. I would not want to wear out our welcome. I have dinner awaiting us at home. Come, Mildred." Bears held out his hand, and his stare let her know he was uncompromising tonight.

She gave a dramatic sigh and rose. "I'll see you tomorrow, Hortence." She gave her friend a hug and then marched past her father in a huff of anger.

Bears nodded to his friends and then followed his daughter. He caught up to her after a few paces and walked beside her as they made their way home. Along the way, they passed numerous townsfolk, and he stopped and introduced her to every one of them as his daughter.

When they finally arrived home, he motioned for her to sit at the table. "That's our dinner." He tried not to grimace at the unappetizing bowls of cold stew with fat globs congealed on top. He sighed, grabbed the bowls, and dumped them into a pan to rewarm them on the stove. When Mildred stood to go to her room, his sharp tone stopped her movement. "Sit at the table, Bright Fawn."

She spun and glared at him. "I don't have to do what you tell me. Just because you think you are my father, doesn't mean you are."

He shook his head as he looked at her. "Have you seen a mirror? Have you looked at yourself?" He smiled with tenderness when his anger evaporated as quickly as it had appeared. "Even if I were as blond as the man who owns the sawmill, I'd still want you as my daughter. You're strong and intelligent and bold. If you felt safe, I think you'd be fearless."

He watched as tears formed in her eyes.

"I know what you're trying to do." He watched incredulousness fill her gaze. "You're trying to push me so hard that I'll send you back. That you'll be proven correct that you are unlovable." He shook his head. "But you're wrong. For I already love you, little one."

She stood there, trembling at his words. "How can you? I've been horrible."

He walked toward her and ran a hand over her head, smoothing down tendrils of black hair that had come loose from her braid during her day of playing with Hortence. "No, you haven't. You've acted as children do who want to test the strength of their tethers. I understand."

"Will you send me back?"

He sank to his haunches, at her eye level. "Never. Watching you laugh and run wild with Hortence fills me with joy. Seeing how you listen to your aunts and uncles as they tell stories and tease each other makes me realize how much I want you to always be with me. I find joy in you every day, Bright Fawn. I hope you'll never want to be sent back, for my house feels like a home because you are here with me."

She started bawling and threw herself in his arms. "I'll make you proud to have me as a daughter," she mumbled against his shoulder. "I promise."

He held her, his big hands stroking the back of her head. "There's nothing you have to do except be as you are to make me proud, Bright Fawn. One day you'll understand that too."

～

Fidelia entered the larger of the two mercantiles in Bear Grass Springs, called the Merc. Although her family had previously conducted most of their business at the smaller General Store situated near the Stumble-Out Saloon, that proprietor had refused to wait on Sorcha after she had wed Frederick Tompkins, insinuating Sorcha was a woman of ill-repute and that her patronage was not desired. In their rage, the MacKinnons, the Tompkins and all their associated friends had transferred their business to the Merc.

Tobias Sutton owned and ran the Merc. A sullen, bitter man, he had begun to make overtures of friendship to his nephew, Frederick Tompkins, and the MacKinnons in the spring. However, such overtures were rarely extended to Fidelia.

As she pushed open the freshly washed glass door, she paused to inhale the varying scents—soap mixed with camphor, licorice, and almond. Farm and ranch items were to the right, while goods for the home were to the left. Foodstuffs were at the back of the store, as that encouraged customers to peruse the items on display and to encourage further sales. She moved to the small stack of fabric, frowning as nothing new had arrived in recent weeks. "Hello, Mr. Sutton," she said with a businesslike smile. "I hope you can obtain the fabrics I ordered in time."

He moved behind his side of the counter until he stood across from her and watched her closely. "I will. I have no reason to doubt they won't be in on the next few shipments." He glared at her. "I fail to understand why you don't keep to the same hours as those other women."

She flushed and took a deep breath. "I no longer work there, and I am no longer an associate. I can shop whenever I choose. And I have no reason to pay the whore tax because I am not a whore." The town's Improvement Committee had implemented a tax on the Boudoir and its residents, fining the women if they shopped in stores outside of very strict hours during the week. It had become a lucrative way for the town to earn money. However, it was also a way for some towns-folk to continue to show their displeasure at Fidelia's acceptance.

He shook his head. "Just because you don't work there don't mean townsfolk don't remember what you were." He watched her closely. "Especially as it appears you are again seeking the Madam's favor."

Fidelia blanched. "I have never sought out the Madam. Not once since I left the Boudoir. Although I have had the misfortune of speaking with her while walking through town in recent weeks."

"Makes folks wonder what scandalous thing you'll do next. Not all stains can be polished clean."

She thrust her shoulders back and met his challenging stare. "Name one scandalous thing I've done since I left the Boudoir." She smiled as he pursed his lips. "Exactly. I live a boring life. One that I happen to like. If you find it difficult to respect me, perhaps I should have my brother-in-law accompany me when I visit your store next?" Her smile spread as she saw Tobias pale at the thought of Cailean chaperoning her.

"No, that won't be necessary."

She shook her head. "I remain confused why you are keen on their approval now, Mr. Sutton. You've never cared to curry their favor in the past."

He glared at her. "That is none of your affair."

"It is when my family is involved. I'd hate to think you planned any mischief for Sorcha or her husband." She frowned as she saw despair and regret flash through Tobias's gaze before he hid it.

He glowered at her and then looked behind her as the bell on the door rang with the arrival of another customer. She looked over her shoulder and bit back a groan to see the miner, Asa Schuman, who had talked with her outside the bakery last month.

"Miss." He doffed his hat and rubbed a hand over his spit-shined hair. "What a pleasure it is to discover you in this fine establishment."

Fidelia nodded. "Hello, sir. I hope you find what you are looking for. I wish you a good day."

The miner glanced at Tobias and followed Fidelia onto the board-walk. "Miss, allow me to escort you home."

"There is no need, Mr. Schuman," she protested. When he walked beside her, she wrapped her arm closest to him around her waist to ensure he would not attempt to place her hand on his arm. She ignored the curious looks of townsfolk as he walked beside her.

"I've heard quite a bit about the man your family considers partner and friend," Mr. Schuman said.

She bit her lip but then blurted out, "What have you heard?"

"Oh, I have friends all over the state. It seems the man your family is so fond of isn't as honest as he portrays himself to be."

"Bea ... Mr. Renfrew is the most honest man I've met," she said as she frowned at him.

He laughed. "Beggin' your pardon, miss, but I doubt you're the best at judging men." He chuckled and then sobered as he noticed her glowering at him.

"I'd thank you for not criticizing me or my friends, especially when you don't know us." She marched away, gasping as he grabbed her arm and spun her to face him.

"Doesn't it worry any of you folk that he stole that girl? That he has no right to her?" Asa asked. "Don't you wonder how she might be sufferin' living with a savage?"

She wrenched her arm free and took a step away from him. "Never touch me unless I've given you permission to." When she saw that he understood, she spoke in a soft voice, although her gaze flashed with anger and disgust. "You have no idea what Millie suffered at that orphanage, and you have no right to spread such vicious lies. And Bears is not a savage. You are." She spun on her heels and raced for the livery.

"Dee, are ye all right?" Alistair asked, standing at the door to the livery, watching her nearly run home.

"I'm fine." She stopped when Alistair stepped forward and shook his head in concern.

"I ken women often say that when they dinna want to talk about what's botherin' them. I hope ye ken ye can speak with me—or any of the MacKinnons—if ye need to."

A tear trickled down her cheek, and she nodded. "I know. I will." She took a deep breath and smiled at him. "I … I find I can't always outrun my past. And that is difficult for me."

"Ye'll never outrun it, Fidelia. Find yer peace with it, an' then it willna bother ye as much." He smiled gently and turned into the barn.

Fidelia took another deep breath and then entered her sister's home. She climbed the stairs to her room, hiding away from the world as she tatted lace.

CHAPTER 5

A girl's scream brought Bears racing from the tack room. He looked around the livery, his heart freezing at the sight of Brutus's empty stall. He ran outside to find Mildred immobile on her back in the paddock, Brutus rearing and snorting as he stood over her. Bears launched himself over the paddock railing and waved his arms so that Brutus would focus his attention on him, rather than his daughter. Bears grunted as one of Brutus's hooves connected with his shoulder, and he watched as Alistair entered the paddock, holding carrots.

Brutus snorted again but picked up the scent of his favorite treat and dropped his hooves to approach his new quarry. Cailean raced from his house and threw in an apple from outside the paddock, and Brutus paused in his pursuit of Alistair to search out the added treat. "Get her and get out!" Cailean yelled.

Bears was already moving toward his daughter, who lay crumpled on the ground near the edge of the paddock. He lifted her to carry her over one shoulder and grunted at her weight as his injured shoulder ached in protest. After he clambered over the paddock railing, he watched as Alistair threw the carrots at Brutus and left the paddock empty, except for the irate horse.

Bears laid Mildred on the ground, happy to see her breathing, and ran his hands over her in a cursory attempt to search for injuries. "I'm going to kill that horse," Bears growled as his hand came away bloody. He pulled back his daughter's hair, and she had a hoof mark near the back of her head. "She must have turned away to protect herself."

Cailean slapped him on his shoulder. "Get her comfortable. I'll summon the doc or Helen. We'll take care of her." He raced away as Alistair approached.

"What can I do?" Alistair asked.

"Carry her inside," Bears whispered. "Brutus kicked my shoulder."

Alistair nodded and picked up Mildred. "Come, wee one. Ye'll be right as rain soon." He crooned to her as Bears raced ahead to prepare her bed.

Bears grabbed a towel to wrap around her head and another to place on her bed. When Mildred was settled, he stayed by her side, waiting for her to wake up, listening as Alistair lit the stove to boil water. "Oh, my little darling, what were you doing? You promised to stay away from Brutus and to stay out of the paddock." He kissed her forehead and then held her hand, searching for any response from Mildred.

"Let me examine her, Bears," Helen said as she bustled into the room, carrying her small medicine bag. "The doc is away at an accident at a ranch two days' ride from here." She met Bears's terrified gaze with one of cool competence. "I will do all that I can to help her."

"I know you will." He rose, giving Helen room to work. He helped ease his daughter to her side and then waited for Helen's reaction.

"The wound doesn't worry me, although it will need to be cleaned and sewn shut. Because she is unconscious, I worry that she suffered a head trauma."

"You mean, you fear she'll never wake up," Bears said. He took a deep breath. "Or, if she does, she'll be addled."

Helen nodded. "But it's too early to know." She waited until a small pan of water was set on the bedside table, and she washed her hands. She motioned for Alistair to remove it. "Please bring fresh water and whiskey." She touched the slight swelling and frowned. "I think this was a glancing blow. There is little swelling." After taking a deep breath, she sighed. "I fear Mildred will wake up screaming with the first stitch."

Bears nodded. "I'll help hold her down."

Helen worked in methodical silence after that. She cleaned the wound and then began to stitch the wound together. As Helen had expected, at the first stitch, Mildred screamed and bucked against the light hold on her head. Thus Alistair sat on Mildred's legs, while Ewan, who had just arrived, held her shoulders, and Bears kept her head still so Helen could quickly finish her work.

"Why do you hate me so much to treat me like this?" Mildred cried out.

"If you'd kept your promise to stay out of the paddock, you wouldn't need stitches," Bears snapped, his fear and anger at her injury bursting forth in a moment of temper. Alistair made a noise, and Bears raised his eyes to meet his friend's warning gaze. He took a deep breath. "We have to heal you, little one. We have to ensure you have no infection and to close your wound."

"Just let me die," she moaned.

"God, would ye no' think she's related to her aunt Sorcha?" Ewan asked. "I ken Sorcha asked the same thing after she was injured."

Helen made a noncommittal noise as she tied off the last stitch. "There you go, Mildred. I expect you to remain in bed for the next few days and to do as your father tells you, since he will be following my instructions."

Mildred closed her eyes in resignation as tears continued to seep out.

Helen motioned for Bears to follow her to the other room, and Ewan remained with Mildred while Alistair cleaned up the pans. "She will have horrible pain for the next few days, but I do not relish giving her laudanum. She is terribly young for such a medication."

"No laudanum," Bears said. "I'll brew her willow bark tea to help with the pain, and she will improve with time."

Helen nodded and gripped his arm. "I fear these will be trying days for you, Bears. Be patient with her."

Bears waited for his friends to leave, absently agreeing for them to bring him food that evening. He reentered Mildred's room and waited for a few minutes for her to open her eyes. When she continued to feign sleep, he lost patience. "I know you're awake, Mildred."

Her eyes opened, and a tear rolled out. "Why do you use that name?"

"Because, if you truly wanted to be my daughter, you would have kept your promise. You would never have been in a paddock with a horse *I* can barely handle." His eyes were filled with panic and fear as he beheld her. "What were you thinking?"

She swallowed as a tear leaked out. "I broke my promise about the paddock. I'm sorry. I ... I sometimes race through it when it's empty because you spend a lot of time there, and it makes me feel closer to you." She flushed. "I know that sounds foolish."

He frowned and left the room. He returned a moment later with a chair and sat beside her bed. "What happened today?"

"I thought it was empty. I swear! I was climbing over the top, and my dress got stuck, and I had to pull on it." She bit her lip. "I thought you'd be mad that I had ripped one of the new dresses Aunt Sorcha had made for me."

"I don't care, little one. I can mend it for you and teach you how to do it too." He smiled as her eyes widened at his admission. "Yes, I sew. I live alone and don't like to ask for favors. I do many things most men don't like to admit they do." His gaze sobered. "What happened?"

"After I freed myself and hopped into the paddock, I raced across it, as I've seen you do, and that's when I noticed the demon horse was inside it. I tried to get away, but he was so fast. And so angry." She shuddered as tears began to fall. "I thought he would trample me to death."

Bears grabbed her hand and held it to his heart. "*Shh*, little one. You screamed. I heard you and ran the instant I knew you were in trouble. And you are well now. You are safe. Promise me that you will never go into the paddock without me."

"I promise," she whispered.

"Keep it this time."

"I will, Father. I promise." She flushed at having called him *father*.

His eyes filled, and he waited a few moments until he could speak. When he did, his throat was thickened with a deep emotion. "I know you have trouble believing me, but you are my daughter, and I love you. There isn't anything I wouldn't do to protect you, little one. I will want you here always."

She sniffled. "I feel like I'm in a fairy tale. Like I'll wake up and be back at the orphanage with Mrs. Marday telling me how I'm not worthy of love and Becky pinching me. I can't believe this is my life now."

"It's how your life should always have been, Bright Fawn. With me. If I hadn't been so proud, I would have gone after your mother and convinced her to come home with me, and we would have lived as a family. But I can't undo what happened. I can only make right how your life will go from now on."

He saw her fighting sleep and gave her hand a squeeze. "Sleep, my daughter, and know I'll be here if you need me."

Bears waited until she was asleep before he leaned forward and kissed her head. He moved into the main room and stood in place as he battled visions of what could have happened with Brutus. After a moment, he reached to take off his shirt. He grunted as he tried to move his left arm and groaned as he finally slipped his shirt off. His chest and left shoulder were black and blue already, and he knew he'd have trouble moving his arm in the morning.

"What did you do to yourself?" Fidelia asked from the doorway. She held two plates of food and watched him with wide-eyed fascination.

He held his shirt by his side and tried to shrug, but that small movement wrought pain and a groan. "Brutus kicked me as I tried to protect Bright Fawn."

"What did Helen say?" she asked, her gaze roving over his muscular chest before focusing again on the large bruise and swelling.

"Nothing. I didn't ask her."

"Fool," Fidelia snapped. She dropped the plates on the table and spun away.

"Fidelia," he called out and then groaned as he heard her walking away. Although the food smelled delicious, he had no appetite. An overwhelming fatigue assailed him, and he lay on the large bed in the front room. Half-dozing as he tried to remain alert enough in case Bright Fawn called out for him, he jerked as soft hands touched him.

"What are you doing?" he rasped, his voice thickened with sleep.

"If you won't be sensible, I'll have to be," she said. She pulled out an ointment that smelled of lilacs and rubbed it into his shoulder and chest. The mixture eased the deep throbbing ache, and he sighed with relief. After she rubbed at his skin for a few moments, she pulled out a strip of clean cloth and put a chunk of ice in it. She eased him to a sitting position and wrapped it around his shoulder, tying it off to hold it in place over the injured area.

"How did you find ice?" he asked.

"Do you really want to know the answer?" When he stared at her impassively, she sighed. "The icehouse owner used to be one of my best customers. I threatened to tell his wife if he didn't give me ice tonight. *Sell* me ice," she corrected. "I refuse to be indebted to him."

Bears groaned in pleasure as the cold further soothed the ache of his injuries. "I am indebted to you and most grateful."

"There is no reason to believe you owe me anything." She moved to rise, stopping only when he grabbed her hand.

"Stay with me. Only for a little while. It's barely the dinner hour, and it's not scandalous." He smiled at her. "Keep vigil with me, as I worry about my daughter." He frowned as his words caused her eyes to fill with tears.

"Why are you such a good man?" She shook her head in consternation. "Why do you look at me as though you want me?"

"I *do* want you. Not as those men at the Boudoir did." He waited a moment and then said in a low, sure voice, "I want you as a man who has honorable intentions wants a woman. As a man who wants a family with a woman."

She shook her head. "You have a family now, Bears. You don't need me."

His eyes flashed with anger. "I'll always need you. And, if you believe my daughter doesn't need a mother, then you are mistaken. She will have plenty of women who will love and guide her. But they all have their own families. Their own duties. I want to share the joy—and the terror—of loving her with you."

Fidelia took a deep breath. "And if there are no more children?"

He shrugged and then groaned, as he forgot that movement wrought pain. "I will be content because we will have each other. I've been alone long enough. I think you have too."

She watched him with guarded eyes. "Someday soon I will tell you everything."

His eyes flashed with hope at her whispered promise.

"And then you can tell me if you still truly want what you've envisioned with me." She leaned forward and kissed his forehead. "I hope you heal quickly, Bears."

He watched her leave, his gaze filled with yearning.

The following day, Bears's shoulder remained swollen and painful. He tried to use it, but the pain was severe. After Alistair saw him struggling to help Mildred to a sitting position, he brought Helen over.

While Alistair entertained Mildred, Helen examined Bears in the main room of his cabin. "Why didn't you mention this yesterday?" Helen asked as she poked and prodded him. She motioned for him to mimic her movements as she raised and lowered her arms, frowning as he winced and groaned through the motions. However, he could fully move his arms, albeit through intense pain.

"I was focused on my daughter. I didn't want you to spend your time on me." He met her glower. "And I was foolish. Fidelia berated me last night when she came with dinner."

Helen nodded. "You have a chance at recovering well because she got you ice. And that liniment." She sighed. "Although I hate to admit there is little more I can do to aid you. I fear you've damaged tendons inside your shoulder, and there's nothing to be done for it. I will see if

I can find exercises you can do to strengthen your arm and shoulder once the swelling goes down."

She frowned as she considered his injury. "This may sound like the opposite of what I should recommend, but continue to move the arm as much as you can. If you don't, I fear you'll lose the ability to move it completely."

Bears's eyes widened in panic. "I will not be a cripple."

Helen smiled. "No, you never would be one. But keep moving it gently. And I'll see what I can find. I may have to write those friends of Warren's in Pennsylvania. They must think I'm a pest, but there's nothing else I can think to do."

"I would think they'd want to meet a woman as curious as you are about the workings of the human body."

Helen laughed. "Few men are as free in their ideas for women as you, Bears." She squeezed his good arm. "If it gets worse, let me know." She called out her goodbye to Alistair and Mildred and left.

After he had donned his shirt, he reentered Mildred's room. Alistair finished telling her about the Isle of Skye, where he was from, and then departed. He smiled at being called Uncle Alistair.

Bears sat, facing his daughter. "How are you feeling?"

"My head hurts, but I'll be fine. I try not to think about what could have happened." She shuddered and then saw the panic in her father's gaze. "I'm sorry, Father. I know this makes you have less faith in me."

He shook his head, his gaze filled with love. "No, it doesn't. It reminds me that you are young and full of life. I must explain to you the reasons why I ask you to do things. Thankfully you learned this lesson without a terrible and permanent injury. What happened was severe enough." He shared a smile with her. "I disobeyed my father plenty of times too."

"Why didn't Fidelia see if I was all right last night?" she asked.

"I hurt my shoulder yesterday, and she was worried about me." He met her curious stare. "By the time she was done tending to me, you were sound asleep."

"I didn't think she liked you." She flushed when her father grinned. "She ignored you the entire time we were at Aunt Annabelle's for my welcome party, and she came later to the house to see me for measurements when you weren't here."

He smiled tenderly at her. "I am grateful you consider the MacKinnons as your family." He took a deep breath. "As for Fidelia, she has had a hard life and is skittish around men."

Mildred bit her lip and frowned. "But I thought she worked in the house of ill-repute. She should know plenty of men."

"Yes, she did, but not in the way that makes a woman believe men are kind. She was so desperate that she worked there until your uncle Ewan won her freedom. She has since learned that she is valued for more than her beauty." He paused as he watched Mildred think through what he said. "Can you understand why she'd be afraid of being hurt again?" When Mildred nodded, he said, "I don't know all that has happened to her, little one. What I do know is that she has had a hard life."

His daughter frowned as she stared at her father. "Why would you want such a woman?"

"She is resilient, kind, compassionate, and hasn't let life turn her into a bitter woman."

"I worry she is making me clothes because she sees it as a way to make you like her." She frowned as her father burst out laughing.

"No, never worry about that. She already knows the high regard I have for her. Her making you clothes could not change my estimation of her."

"What if she's making me clothes so that I'll like her?" Mildred asked.

"Do you feel like she's trying to manipulate you?"

"No," she whispered. "She seems to like me. She watches me funny sometimes." She shrugged. "Like I'm a gift she can't have."

"You're very astute, little one. I believe she yearns for what I desire, Bright Fawn." He waited until she nodded, as though asking him to answer her question. "She yearns for family. For a sense of truly belonging."

Mildred let out an *oof* of air at his words. "You feel that way too?"

His soft smile was as a caress when he looked at her. "Yes. I've always been seen as different. As not quite worthy because I am not a white man. Or not wholly a white man."

"And she doesn't see you as different?"

He shook his head. "No." He gripped her hand. "It's why I'm willing to be patient. Why I'm hoping she will be a part of our family someday. Why I hope you will see past who she was to who she could be. For you and for me."

"You see me as more than anyone else ever did," Mildred whispered. "Even Mother looked at me as a burden sometimes."

"No, you have never been nor will you ever be a burden. You are my life's greatest blessing, daughter."

~

"How are you tonight?" Fidelia asked in a soft voice from the doorway.

Bears stood at the opening to his daughter's bedroom, watching her as she slept. He closed his eyes as his prayer for Fidelia's presence had been answered. He turned to face her. "I'm well. Mildred improves. She will be fine with little to show for her misadventure except for a scar and a healthy respect for the paddock. I gave her some tea for her pain, and she is sound asleep." He pulled the curtain to cover the doorway, and a soft snore could be heard.

"I heard Helen came to examine you today," Fidelia murmured as she entered his home with two plates of food. He stared at the plates, glancing at the stew bubbling on the stovetop. However, he would not speak against her bringing him food, as it encouraged her to continue to visit him.

"She did, and she said that, because of your common sense and your fine liniment, the damage to my shoulder will be minimal." He met her doubtful stare and sighed. "She admitted there was little more she could do that you hadn't already done and praised your resourcefulness in obtaining ice. She also mentioned she'd contact friends of Warren's in Pennsylvania to see if they had any ideas."

Fidelia frowned. "What is wrong?" Her hands rose of their own will and stroked his injured side in a featherlight touch.

He closed his eyes in pleasure at her caress. "I might have injured ligaments or tendons." He opened his eyes. "But I would have done nothing differently."

"Of course not. You had to protect your daughter." Her eyes filled. "It's such a wonder to see how you care for her."

He shook his head. "I don't understand how that is wondrous. It's how a father cares for his children."

She sniffled and swiped at her damp cheeks. "Perhaps how your father cared for you. Perhaps that is what is normal to you. But that's not what was normal for Annabelle and me. We were more familiar with our father's anger and the back of his hand than his regard."

Bears nodded, as though urging her to continue speaking. His silence eased an ache in her that he would judge her for her father's disregard.

"I was older, and I tried to shield Annabelle. She was young and bright and beautiful." Fidelia shrugged. "And believed in the good of everyone." Her distant gaze focused on Bears. "Look at how she is now, still believing in her friends. In me."

"She has every reason to believe in you, Fidelia." He smiled at her, took a step closer to her.

Her eyes filled with tears, and she gave a subtle shake of her head. "My father ... My father never liked me. He said I was too like my mother. I had too much of an independent spirit and that I had to have it beaten out of me. My mother tried to protect me until she died. But then I only tried to protect Annabelle." She paused and flinched, as though remembering distant scenes.

"What happened?"

"He was a drinker and a dreamer and hated the life he had. It wasn't the life he had envisioned, but he didn't care to do anything to change it so that his life would alter in any measurable way. I had a fine hand at sewing, and Anna was a baker." Fidelia smiled. "Some things never changed."

Bears reached forward and clasped her hand. "What did he do to you?"

She closed her eyes, but she clung to his hand as though it were a lifeline. "He threw me out when he realized I would not remain his pure, innocent daughter forever. He never wanted me to speak to a man, never mind kiss one." She met Bears's patient gaze. "When he discovered I'd done more than kiss Aaron, he beat me and threw me out. He forbid Anna from ever speaking to me. He destroyed my reputation in town so no one would purchase any of my fine linens or have me do work for them. I had no choice but to leave."

"And Aaron?"

"Was not the man I thought he was, when I was drunk on our romance and the thought of defying my father." She quietly sobbed, and Bears pulled her into his arms, easing her head onto his uninjured shoulder. She clung to him, gasping an apology as she inadvertently caused him pain when she gripped his bruised arm.

"*Shh*, let me hold you. Let go of this pain, Stitch. You have no need of it. For it's not the woman you are now," he murmured as he rocked her in his arms.

"There's more," she stuttered out.

He made soothing noises. "I know. And I want to hear all you want to tell me, but only when you are ready to. If that's not tonight, I understand."

She rested against him with a grateful groan, her hands moving over his back as though learning the shape of him. "It's been so long," she whispered against his neck. When he remained quiet, she continued. "So long since a man has held me with no expectation of anything more from me."

"I wonder if a man has ever held you with no expectation except for the sheer joy of having you in his arms," he said as he kissed her neck. "For it is a joy to finally hold you and to know you are no longer afraid of me."

She backed away and met his gaze. She felt his arms drop from around her, and she shook her head, moving forward so that he would keep her sheltered in his embrace. She raised her hands to cup his cheeks. "You might have no expectations, but I dream of your kiss."

His gaze sharpened, and his hands formed fists where they rested against her hips. "I don't want to ruin what is growing between us."

She stood on her toes and nipped at his chin. "You won't. You couldn't." Her eyes gleamed with residual sadness but also a dawning joy. "Because you've shown me that this is my choice, free of spite or desperation. This is what I truly want." She waited, and then her smile faded as he failed to act.

"Kiss me," he whispered, his gaze as intense as she had ever seen it.

Her grip on his cheeks tightened, and she tilted his head down to meet her lips as she stood on her toes. She groaned an instant before their lips met because his hands, no longer fisted, held her hips and tugged her closer. She pressed her lips to his and kissed him.

"More," he rasped. "Open for me." When she gasped, he kissed her deeply as he hauled her so that her front was plastered against his. After many long minutes, he broke away, gasping. "I ..."

She shook her head and covered his mouth with her fingers. She shivered as he kissed them. "Don't say you regret that. Don't say that you thought a whore could kiss better." She shuddered at the anger that flared in his gaze.

"You are not a whore, and you kiss like my wildest fantasy," he whispered. "Never speak poorly about yourself to me. I do not like it."

Her eyes filled with tears. "I have not kissed anyone since Aaron. I did not allow the men ... the men at the Boudoir to kiss me."

Bears nodded. "Then this was as special for you as it was for me." He raised her hand and kissed it.

"Anything we do will be special because it is between us, Bears. No one else."

He watched her closely. "I will never know what it was like to live the life you lived. To make the sacrifice of your body the way you did." He watched as she swallowed and flushed. "I want you to know I will never use your time at the Boudoir against you. I will never make you feel less worthy because you did what you had to do to survive."

She blinked away tears. "I do feel less worthy."

He cupped her cheeks, stifling a moan as the movement caused pain in his injured shoulder. "I hope, with time, that feeling will disappear." He watched her a moment before swooping down to kiss her again. "I hope someday, you will let me love you."

She stilled. "You want to make love?"

He tilted his head to one side as he saw panic in her gaze. "Yes, I would. But I mean what I say. I hope you will let me love you. That you will finally realize that you are worthy of love."

She pushed herself into his arms again and held him tight as she fought deep shudders. "You make me want to dream again. To hope again."

He made soothing noises. "You already dream and hope. Annabelle helped teach you the way again, and I suspect you were always an astute student."

She leaped from his arms as Mildred called out. "I shouldn't be here. What was I thinking? Kissing you with your daughter in the next room?"

Before she could race from his home, Bears grabbed her hand and stilled her retreat. "Thank you for sharing yourself with me tonight. Thank you for having faith in me and for trusting me enough to share your fears with me. Thank you for being brave." He caressed her cheek once before entering his daughter's room.

He absently heard the door close with Fidelia's departure as he focused on his daughter, ensuring she fully recovered.

CHAPTER 6

The following day at the bakery, Fidelia stood at the sink, staring out the window. She held a pan in one hand and the sponge in the other but did nothing to wash it.

"Are you hoping, if you hold it in the sink long enough, that it will magically clean itself?" her sister asked.

Fidelia jumped and began to scrub the pan. "I'm woolgathering."

Annabelle chuckled, as did another female. Fidelia turned to see Jessamine in the room.

"When did you arrive?" Fidelia asked.

"About five minutes ago. Right after you picked up that pan and stared out to the street. Is there anyone you hope will walk by?" At Fidelia's blush, Jessamine smiled. "Do tell. The life of a small-town reporter is rather boring."

"It is not. You have more tall tales than you could ever use," Annabelle said with a chuckle.

Jessamine groaned. "Had I known that I would regularly report on the appearance of a lifelike man who is eight feet tall in the woods, I would have remained on the East Coast." She ignored her sister-in-law's shake of her head in disagreement and focused on Fidelia. "Who are you hoping to see? Certainly not Walter Jameson. I have sources who confirm he is back."

Fidelia dropped the pan, and it clanged in the ceramic sink. She gripped the edge of the counter and bent over, as though she had suffered a body blow. "I had hoped he was gone for good, after the sheriff had a warrant for his arrest."

"It seems the man who wanted him arrested for fraud died of pneumonia in Helena. Without that man threatening him, there is no reason for the warrant. Or so says my source. Thus Walter feels free to come out of hiding."

"He'd better hope that none of the MacKinnons see him," Annabelle said.

"Or Frederick," Jessamine said as she nodded. She shared a glance with Annabelle as they watched Fidelia.

"Dee?" Annabelle set aside the bowl of cookie dough she had been mixing and approached her sister. Fidelia appeared as though she were about to fall over, and Annabelle pushed her onto a stool. "We all worry about Walter, especially after his treatment of Sorcha and Helen." She shook her head in confusion. "Why does he upset you so?"

Walter Jameson, Helen's brother, had verbally and physically abused Helen before her marriage to Warren. Last November, he had scared Sorcha's horse, intent on causing it to rear. Sorcha had fallen from the horse, breaking her leg and nearly crippling her. Then earlier this summer, he had kidnapped Sorcha, and tortured her with a knife as he tormented her about the fickle nature of Frederick's love. Frederick had found Walter harming his wife and forced Walter to flee his illegal camp on Frederick's land. Since then, Walter had been in hiding.

Jessamine studied Fidelia as a reporter, not as a friend and relative. "He's the one, isn't he?" When Annabelle stared in confusion, Jessamine shook her head and focused on Fidelia, sitting in ashen silence, quaking on a stool. "He's the one who beat you."

Annabelle gasped and watched her sister with wide, horrified eyes.

Fidelia gave a short jerk of her head. "Yes. He took great pleasure in hurting me. In reinforcing the Madam's belief that I would never be anything but a whore and that I was unlovable."

Her sister grabbed her hand and squeezed it. She waited until Fidelia raised despair-filled eyes to meet her angry gaze. "You know by now how much he lies. For *I* love you. I always did. I never stopped. And all of the MacKinnons do too."

Fidelia nodded, her gaze distant. A tear tracked down her cheek. "I wanted to believe I could start over again. That I could believe in love once more. I should have known I needed to move to a new town."

"No!" Her sister's hold on her hand tightened. "I couldn't bear to be parted from you. Not unless it's what you truly wanted. Not what you felt forced into doing." Annabelle fought tears as she witnessed her sister's ongoing torment. "The townsfolk purchase your linen and lace, and pay a good price for it. They don't barter the price down, and they value what you offer them. You are an essential part of our family."

"I'm tired of living a half-life," she whispered.

Jessamine gave a small *"Aah"* and walked to the front of the store. When she returned, she pulled out stools for her and Annabelle. "I closed the bakery for a little while. This seemed more important than selling buns or cookies." She smiled at Annabelle's grateful glance. "You want to love again? To marry?"

"Perhaps," Fidelia whispered.

"Oh, Dee," Annabelle began, all smiles now.

Jessamine kicked Annabelle in the shins to prevent her from becoming overexuberant and gave her a warning shake with her head. "Fidelia, you have to know that there will always be those who will disapprove. I've found that, no matter where I live, someone will disapprove of what I do. I'd rather focus on those who truly know me and who wish me well."

"What would the family think of the man you care for?" Annabelle asked in a gentle voice.

Fidelia rolled her eyes and scowled at her sister. "You know it's Bears. I'd think you'd be delighted that we have stopped dithering."

Annabelle stroked a piece of chestnut hair from Fidelia's temple and smiled at her sister. "All I care about is that he is a good man. A man who understands the importance of family. A man who will treat you well and not ever judge you for the hard decisions you had to make in the past."

Fidelia met her sister's worried gaze. "Bears is that man. I see how he is with his daughter, and I yearn." Her voice broke on *yearn*. "But some things will never be."

Jessamine shifted uncomfortably. "What do you mean, Fidelia?"

Fidelia looked around and seemed reassured they were alone in the quiet warmth of the bakery kitchen. "I can never have children. I … I had to do too many things while I worked at the Boudoir to ensure I never had children then that will ensure I never have a baby now." She hung her head in shame. "At the time, it seemed a relief. Now it only brings me sorrow."

"Oh, Dee," her sister whispered, embracing and holding Fidelia as she cried. "I'm so sorry. I never knew."

Fidelia sobbed for a few minutes and then eased away from her sister. "I rejoice in Skye. In Angus," she whispered on a stuttering breath. "But I will always mourn every time I see them."

Jessamine's cheeks were wet as she watched the sisters. "Of course." She paused a moment and whispered, "Have you told Bears?"

"No. I've hinted that I may not be able to have children, and he says he doesn't care. But men always say that when they want to get you into bed. It's later on, when the novelty wears off, that you realize they were never sincere."

"Give me one instance, *one*, when Bears lied or misled you—or any of us," Annabelle demanded. She waited a few moments as her sister stared at her blankly. "Bears is not like other men. He's not like the men you've known, Dee. He's like our husbands. He's honorable. He stands by what he says."

Jessamine nodded. "If he says he wants you more than he wants a baby, you have to have faith that he speaks the truth. Otherwise, you dishonor him and whatever might be growing between you."

Fidelia's gaze sharpened as she focused on Jessamine. "You and Ewan," she breathed.

Jessamine shook her head. "This discussion isn't about me. But, yes, we can't have a child." Her eyes filled. "And no matter what Ewan says, I'll always feel like a failure."

Fidelia stared at her, dumbfounded. "You're the farthest thing from a failure I've ever seen. You're a successful reporter, a wonderful friend, sister, and wife. You'll be a mother someday, Jessamine."

Jessamine shook her head, blinking to hold back the tears. "It's what I want more than anything in this world. Except for Ewan. And that's when I realize he isn't lying to me, when he says he wants me more than the future hope of a child." Her tremulous smile filled Fidelia with hope.

Fidelia sighed and rubbed at her forehead. "For now, I must find a way to avoid Walter. For he's always considered us in a game of cat and mouse. And I find I no longer care to be the mouse."

Mildred poked her head into the bakery and sighed at the scents wafting around. She closed her eyes, taking in the smell of almond and vanilla and fresh baked bread. She gasped and opened her eyes when her aunt called out, "Don't just stand in the doorway. Come in." She saw Fidelia smiling at her.

"I didn't mean to bother you." Mildred stood, hopping from foot to foot and looking at the floor.

"Why would a visit from my favorite ten-year-old ever be a bother?" Fidelia smiled invitingly and motioned for Mildred to join her in the kitchen at the counter. "Come, Millie. Annabelle always has extras." She turned and pulled out a plate of imperfect snickerdoodle cookies.

"Oh, those look delicious." Mildred licked her lips and then hunkered down, like a vole about to be chased by a determined hawk. "I shouldn't."

Fidelia studied her with her head cocked to one side. "Why not? If you eat one, it won't ruin your dinner. And I'm offering it to you."

Mildred watched her with wide eyes as she snatched a cookie, pulling it to her with a stealthy speed. She nibbled on a corner of it and sighed. "Delicious. Just like I thought."

After pouring a glass of cold milk for her, Fidelia sat on a stool across from the child and frowned. "I thought you understood that none of us would use food as a weapon against you. That we'd never tease you with it."

Mildred moved to hop off her stool and to run away.

Fidelia's hand shot out and gripped Mildred's arm. "No, Millie, don't. You can't outrace your demons. You must face them." She met Mildred's defiant stare.

"Is that why you hide in your room and refuse to face the towns-folk? Because you face your demons?" Mildred asked. "I've heard people say you should stay hidden. You shouldn't flaunt yourself here among us." She flushed as Fidelia paled and dropped her hand from her arm.

"I see," Fidelia whispered in a low voice. "I knew it was too much to hope you'd accept my friendship." She rose. "I wish you a good day, Mildred."

Mildred stood, clutching the cookie to her. "I ... I ..." She turned as Annabelle entered.

"Oh, Mildred! How wonderful that you've come to visit us. And on a day when we have extra cookies." Annabelle pulled her close for a hug. "I'm so glad Dee gave you milk to go with your cookie. Dee's always thoughtful in that way." She smiled from her sister to the girl and frowned as she belatedly noticed the tension between them.

"Thank you for the cookie, Aunt Annabelle," Mildred whispered. "I have to go home." She ran from the room, the front door slamming shut behind her, as she fought a wave of shame and regret at what she'd ruined.

~

Ewan strolled into the livery to see his brothers. He saw Bears working in a stall, pushing hay around with one arm and called out a hello as he pulled out the stools. His brothers saw his actions, and they knew it meant he needed to have a chat. "Bears," Ewan called out. "You might as well join us."

Bears set aside the shovel and joined them near the paddock doors. He leaned against a post, his gaze guarded. "What is it, carpenter?" He rubbed at his aching shoulder as he frowned at Ewan.

"How is Mildred?" Ewan asked.

Bears smiled. "Better. She's spending the day with Hortence, and I know they'll get into some mischief." His smile warmed at the thought. "She no longer has a headache."

"Aye, 'tis good then. She's no' damaged by what happened," Ewan said.

"She has nightmares most nights but calms after I wake her. Hopefully they won't last long." Bears looked at Ewan. "I know you didn't come here to inquire after my daughter's health."

"Walter Jameson is back in town," Ewan said. "I saw him as I drove my team back from the sawmill. Took everythin' I had no' to divert my horses and run him over."

Cailean gave a sound of disgust. "Needs to be something more subtle. Besides, didn't we promise Frederick we'd let him handle this?"

"Frederick's on the ranch. We're here," Alistair said, sharing a glower with his brothers.

"If the man turns up dead after returning to town, we'd be the major suspects." Bears stared at the brothers. "You can't kill the man, no matter how much you'd like to."

The three brothers grumbled, kicking at the hay on the ground, but reluctantly agreed with Bears's statement.

"What do you suggest?" Cailean asked.

"Discover why he's back. And then ensure what he wants is denied him." Bears looked at Ewan. "We already destroyed Walter's attempt at a mine on Frederick's ranch. He has no ready source of income because that man in Helena died, and few will be bamboozled by him again in Montana Territory. I'm surprised he returned here at all."

Ewan canted forward and frowned. "Why *did* the man return? It makes no sense. He has no loyalty to his mother, an' we all ken how little he cares about his sister. Plus Helen is protected by Warren and all of us now." His frown deepened. "Why risk our wrath, an' the knowledge that he has no prospects here, to return?"

"He must want something or someone here. An', if that's Sorcha, he will no' have her," Alistair said in a low growl.

Bears shook his head. "He could have had Sorcha twice, when she fell from the horse and when he later kidnapped her. Walter could have taken her and disappeared, and we might never have found them." He ignored his friends' noises of protest as Bears was the best tracker in the area. "Someone else fascinates him enough for him to return."

"Aye, an even if it's no' a MacKinnon, I say we keep an eye on our womenfolk and our children. An' ourselves. We MacKinnons, an' anyone associated with us, are no' popular with that man," Ewan said.

"And he has a penchant for violence," Cailean murmured, nodding in agreement with Ewan's statement.

A few days later, Fidelia worked in the back of the bakery alone, cleaning up after another successful day. She wiped down the counters and turned to ensure the ovens were off. She then picked up a broom and began to sweep the floors. She looked to the back door, hoping Mildred would come by again. Hoping that they could somehow repair their damaged fledgling relationship. "A dress won't do it," she said to herself. She sighed as she continued to work, the ache in her heart intensifying as she thought through her interaction with Mildred a few days ago.

When the back door opened, she turned to smile at who had entered and then froze. "What are you doing here?"

"Isn't it my luck you didn't lock the door today?" Walter said, shutting the door behind him and sauntering toward her. "I've had to bide my time, waiting to see you again."

Fidelia gripped the broom as though it were a club and held it in front of her. "You are not welcome here, and you are trespassing. You must leave." She shivered at his laugh. The memory of just such a laugh brought her back to the nights she was in her crib at the Boudoir, and he had laughed in the same manner as he beat her.

"Why should I care about trespassing? I already know every member of your family—or your so-called family—wishes me harm. I have to skulk around in my own town as though I were a criminal!" He took a step toward her, and she swung out with her broom. He sidestepped the swipe and laughed again.

"Stay away from me!" she screamed.

"Do you really believe anyone in town will concern themselves over your well-being?" He shook his head in mocking commiseration. "You're a whore. You'll always be a whore, and you'll never be worth anyone's regard. I'm surprised you aren't restricted to the whore's shopping hours."

"I am a decent woman," she whispered. "I sell my linens and lace …"

"And I'm sure you throw in a petticoat or two for your best customers. Tell me. Where do you meet them now that you aren't at the Boudoir? Do you have a special place in the woods you like to use as your rendezvous?"

Her body quivered with anger. "No. I am not a whore," she repeated. When he took a step toward her, she screamed in rage and whipped the broom at him, hitting him across the head.

He was momentarily stalled by her action, but then he shook his head, and his gaze sharpened, filled with hatred. "You will regret ever treating me in such a fashion." When she raised the broom again, he leaped forward and grabbed it, ripping it from her hands and throwing it to the floor behind him. "I had not realized you missed my attentions."

She trembled at the promise of pain in his voice. "No," she whispered and backed up a step. She continued to back up until she hit the wall.

He struck her in her belly and sneered at her when she gasped and fell to the ground. "That is where you belong, on your knees, begging me for mercy."

Fidelia gripped her stomach and gasped for air as tears poured out.

"Fidelia, I forgot to ask you," Jessamine said as she opened the rear door and walked in. She stopped as she saw Fidelia on the floor, Walter standing over her. "You!" Her tone was filled with rage. "You have no right to even look at her."

"And you have no right to interfere in things that are none of your concern," he snarled. He pulled back his boot as though to kick Fidelia, and Jessamine let out a scream as she launched herself across the room. She hit him so hard that she knocked him off-balance, and he careened into the still-cooling ovens.

"Fire!" he screamed as the skin on his hand, arm, and shoulder burned. He ran from the bakery, most likely in search of something to cool his burns, leaving the two women alone.

"Fidelia," Jessamine whispered as she knelt by her friend. "What can I do?"

"Don't tell anyone," Fidelia gasped out.

"No, I will not agree to that. They need to know." Jessamine put a hand under Fidelia's arm and heaved her up. "Come. Let's go to my house, and I'll get Helen."

They made the slow walk to Jessamine and Ewan's nearby home, and Fidelia rested on the bed in the spare bedroom while Jessamine ran to find Helen. Fidelia held a hand to her belly where Walter had kicked her and curled onto her side. When a soothing touch brushed hair from her brow, she sighed with relief.

"What did he do?" asked a man with a deep baritone voice.

Her eyes opened to find Bears staring at her. He knelt by the bed, and he continued to run his fingertips over her brow, down her cheek to her neck and then to her shoulder and back up again.

"How did you know?" she whispered.

"Bright Fawn saw. She didn't know what to do. So she ran to find me. By the time I got there, you were gone. I found Jessamine, and she sent me here. Jessamine informed the family and Warren that Walter has attacked you. They will ensure that those we care about are protected." His gaze was filled with anger and remorse. "Why didn't you tell me?"

"That I'm his target?" she whispered. "That he never lets me forget I'm a whore?" Her voice cracked at the words.

He muttered his disagreement. "That is his truth. Not yours. He has no regard for any woman."

She met his gaze. "Why would your daughter run to you for me?" She moved into his touch and sighed at the pleasure of his soft caress.

"She knows you are precious to me." He met her shocked gaze. "I see no reason to hide how I feel from my daughter, when my hope is that someday she will feel the same way about you."

Fidelia began to cry and leaned forward. "I need you to hold me," she whispered.

"Scoot back," he said. When she felt the wall behind her, he climbed onto the bed and then tugged her so she lay on his chest. He wrapped his arms around her and kissed her head. "You are cherished." He held her as she cried on his shoulder. He shook his head as Helen stood in the doorway on the verge of entering the room. Helen nodded and moved to wait in the living room before interrupting them again.

When Fidelia had calmed, he murmured, "You're the reason Walter returns to town. You're the reason he doesn't leave Bear Grass Springs."

"Yes." Her hands gripped Bears's arm, as though fighting the truth or clinging to a sense of safety. "It's why I've disliked going to social outings. It's why I rarely leave the house or the bakery. I fear seeing him."

Bears kissed the top of her head. "You can't allow him to steal your joy of life. You are a woman meant to laugh and to smile and to dance." His hold on her tightened as she gave another small sob at his words. "You were meant to shine, Fidelia, not to stand in the corner and hope to be ignored."

"I've spent too much time in the limelight as it is."

"No, just the wrong sort of light." He paused. "Is he the one who beat you?" His hold on her tightened at her nod. "Is he the one who paid for your laudanum?"

"Yes," she whispered.

"I always knew you couldn't have afforded it on your own." He kissed the top of her head again.

"The Madam convinced wealthy men to pay for laudanum for their favorites, so we would be more docile." She shuddered. "But I was never docile enough."

"What do you mean?" His hand stroked her back, and she slowly relaxed against him.

"Walter wanted the one thing I would never give him." She waited, and Bears grunted his understanding.

"A kiss," he said.

"Yes, and he beat me until he thought I would submit. He didn't realize he would have to beat me to death." She pressed her face into Bears's shoulder, as though banishing those memories.

"Why was it so important to deny him that?" Bears met her gaze when she stared at him in disappointment. "I would have had you spared any pain, Fidelia."

"They demanded every other part of me, Bears. That was mine and only mine to give. And I refused to give that." A tear rolled down her cheek. "That one small defiance reminded me how I was more than what they said I was."

He nodded. "Yes, you are so much more." He kissed her forehead. "Helen is here, and she would like to examine you. Would that be all right with you?"

Fidelia closed her eyes in resignation. "There's nothing she can do. I have suffered many such blows, and it just takes time for the bruises to heal." She opened her eyes to see the anger in his gaze. She cupped his cheek. "I will be fine, Bears."

"You might be, but I don't know if I will be. I hate the thought of you harmed in any way."

She looked at him and saw the deep concern in his gaze. "I will see Helen. Not because she can do anything but because it is important to you. To Anna." She leaned forward and kissed him softly on the lips. "Thank you, Bears."

His eyes had closed as though in bliss at her soft kiss, and he ran his fingers over her cheek again. "Always, Stitch. Always." He slipped out from under her and called for Helen.

When Helen entered, she closed the door behind her. "What would you like me to do?"

Fidelia watched her with wary humor. "There is little for you to do, and I hate to waste your time."

Helen waved away that concern and urged Fidelia to sit up and to strip off her dress. Soon Fidelia was only in her shift. "Does it feel better to have your corset off?" At Fidelia's nod, Helen smiled. "I have some of your favorite liniment. Why don't we use that and see if it eases the pain?" She frowned at the panic in Fidelia's gaze.

After a moment, Fidelia nodded and lifted her hips so her belly was exposed. She watched as Helen's gaze narrowed when she looked at Fidelia's midsection. Silver stretch marks, like an unfinished spiderweb, spread across her belly. When Helen looked at Fidelia with a questioning gaze, she nodded. "I see," Helen murmured. "Does anyone else know?"

Fidelia shook her head.

"What is discussed between us is confidential, Fidelia." She smiled as Fidelia relaxed. After applying a generous amount of the ointment, she lowered Fidelia's shift. "Where is your child?"

Fidelia again shook her head. "I don't know. I imagine somewhere near Albany." Her voice broke, and then she shrugged. "I have no right to mourn."

Helen *tsked*. "Of course you do. You made a very difficult decision." She paused as she met her friend's guarded gaze. "I wish you'd share what happened with your sister. With those who care for you."

Fidelia began to speak, about to spout an instantaneous denial as she was accustomed to. However, she paused and then whispered, "I will. It's time."

Helen squeezed her shoulder and pulled a sheet over her. "Rest. You'll feel better in a day or two."

That evening, Bears sat at the round table in Cailean MacKinnon's kitchen with a cup of coffee in front of him. He had never been a man to drink strong spirits, but he was tempted to ask Cailean to bring out the whiskey.

"Ye dinna want it, Bears," Ewan said as he sat beside him. "Whiskey never brings clarity."

"Aye, but it may prevent him from killing the man," Cailean said, watching his friend and partner stare with murderous intent at the table. He sat across from Bears and frowned. Bears did not respond to their teasing.

Alistair poured himself a cup of coffee and sat on Bears's other side. "Now ye ken how we've felt about Walter."

Bears looked at them and frowned. "I've always thought he was worse than the lowliest varmint that needed to be exterminated. The difference is, I never thought it was my responsibility to stop him." He glowered as he stared at his friends. "I should have realized it was. I should have followed his trail this summer, found him, and ..."

Warren entered the kitchen, doffing his hat as he entered. "I'll forget I heard you saying such things." Warren gave Bears a warning glance, although his gaze was filled with understanding. After Sorcha had been rescued this summer, Bears had tracked Walter a short distance. Frederick had decided there was no reason to find Walter at that time, as he would resurface all too soon.

Warren looked at the men he considered family sitting around the table. "The man's gone aground again. I can't imagine many in town would shelter him." He sat next to Cailean and waved away the offer of a cup of coffee. "I've had too much coffee for one day."

"There is no' such thing," Ewan said with a grin before focusing on the topic at hand. "Where would he go?"

"Helen's visited her mother," Warren said and nodded as the men shuddered at the thought, "and he's not there." He saw Bears frown. "And, no, she did not travel there alone. I was with her."

"He has no friends in this town," Cailean said as he looked at his brothers.

"I'd look for him at the Boudoir," Bears said. "The Madam is in financial difficulties. She's never had trouble in the past, misplacing her scruples with regard to her girls' safety, if it meant she'd earn a few more dollars. I imagine Walter has sweet-talked his way into her good graces with another grand scheme."

Ewan frowned. "The Madam is no' a dumb woman. Nor is she gullible. Besides, Walter's past shenanigans to sell Helen to the Boudoir were short-lived."

Warren stilled, sitting straighter, anger filling his gaze, but he kept quiet as he recalled the night he saved his future wife from the virgin auction at the Boudoir.

Bears shrugged. "True, but the Madam is a woman who reacts to strong men. And she believes Walter is strong." He nodded as the MacKinnons and Warren grumbled. "We already know the Madam has shown bad judgment before."

Warren nodded. "We know Walter's a bully and the worst sort of man because he picks on those who are weaker than he is. And he places the Madam in that category."

"Why should the Madam want anything to do with him?" Alistair asked.

"As Bears said, if the rumors are true, she is short of funds." Cailean looked at Warren. "How trustworthy is the new banker?"

Warren stared in confusion at Cailean. "He's better than Finlay."

Ewan snorted. "That is no' sayin' much." They all muttered their agreement as they thought about the previous banker who'd been run out of town after he had tried to fleece the town's Improvement Committee. Ewan stared at his eldest brother. "What bothers ye, Cail?"

He looked at the men around the table. "You know I consider all of you family. So what I am telling you now is in confidence." Each nodded in agreement. "Fidelia has money. Money set aside by Annabelle from their father." He looked at Warren, whose expression remained impassive. "I fear Walter has found out that Fidelia has such funds and is bartering his ability to get her to return to the Boudoir for the Madam's good graces."

Bears tightened his grip on his mug until it looked as though he'd crush it between his hands. "I should have tracked him down and killed him. No one would ever have been the wiser."

Warren sighed and covered his eyes. "Again, don't say such things in front of me."

Cailean gritted his teeth together. "Fidelia's never going back there. It would kill Belle."

Bears nodded. "And Fidelia would end up dead if she returned." He looked at the men around the table, men he considered family. "*She* is his target. *She* is the reason he returns to town." He saw the MacKinnon men and Warren nod their heads in understanding. Bears lowered his head and ran a hand over his scalp, thinking through all they had discussed. "The problem is, apart from Fidelia being his focus, this is all speculation. We don't truly know where Walter is or what is going on between him and the Madam."

Ewan shrugged. "I can visit the Boudoir. Talk to the girls. Ezekial has allowed me in the last few times I've visited. The Madam realized that my visits led to publicity in Jessamine's paper and to an increased interest in her establishment due to it." He looked around the table at the men gathered here. "Jessie willna mind, no' when she understands why I must go there."

The men nodded their agreement with Ewan's plan. Cailean spoke. "Aye, thank you, Ewan. And, as I don't need to say, we must ensure Walter has no opportunity for more mischief."

Bears met his friends' gazes. "Never again will Walter harm Fidelia."

Warren looked at Bears. "*Never* is a long time, Bears. Do what you can to keep her and Mildred safe."

~

After she had recovered enough to travel home later that afternoon, Fidelia returned to Cailean and Annabelle's home and rested in her room. She heard the gentle murmur of voices from the kitchen down-

UNBRIDLED MONTANA PASSION

stairs, and she imagined the men having an informal clan meeting as they discussed the problem of Walter Jameson. She wished she had the desire to join them, but a lassitude filled her, and she yearned for time alone.

Memories from her time at the Boudoir flooded back, and she curled into herself, as though protecting herself from them. The laughing, mocking men as they looked at her like she were a prize mare. The faked display of pride when men fought over her. The feigned pleasure anytime a man touched her. She shuddered and curled farther into herself. The terror and pain when Walter visited. His penchant for using fists, boots, and buckles in an attempt to break her will.

"No, no, no," she whimpered as tears streamed down her face.

At the soft touch to her cheeks, she stifled a shriek. "Are you having a nightmare, Fidelia?" Mildred asked as she peered over her.

Fidelia sobbed and shook her head and then nodded. "A waking one."

Mildred frowned. "I didn't know you could dream while awake."

"Of course you can, Millie." She swiped at her face. "Why are you here?"

Mildred flushed. "I was worried about you. Father said you would be all right, but I wanted to make sure." She bit her lip. "And I'm sorry. I'm so sorry about the things I said."

Fidelia watched her, tears slowly leaking from her eyes. "Why did you?" She looked at the girl she had hoped would consider her a friend. Perhaps even family one day. "Why hurt me?"

"I ... I learned while at the orphanage and from that man who said he was my father that, if you strike out, you protect yourself," Mildred whispered, referring to Bertrand March. "That, if you hurt someone before they can hurt you, you won't hurt as bad." She shook her head. "But that didn't work. I hurt something awful after I saw what my words did to you, Fidelia."

"Why?" She watched the girl intently.

"Because you'd only ever shown me kindness. You had accepted me. And you like my father." She took a deep breath. "What if you turned away from him? He'd be sad." Mildred's eyes filled. "I don't want him to be sad."

"Words can hurt worse than any blow, Millie," Fidelia whispered.

A tear tracked down one of Mildred's cheeks. "I know. And I'm sorry." She hung her head in dejected silence. "Will you be my friend?" When Fidelia remained quiet, she looked up to meet her gaze. "I don't care about the dress! You can give it to someone else. I understand if you don't want to make it for me. I don't deserve it now."

Fidelia held out a hand and made a *shush*ing noise, but Mildred continued to plead with her.

"I … I want to visit you at the bakery. To eat cookies. To tell you about my day and …" Mildred's gaze implored Fidelia to believe her.

Fidelia nodded. "To feel like you belong," she whispered. "Annabelle's bakery makes all of us feel like we belong." She raised a hand and held it to the side of Mildred's face. "I want to be your friend. I want you to visit me and to tell me about your day. About your hopes and dreams and frustrations. And I want to make you that dress. Thank you."

Mildred's eyes filled again. "I'm so sorry the bad man hurt you. I ran as fast as I could to get Father. I didn't know what else to do. I'm sorry, Fidelia."

Fidelia shook her head. "You did nothing wrong, Millie. You did everything you could to help. Thank you." She watched as Mildred studied her with wide eyes. "You didn't hurt me, not on purpose. The bad man hurt me. And he wanted to." She smiled at Millie. "We will unintentionally hurt those we care about, when we lash out in frustration or fear or pain. It's when we intentionally hurt others, Millie, that shows how cruel we are. Don't be like the bad man."

Millie fell forward and into Fidelia's arms. "I don't want to be!"

"It's okay, Millie." Fidelia made soft crooning noises and urged her to climb onto the bed with her. She held Mildred in her arms as she cried and then as she slept.

When Bears looked in, he stopped short at the sight of Mildred asleep in Fidelia's arms. "I thought to check on you before heading home. Annabelle didn't mind." His gaze roved over the sight of Fidelia holding his daughter. "I didn't realize Mildred was with you."

Fidelia stroked a hand over Mildred's back. "She was worried about me. She thought I'd be upset that she didn't do more to help me."

"She did what she could," Bears murmured.

"Yes. The last thing I want is for her to interact with Walter. I don't want him to ever focus on her."

Bears nodded, and he clenched his jaw. "I agree." He reached forward and traced his fingers over Fidelia's cheek. "But I don't want him focused on you either."

They shared a long look, and then he took a deep breath. "I should get her home." He picked up Mildred, cradling her in his arms, studying Fidelia again. "Come visit us soon, Stitch." At her nod, he broke his stare and departed.

She watched as the door closed and curled on her side. Rather than being haunted by memories of the past, dreams of the future filled her mind.

CHAPTER 7

Fidelia poked her head into the café a few days later and paused as the café kitchen was empty. She entered on silent feet and set the basket of treats for the evening crowd on the kitchen table. Holding her hands over the warm stove, she closed her eyes and relaxed a moment, before venturing back out into the cool, early October weather. It was a beautiful day, with a gentle breeze and the trees changing color. She knew that, all too soon, winter would arrive. She jumped at a noise behind her, spinning to find Harold entering the back door.

"Hello, Fidelia," he said, watching her regain her composure. He frowned as she flushed and looked down. "Irene is not feeling well today."

"Why didn't you tell one of us? We would help you." She took a step toward him, as though to rush to Harold and Irene's small house behind the café that Ewan had built for them, in search of Irene.

"There's no need. She suffers from headaches now and again, and today is one of those days. She'll be right as rain tomorrow." He shrugged. "Or the day after."

Fidelia looked around the kitchen. "The café isn't open today, is it?"

He shook his head. "No, and Irene will tan my hide because I forgot to tell Annabelle to cancel our order today." He looked at the overflowing basket of breads and cookies. "I wonder who I'll find to eat all of this?"

She shrugged. "You'll think of something." She paled as she saw his contemplative gaze. "I'm not bringing this to the Boudoir."

He gaped at her and then gave a choked sound of embarrassment. "And I'd never ask you to. I was wondering how much I could peddle it to the owner of the Stumble-Out for. He's been bellyachin' that his customers leave to eat at my café and don't come back as thirsty as when they left. Perhaps he'd like to buy it from me to keep his customers in one place today."

Fidelia laughed as she relaxed. "You'll always be a businessman, won't you?"

He grinned at her and motioned for her to sit down as he moved to the coffeepot on the stove. "Of course. It's in my blood, and I don't know what I'd do if I wasn't trying out some new business idea."

"I'd think the café kept you busy enough," she said. When he'd poured her a cup of coffee, one for him as well, he settled across from her.

"Well, it was a challenge in the beginning, and I used to take great delight in writing outlandish things on our blackboard as a form of advertisin'." He slurped up some coffee as Fidelia giggled. "Irene put up with me because she realized I needed to be creative and because she enjoyed seein' what I'd write each day."

"Why don't you do that now?" Fidelia asked, her fingers wrapped around the warm coffee cup.

He shrugged. "I ain't so stupid as to try to upstage that reporter." He tilted his head in the direction of Jessamine's print shop. "She's got a way with words."

"As do you," Fidelia said loyally.

"Well, there's my way, and then there's the proper way. The townsfolk are taken by her stories, so I cede the stories to her." He noted Fidelia's dubious expression and nodded. "Unless I'm in the café talkin' with my customers." He watched her closely. "Seems your past caught up to you, Fidelia."

She closed her eyes and let out a long sigh. "It did," she whispered in a defeated tone, before straightening her shoulders as though she were readying for battle. "I don't know what to do to make Walter understand I'm free of him. Free of the Madam."

Harold shook his head. "Ain't nothin' you can do for a man like that. For a woman like the Madam. They will always ignore what someone wants, especially if it goes against their selfish wishes. It's their nature." He watched her with compassion. "It don't make it right, but it helps to understand them better."

"I hate that I jump at the smallest sounds again," she whispered.

He watched her with a deep understanding. "You were just beginning to believe that you had a place in this world, free of spite or hurt. And then *he* returned."

A tear tracked down her cheek.

"And hurt you all over again."

"Yes," she whispered.

He leaned forward and clasped one of her hands. "But you ain't alone this time, Fidelia. You have your sister and men who consider themselves your brothers." He paused as he watched her a long moment. "You have a man like Bears."

Another tear coursed down her cheek. "I worry, in the end, I'll still end up alone. Back in the Boudoir. And it will be so much more bitter because I know what this life feels like." At his curious stare, she whispered in a barely discernible voice, "Friendship. Having a sister again. Family."

"This isn't no dream, Fidelia. I'd think of the time you were at the Boudoir as the nightmare you overcame." He sobered. "And they'd have to come through me to get you back there."

A fresh batch of tears poured out to drip onto the front of her dress. "Thank you, Harold."

He nodded. "You might have trouble seeing it, but you're precious to all of us. Watching you blossom has brought us great joy. We protect those we love." He paused a moment and said, "It's why

Jessamine was not worried when Ewan visited the Boudoir to see if the Madam's in cahoots with that no-good rascal." At Fidelia's inquisitive stare, he nodded. "And it appears the Madam is. It's always good to know your adversary."

Fidelia pulled out a handkerchief and scrubbed at her face, before blowing her nose. She opened her mouth to speak but couldn't form any words.

He nodded his understanding and then tapped his fingers on the table. "Now, if you could figure out what to do about my darned horse, Brutus, that would be a true service. He ate another pair of pantaloons yesterday." He smiled when she giggled, just as he'd hoped she would. "Seems I wasn't paying attention as I spoke to Bears, and Brutus reached out and got ahold of my britches."

"I'd pay more attention, or he might get more than your britches," she teased.

He laughed. "I wouldn't put it past that beast. I keep threatening him that I'll send him east for glue. I just might." He shook his head.

"I'd set him free before taking such a drastic measure," she murmured as she rose. "Some aren't meant to be caged."

He watched her and nodded when she slipped from the café. "Quite true, Fidelia. Quite true."

Nearly a week later in early October, Fidelia poked her head into Bears's cabin and frowned when she found it empty. She entered and began to tidy the small space, although it was not messy. She washed the single cup in the basin and then wiped down the kitchen table. After looking around for something else to do, she sat with a huff in the rocking chair. As time spun away, she sang to herself, the songs her mother taught her as a little girl. Of men going to sea to fish. Of women yearning for their loves to come home. She imagined she could smell the briny salt air, could hear the seagulls calling and the crash of the waves. When the song ended, the spell was broken, and she was back in Bear Grass Springs.

However, now that she looked around Bears's home and realized she was waiting to tell him her deepest truths, a sense of calm settled over her. She no longer yearned for a time that never truly existed. She yearned for what she could have if only she were brave enough.

"I never knew you sang," Bears murmured from the doorway.

She smiled and turned her head to find him leaning against the doorjamb, watching her. "I do when I am happy."

His bright smile made her breath catch, and she reached out a hand to him. He grabbed a kitchen chair and set it so he could sit facing her. "Why are you here, Stitch?"

She bit her lip and flushed. "I heard that Mildred was spending the night with Hortence. I thought I would visit."

He raised an eyebrow and waited.

"I wanted to speak with you." She looked deeply into his eyes and grasped his hand. "I want to first tell you everything. Then I will have to tell Annabelle." She swallowed. "I fear losing your regard. Or hers."

"Trust me."

She nodded. "I must, or I wouldn't be here." After a long silence, she spoke in a low voice. "I told you what it was like, living with my father. After a while, even though I wanted to protect Annabelle, I also yearned for some sort of affection. For a sign that I was worthy of love." She closed her eyes. "I was young and stupid and believed that men meant what they said."

After a long pause, she continued. "Aaron and I had known each other for years. He was a fisherman. Loved the sea. Never wanted to leave Maine. However, when my father found out we'd … been together, his father insisted he act honorably. Aaron convinced me to run away with him. That we'd be like Romeo and Juliet, but this time there would be a happy ending."

She gave a snort of disbelief. "I should have known then that things would be disastrous. Never have faith in a man who cites a Shakespearean tragedy and claims that he'll have a better outcome." She met Bears's gaze, and she saw her attempt at humor failed, as he continued to watch her with patience and understanding. "We fled Maine and took the train to Albany. He thought he could find work there, or we'd go to New York City. But, by then, I was pregnant, and he found me to be a burden."

"Where is he now?" Bears asked.

She shook her head. "He died. From diphtheria. Leaving me alone and on the verge of giving birth. I could sew and knit, but few were interested in my skills, and I couldn't earn enough to support myself or a baby. Even fewer had sympathy for an unmarried woman who had been living in sin. I tried to leave Albany, intent on reinventing myself as a widow in another town or city, but, when I was at the train station, I went into labor."

Tears leaked down her cheeks. "I used all of my meager savings to pay off the midwife. And then I had nothing. No way to support my baby boy. No way to ensure we didn't starve."

She hung her head.

Bears put his fingertips under her chin, urging her head up. "You have no reason for shame, Fidelia. What happened?"

"I gave my baby to an orphanage. I didn't know what else to do. They assured me that families were always looking for babies and that he'd find a good home." She fought a sob. "I pray, every day, that he is well. That he is loved. That he knows how much I love him."

She took a deep breath. "So then I was child-free but still penniless."

"You were heartbroken. You'd lost the support of the man you thought you'd loved. You'd been forced to give up your child. You'd lost your sister." He shook his head. "Don't make light of what you lost."

"I couldn't find enough work. And winter was coming. I had no way to pay for a train ticket south. I had nothing." She shivered. "I met the Madam as I begged on a street corner, starving. She invited me to her home and fed me a wonderful meal. She convinced me that the life in the whorehouse was the life for me. I would always have a warm bed. I would always have food."

"How did you wind up in Montana?"

Fidelia shrugged. "I don't know. The Madam wanted to find a place where there wasn't much oversight, and she had heard fantastic stories of rich whorehouse owners in towns near mining strikes. She had a wealthy benefactor at the time, and she fleeced him of enough money for a few of us to travel west." She shrugged. "She thought I was beautiful enough to be worthy of the expense."

Bears shook his head. "I doubt that. I bet she made you work off the price of your ticket." He saw the agreement to his statement in her gaze. "So somehow you ended up here."

"Yes. And, for whatever reason, I continued to send letters to my father. I lied about my circumstances. I wanted him to believe I had a wonderful life. I wanted him to believe he'd been mistaken about me."

"And, because of those letters, you brought Annabelle back into your life." He smiled. "And all the rest of us."

She nodded. "I treated her horribly when she first arrived." Her voice was filled with remorse and regret. "I envied her everything she had."

"What does she have that you don't, Stitch?" He caressed her palm.

"She has a family and a child. A home. A business. The respect of the townsfolk." She shrugged.

"You could have all that too," he whispered. "A family. A child. A home. A man who loves you." He smiled at her. "You already have a business." He gave a small grimace. "Those who matter respect you. Admire you even."

"I can't have more children, Bears," she whispered. "I ... During my time at the Boudoir, I used potions and poisons, and I killed any chance of having another child."

His eyes filled with sorrow. "I will never lie to you." He waited until she nodded. "I would like to have known what it is to wait in fearful hope of a child. With you. But I don't need another child. I have Bright Fawn. And every girl needs a mother."

Fidelia raised her hand and cupped his face. "I ... I don't know if I would be any good as a mother, Bears."

He smiled. "Look how you are with Skye. With Angus. With Hortence. You are patient and kind and loving. They already clamor to be with you, but you shy away from them because you fear you will make a misstep. Trust in yourself the way they already trust in you." He smiled. "Look at your relationship with Mildred. She's never fallen asleep in my arms."

She leaned in and kissed him. "I love you, Bears." She looked deeply into his eyes and saw the answering emotion in his gaze. "I have for some time."

His eyes shone with his love, and he nodded. "Come lie with me." He shook his head as she froze. "No, just lie with me. Let me hold you after you tell me how you love me. Please."

She rose on unsteady feet, and he held her shoulders until she was steady. When she moved to the bed, he pulled the curtains over the two windows of his cabin. He pulled out his shirttail, unbuttoned the top few buttons, and kicked off his boots. He crawled into bed fully clothed and waited for her to do the same.

"You truly mean it," she whispered.

He smiled. "Of course I do."

She giggled and shook her head. "I refuse to sleep in my corset." She shucked her dress and corset and climbed into bed in her shift and drawers. "Somehow this feels more scandalous than if we were naked."

He chuckled and wrapped an arm around her waist. He lowered his head and nuzzled the soft skin at her nape. "I love you, Fidelia. I will never rush you into giving more than you are prepared to."

She smiled, raising his hand to kiss it. "I'm coming to realize that. I love you so, Bears." She sighed with contentment as his arm around her waist tightened.

"Sleep, love. I'll wake you before dawn, so you can sneak home without causing a scandal."

She murmured her agreement and slipped into a sleep filled with dreams of a future with Bears and Mildred.

Fidelia eased open the kitchen door to Annabelle and Cailean's house and stilled when she saw her sister sitting at the kitchen table, a cup of coffee in front of her. "Anna?" she whispered. "Has something happened?"

Her sister glared at her. "Yes. My sister went missing last night. ... I had no idea if you were well or in the hands of that monster."

Fidelia blushed. "I'm sorry. I didn't think to ..."

"That's just it. You never think I'll be worried about you. That I would care that you've been harmed." Annabelle watched her sister with disappointment. "I've tried to support you, Dee. I've done everything I know to show you my love. But it will never be enough, will it?"

Fidelia grabbed her sister's arm before she could race from the room. "No, Anna, it is enough. It's always been enough." She fought tears as her sister stared at her without emotion. "I'm sorry."

"For what? For believing I'm a fool to care for you? For believing I wasn't worth the bother to inform you were well last night?"

Fidelia closed her eyes. "For everything."

Cailean entered the room and glared at her. "So you're well."

She shook at the animosity and anger in his voice. "I'm sorry. I was with Bears. We started talking and then ... and then ..."

"And then you slept with him." Annabelle rolled her eyes and rose. "It's just like with Aaron. Once you find a man, you'll forget all about me."

"No!" Fidelia moved to hold on to her sister's hand, but Cailean blocked her from touching Annabelle. "Please, Cailean. Please, Anna. Let me explain." Tears dripped off her chin.

"I'm exhausted, and I have no need to hear excuses," her sister said. Yet, when she shared a long look with her husband, she sighed as she pulled out a chair and sat on the opposite side of the table from Fidelia. Once Annabelle sat, Fidelia did too.

"I ... I went to see Bears last night to tell him everything. To explain about leaving Father's house. About Aaron." She took a deep breath. "About giving my baby to an orphanage." She saw her sister jolt as though she'd been poked by a hot iron. "I told Bears everything, and then he wanted to hold me. I fell asleep in his arms. We did nothing, I swear!"

Annabelle watched her sister with deep sorrow in her gaze. "Is this why you've always held yourself apart from Skye? Because your wound was always too fresh?"

Fidelia nodded. "And because I can never have another. I don't know where my baby is. As I told Bears, I pray every night that he is happy and well loved. That I did the right thing. But I miss him every day."

"What did you name him?" Cailean asked, his concern replacing any animosity.

"Benjamin," Fidelia whispered. "I always liked that name." She shared a look with her sister, while Annabelle fought tears. Fidelia had always dreamed of naming her son Benjamin when the sisters made up stories of their futures together in Maine, whereas Annabelle's son would have been named Grant.

"And Aaron?" Anna sniffled. "Did he really die?"

"Yes, of diphtheria. But, by then, he didn't want me. He'd refused to marry me. Thought a pregnant woman was a burden he shouldn't have to suffer."

"Bastard," Cailean muttered. "I hope you choose better next time."

She watched him and nodded as she rubbed at her cheeks and her chin with the sleeve of her dress. "I know I have. I've chosen Bears." She paused as she took a deep breath. "I love him."

Cailean stared at her steadily, while Annabelle smiled. "Good," he said. "Although you won't always find it easy to be with someone many consider an outcast."

Fidelia gave a snort and rolled her eyes. "I'm an outcast. I know exactly how that feels." She watched them. "Besides, I doubt we'll marry."

Cailean glowered at her. "Why would you say that?"

"There's no need as we won't have children," she whispered, her gaze lowering to focus on the wilting bundle of flowers at the center of the round table.

"There's every need, and, if you aren't sensible enough to know it, I won't sit here and spell it out for you," Cailean said with a roll of his eyes. "I'm to bed. I want a little sleep before I have to face the dawn."

He looked outside and glowered at the light already highlighting the mountains. He trudged upstairs, leaving the sisters alone.

"I'm sorry, Anna," Fidelia whispered. When her sister just stared at her, she said in a low voice, "I'm sorry I treated you so poorly when you arrived. I'm sorry I was envious of your good fortune. I'm sorry I've not been as good an aunt to Skye as I should be." She lowered her head.

"She's young. She won't remember her aunt who kept her at a distance. She will remember her aunt who loved her and played with her. Who taught her songs of Maine and how to knit and tat lace. Be *that* aunt for Skye." Annabelle's eyes filled. "Trust in me and family again, Dee."

Fidelia nodded. "I will try. There will be times when I fail, but I will always try." She gripped her sister's hand. "I never meant to worry you last night. I should have told you that I was going to see Bears. But my fear and anxiety about telling him what happened overrode any thought that you would be concerned. And I didn't plan to stay the night. Forgive me."

"I will always worry about you. You're my sister." She smiled. "And I'm so happy you will be with Bears."

Fidelia couldn't hide her contented smile. "I never knew a man like him existed. It seems too good to be true."

Annabelle smiled. "It's not." She looked at her sister and shook her head. "I can see you slept well last night, but I'm joining Cailean. I need some sleep before Skye wakes. Thank God the bakery is closed today."

"Sleep. I'll watch her." She smiled at her sister. "Things will be different from now on."

CHAPTER 8

The Bear Grass Springs' Town Improvement Committee had voted to use all the proceeds from the bake sale at the October Harvest Dance to bolster the coffers of the community's school. It needed new school primers, a window replaced, and funds for wood and coal during the school year.

Fidelia followed Annabelle and Cailean into the Odd Fellows Hall and marveled at how the women on the decorating committee managed to make every party look the same. Streamers hung from the rafters, while the punch and food were along the far wall. The small group of musicians stood off to one corner, and men huddled around the two kegs brought in from the Stumble-Out Saloon.

"I wish we could have more of Karl's *glogg*," Cailean murmured, smiling at a few customers he knew from the livery.

"That's only for Christmas," Annabelle said. "Besides, Karl is busy with baby Mette and Leena. He doesn't have time to make us punch."

"I hope he has time by the New Year's Dance," Cailean muttered.

"I'd prefer it to the sweet punch," Leticia whispered, then took a sip of Mrs. Guerineau's punch. The recipe came from an old plantation mixture her mother had taught her when she had lived in Louisiana.

Now it was a staple for events in Bear Grass Springs. "I almost envy the men their whiskey and beer."

Fidelia rolled her eyes and giggled. "Can you imagine what would be said if the townsfolk saw us drinking spirits?"

The three women began to laugh. "How are you feeling, Leticia?" Annabelle asked.

"Tired but well." She stroked a hand over her belly. "It's hard to believe I'll have another babe by Christmas." She shared a smile with Annabelle and Fidelia. "Alistair is nervous but excited."

"He's a smart man," Fidelia said and then backed up a step to make room for Ewan and Jessamine, who joined them.

Jessamine watched the room with a roving eye as she searched out a story for her *News and Noteworthy* column.

"I'm sure a miner will start a brawl for ye, darlin'," Ewan murmured.

"I'm sick of reporting on miner brawls. There's nothing new in that sort of story," Jessamine grumbled.

"You could report on the fact that the teacher, Mr. Danforth, is starting the school year later this year and insists he only needs to have the school open for twelve weeks," Leticia said with consternation.

Jessamine glowered. "I've already written three stories on that topic, and I've been informed by many of the townsfolk that they'd rather read about a tall tale than my bellyaching over the teacher. That he's within his rights to teach the minimum amount required."

"I wonder if they'll still feel that way when their children can barely read and can't find a good job," Annabelle said. "Although too many still wonder at the benefits of education."

Leticia sighed. "As it is, school won't start until November. Hopefully we'll have a mild winter so the children can travel to school with ease."

The women stood in silence as they contemplated the schoolteacher who had been welcomed with such high hopes a few years before but had proved to be a disappointment.

Jessamine looked around, still in search of anything worthy to report, and her eyes widened as she glanced toward the entrance to the Hall. "That's a story," she murmured.

The MacKinnons turned and stared at Bears as he ushered in Mildred. He saw them and nodded as he approached them. "We thought we'd join the festivities," Bears said. He watched as Mildred raced away to play with Hortence and to meet other children. His gaze followed her, but he looked at Leticia as she spoke to him.

"She will be fine here, Bears. We all watch out for them." She smiled at the fear in his gaze. "And Hortence is fiercely protective of her new friend."

Bears relaxed at her words and accepted a glass of punch from Alistair. He shook his head at Ewan's offer for a glass of whiskey or beer. "What happens at these events?"

"We stand around and talk with each other. Then we eat some food and dance." Cailean shrugged and accepted Skye from Annabelle. "It's a way for the townsfolk to come together."

Bears turned as the music began to play and frowned. "I only know how to dance the waltz."

Ewan grinned at him. "Well, ye're in luck. They play a lot of waltzes. They like to give the miners a chance to dance with the bonny lasses here."

Fidelia shook her head as Asa Schuman approached her, and she moved into the corner by the wall. She paled as Asa returned to his friends and glared over his shoulder at her.

Bears eased to her side and dropped his hand so that their fingers touched. "Will you dance with me?" he whispered.

"Yes." She flushed at the desire she saw in his eyes.

He smiled. "When it is a waltz." He met her amused stare and then focused on Helen and Warren as they joined their group.

"Will Sorcha be here today?" Helen asked. "I've missed seeing her."

"Aye," Cailean said. "She wrote saying she, Frederick, and most of the men would come for the celebration. The men always complain they don't have enough opportunities to dance with pretty women." His smile broadened as he saw his baby sister enter on the arm of her husband. Sorcha wore an attractive dark-blue wool dress that hid the advancing stage of her pregnancy. She gripped Frederick's arm as though her balance were more precarious than usual. Their ranch hands fanned out behind them to greet acquaintances and to partake of punch and stronger libations.

Sorcha hugged everyone and stood beside Fidelia. "I dinna think we'd make it in today. Cannin' vegetables takes much longer than I thought it would!" She embraced Irene and Harold as she laughed.

Frederick greeted his grandparents and smiled at his extended family. "The fall roundup went as well as we could have hoped. Peter and Cole are on their way to Chicago for the livestock auction." His brothers each owned one-third of the ranch, although they spent little time on it. They preferred to travel to Chicago each fall to auction off the cattle and then winter in Texas. They would drive a herd up in the spring.

"Will they drive another herd up north next year?" Bears asked with a frown.

Frederick shook his head. "They aren't sure. The land is getting parceled off, and there are too many fences now. If they do it this next spring, I think it will be for the last time."

Frederick watched as the women formed a circle around Sorcha and Fidelia, and he eased away with Bears and the men, while his grandfather, Harold, joined them. "I have a concern," Frederick said.

The MacKinnon brothers' attention focused on him. "What?" Ewan asked.

Frederick lowered his voice. "I want Sorcha to be in town when she gives birth. I worry it will happen in the middle of a blizzard, and she'll have to depend on me and Slims and Dalton." He watched as Sorcha spoke with Helen.

Warren nodded. "I'd prefer it if my wife didn't have to travel such distances in winter."

"We'll make room for you in our home," Cailean said. "Whenever you want to move to town, know there is space for you."

Frederick let out a deep breath and relaxed. "Thank you."

"Ye are a good man, Frederick, an' ye care well for our sister. Thank ye," Alistair said.

Bears's head jerked up, and he tilted his head toward the men playing music. "That is a waltz, isn't it?"

Ewan laughed. "How are ye to dance with yer woman if ye dinna ken it's a waltz?"

Frederick nodded at Bears. "Ignore him. And, yes, it is."

Bears moved into the crowd of women and held out his hand for Fidelia. She smiled at him and walked with him onto the dance floor, sighing with pleasure to be in his arms again after a few days without seeing him. She absently noted Warren and Helen dancing near them. "I've missed you," she whispered.

"Don't stay away again," he murmured.

She nodded and then gasped as she was yanked from Bears's arms. She glared at the man who held her arm like a manacle and then recoiled as he spit on her.

"You are a whore and should not be allowed here!" Walter Jameson yelled.

The lyrical music ground to a halt, and everyone in the Hall turned to stare at the spectacle on the dance floor. Bears lunged for Walter but was held back by Warren, who had been next to him. The sheriff stood to one side, alert and ready to intervene, should his authority become necessary.

"No, Bears," Warren murmured. "No." Warren wrapped an arm around Bears's chest and held him in place as Bears struggled to free himself.

Bears stood with his fists at his side, his arms held down by Warren's strong hold on him. He watched Fidelia kick Walter and wrench her arm free. She then pulled a handkerchief from her pocket and swiped the spit off her face.

"You have no right to speak about me in such a manner," she said as she faced Walter.

"I have every right. The people of this town have the right to know that you have played them false." Walter watched her with a triumphant gleam in his gaze. "You've led them on to believe that you are an honorable woman, eager to repent after giving up your lascivious ways. I know for a fact you've carried on as you did in the Boudoir."

She shook her head. "You're mad."

"I saw you at this man's house. Alone!" He pointed at Bears.

Bears watched him with an impassive expression, although his eyes shone with loathing.

"I saw her *kiss* him," Walter said, with envy tinged with hate. "On the lips."

"You witnessed a kiss, and you consider her worthy of your contempt?" Bears asked. "Did you bother to discover why she kissed me?"

"There is no reason for a woman like her to kiss a man like you!" Walter snapped.

"Of course there is," Fidelia said as she stood tall and again boldly faced Walter. "He asked me to marry him, and I said yes. I sealed that promise with a kiss."

Loud gasps were heard in the crowd, and then a resounding applause echoed through the Hall.

"About time!" someone called out.

"A perfect match," another shouted.

"Lies!" Walter screamed.

Fidelia shook her head, and Bears, who had been freed from Warren's hold, took her hand. "I do not lie," Bears said, then moved Fidelia behind him, protecting her. He leaned forward and whispered into Walter's ear.

Walter paled and took a step away.

Bears's eyes shone with menace. "Heed me."

Walter spun on his heels and stormed away.

Fidelia let out a deep breath and leaned into Bears. "Hold me," she whispered. A fine quivering moved through her, and he held her as she calmed after facing her nemesis.

He whispered in her ear, "Will you?"

She giggled. "Yes."

Warren approached. "I have no desire to ever know what you whispered to Walter." He shared a long look with Bears. "But I appre-

126

ciate your ability to get him to leave."

Well-wishers soon surrounded the couple. A few held back, as they found it hard to reconcile a marriage for a woman who used to work at the Boudoir with an upstanding man of the town. A few others found it difficult to envision a white woman married to a half-Indian man. However, people with those reactions were vastly outnumbered.

Mildred made her way to them and watched them, wide-eyed.

Cailean motioned to his brothers, and they formed a circle around the couple, facing outward, engaging the townsfolk in idle chitchat so that Fidelia and Bears could speak privately to Bears's daughter.

"Are you really going to marry?" she asked.

"Yes," her father said as he sank to his haunches. "I had hoped to speak with you privately, but that wasn't possible."

"He's a bad man," Mildred said, pointing to the door where Walter had left the Hall. "He had no right to treat you like that, Fidelia."

Fidelia held out a shaking hand and rested it on Mildred's shoulder. "I'm so happy we'll be family."

Mildred nodded and then hugged her father. "I'm happy for you, Father." She spun away and raced off to play with Hortence again.

Fidelia watched her with longing in her gaze, and Bears linked his hand with hers. "Give her time," he whispered.

Annabelle approached her sister and Bears. "When is the wedding?" she asked with a broad smile.

"As soon as possible," Bears said with a smile, while Fidelia flushed.

Ewan joined them and patted Bears on his shoulder before hugging Fidelia. "Ye canna remain in that small cabin." He frowned as though figuring out a puzzle. "I have an idea." He walked away and approached his foreman and good friend, Ben Metcalf.

"Come. Waltz with me again," Bears whispered to Fidelia. She nodded and smiled at him, walking into his arms and sighing with contentment when they twirled around the dance floor together.

A few days after the impromptu betrothal announcement, Fidelia worked alone in the bakery kitchen. Annabelle had gone home with Skye, and Fidelia wanted to tidy the kitchen a little more for the following day before joining her sister at home. She looked outside at the bright, beautiful fall day and yearned to walk into the woods. She closed her eyes as she envisioned sitting by the stream. Breathing in the fresh air of the pine forest. Having a moment alone that wasn't in the solitude of her bedroom or the back room of the bakery. However, with Walter's return, she had no desire to give him the added opportunity to find her alone and vulnerable.

"You always did spend too much time daydreaming."

She jerked and stared at the door she was certain she had locked after Annabelle's departure.

"You have no right to be in here," Fidelia said, her hands gripping a dishcloth.

The Madam, dressed in a shimmering aquamarine dress that changed hues as she moved, sauntered toward her. "I have every right to visit you, Charity. Especially when I hear that you have the perverse notion to marry a man such as that half-breed." Her eyes shone with hatred and enmity.

Fidelia stood tall and stared at the Madam in confusion. "Whether or not I marry Bears does not change the fact that I will never return to the Boudoir. *Never.*"

She gasped as the Madam strode to her and slapped her. "You thankless girl. I saved you when others spat on you while you begged. I gave you food and shelter. I prevented you from meeting your maker all those years ago. Where is your loyalty? Where is your appreciation for all I did for you?"

Fidelia held a hand to her cheek but stood her ground. "You were thanked by every man who paid coin to abuse my body," she rasped. "You were paid every time you laughed as I screamed in pain. Every time you reveled in my misery, you were paid. Any debt you perceive owed to you is in your imagination. My debt is paid in full."

The Madam reached forward again but jerked back when Fidelia thwacked her with the dampened drying cloth. The Madam yowled in pain and stared at her in confusion, since Fidelia had never fought back before. Previously she had sidled away and avoided the Madam but never stood her ground. This time Fidelia stood tall and glared at the Madam.

"How dare you presume you have the right to enter this bakery and threaten me in any way?" Fidelia said. "I'm not alone anymore, Madam. There are many who will protect me."

The Madam glared at her. "I want what's mine. What you've kept from me." When Fidelia shook her head in confusion, the Madam said, "The money that your father left you while you were living at the Boudoir. That is rightfully my money."

Fidelia laughed. "How do you come to that conclusion?"

"I spent money I didn't have to entice worthless men to your bed. I made you into the most sought-after whore in Bear Grass Springs. You would have been dead from disease if I hadn't protected you, like Sincerity." She saw Fidelia's eyes cloud at the mention of the woman who had died soon after they had arrived in Montana. "You owe me."

Fidelia shook her head to push aside those sad memories, then smiled. "I'm sure the lawyer would be fascinated by your definition of a *debt*. And of what's *yours*." She saw the Madam blanch at the thought of visiting Warren Clark, a man who held her in low esteem for the Madam's attempt to auction off the woman who became his wife nearly two years ago.

"He must uphold the law," the Madam said with a jut of her chin.

"Yes, he must. However, we never had a contract between us. You've always been afraid of what a written contract could mean. Thus, it's your word against mine." Fidelia smirked, as though just pronouncing *checkmate*. "Fortunately for me, more in the community would believe me over you."

The Madam turned beet red and spun on her heel. At the back door, she hissed, "This isn't over!" She slammed the door shut behind her.

Fidelia took a deep breath and grabbed the key before locking the rear door. She then opened the front door, making sure to lock it too, and exited onto the boardwalk. After taking another calming breath and focusing on the beautiful day, she walked across the street and down the boardwalk to Warren's office.

Hesitating only a moment, she pushed open the door and entered. "I apologize for bothering you without an appointment," she blurted out.

Warren stared at her a moment, before rising and motioning for her to sit in the chair across from his desk. He patted at his finger-mussed hair and smoothed down his shirtsleeves, then pulled on his jacket. "Forgive me. I was lost in this report." He focused on her and smiled softly. "What is it, Fidelia?" He frowned as he looked at her. "Did Walter do that?" he asked as he nodded at her reddened cheek, his eyes lit with ire.

She hastily raised a hand to cover her abused cheek. "No." When she saw doubt in his gaze, she whispered, "The Madam."

He leaned back in his chair and let out a deep breath. "Perhaps you should explain everything." He gave Fidelia a nod of encouragement and waited for her to speak.

She took a deep breath. "I'm certain you are aware of the money my sister set aside for me. She must have spoken with you, if she were successful in saving me a portion of that inheritance, before she married Cailean."

Warren nodded and frowned. "Yes. It was set apart, specifically for you. What bothers you?" When Fidelia took another deep breath but remained silent, he said, "Unless a contract is written up, like the one Annabelle had Cailean sign, the money will become your husband's on your wedding day."

"What about a woman's right to own property?" Fidelia asked with a frown.

"There's the law, and then there's what occurs." He gave her a chagrined shrug. "The Married Women's Property Acts are intended to protect women so that they do not lose everything when they marry. But I fear they are often laxly enforced." He watched her intently as she seemed to relax at his words. "I would help you in any way I could, if it were necessary." He paused and seemed to be choosing his words with care. "Are you worried Bears will spend your money?"

Fidelia shook her head. "No, although I should tell him about it." She clenched and unclenched her hands. "The Madam knows I have money from my father and believes it is rightfully hers." She nodded as Warren stifled his laughter.

"How does she come to that deduction?" Warren held a hand over his mouth as his eyes shone with merriment.

"She believes that, while I was living with her, everything that was mine belonged to her. Because she paid for my food and lodging." Fidelia bowed her head in shame when she spoke of her time in the Boudoir.

"Hogwash," Warren said as his amusement changed to anger at Fidelia's mention of her time at the Boudoir. "If the Madam were dragged in front of a judge, she'd argue that you were an honorable employee and that you received wages. No employer has the right to garnish the inheritance of any of his or her workers. Not even the Madam." His eyes now shone with righteous anger. "Don't allow her to control you again, Fidelia. Not even in this small way."

Fidelia let out a deep breath and relaxed. "Thank you, Warren. I thought there was nothing she could do, but I don't know the law."

Warren rested his elbows on the desk and smiled encouragingly at Fidelia. "If anything, I'd remain on guard for Walter. He wants money, and he'll do anything he can to obtain it. I'd bet my father's wealth that he's in cahoots with the Madam in some way."

Fidelia's eyes widened, and she paled. "Oh, no," she breathed. She sat frozen for a moment and then looked at him beseechingly. "Would you do me the favor of walking me home?"

Warren rose. "Of course. I was just thinking it is too nice a day to remain cooped up inside. Soon enough, we won't want to go outside due to the winter weather." He opened the door for Fidelia and followed her out.

After the short walk to Cailean's house, she gripped his arm in thanks and entered the livery. The barn was quiet, with horses nickering. Brutus huffed and kicked at his stall a few times when he saw her but soon quieted after she passed his stall. She walked to the tack room and stood there a long moment, watching as Bears polished tack and sang in a low baritone.

"You sing too," she whispered.

He looked up and smiled. "Stitch. I didn't expect to see you today." He frowned as he noticed the tension in her stance. "What happened?" His alert gaze looked for some injury, and he frowned when he saw the fading redness on one cheek.

"I visited with Warren."

He moved toward her, rubbing his hands over her arms. "Why should the lawyer upset you?"

She threw herself in his arms. "He didn't," she said as she nestled into his arms. "Hold me." She wrapped her arms around his waist and sighed as he enfolded her in his strong arms. "I have to tell you something."

He murmured into her hair and kissed her, waiting for her to speak.

"When my father died in Maine, he left his estate to Annabelle. He believed I deserved none of it." She sniffled as a tear leaked out. "Even though he didn't know I was a prostitute, he considered me unworthy of anything."

"*Shh*, my darling. He isn't worth your tears," Bears whispered as his hands caressed her back.

She took a stuttering breath. "Annabelle found a letter I'd written Father. And she found me. Here." Fidelia pushed away and met his gaze. "And insisted that half of what she'd received from the sale of the land and house in Maine was mine." Another tear leaked out and trailed down her cheek.

"Why do you continue to believe you are unworthy?" Bears whispered.

"I was horrible to her when she arrived." She closed her eyes as she blushed. "I was so ashamed to have my baby sister see me for what I'd become."

Bears huffed his disagreement. "She always saw you as her beloved sister."

"Which was almost harder to bear when I felt such a failure." Fidelia opened her eyes. "She had Cailean sign a contract before they married to ensure the money remained mine. Warren confirmed it is all still there, set aside in the bank."

Bears frowned. "Then what did Warren say to upset you?"

She shook her head. "It wasn't Warren. It was the Madam. She claims that what I had during my time at the Boudoir is hers. That I owe her my inheritance for everything she did for me."

He scowled. "She should pay you." He cupped her cheeks and looked deeply into her eyes. "I knew about the money. I've known about it since the day Walter returned and injured you. Cailean told the men of the family about it in confidence."

"Why?" she sputtered, her eyes round.

"There was concern then that Walter and the Madam would attempt to force you back to the Boudoir for the purpose of taking that money. I see we were correct in our concern." He met her wary gaze. "I don't want your money."

"It will be yours soon enough," she whispered. "When we marry, it becomes yours."

"No," he said and swooped forward, kissing her passionately. "I want you. Nothing more."

"I don't understand." More tears leaked out, and she moved her face into his palm as he swiped the tears away.

"Money will never compare to you, Stitch. You could come to me as an heiress or as a pauper, and it would never change how much I want you." He smiled. "Besides, I know I profess to be a humble worker in the livery, but I do have some money set aside by my father. The MacKinnons have it in trust for me because they were worried about Finlay."

She pushed herself into his arms and clung to him. "Why don't they sign it over to you now?"

"I'll ask them to, now that we are to marry. I should have done it once I found Bright Fawn." He kissed Fidelia's head. "It hadn't mattered to me before. I had a house, a job I enjoyed, and I never went hungry. What more did I need?"

She kissed his chest. "Me."

His hands tightened around her. "Yes, you." After a long moment, he murmured, "I could speak with Warren about signing a similar agreement, as Cailean did. To ensure the money remains yours."

She shuddered. "No. I want no individual claim on it. If Walter and the Madam think it's solely mine, they might continue with their plotting." She arched back and looked at him with terror-filled gaze. "I can't go back there, Bears."

"Never, my love," he whispered. "I won't let that misfortune befall you again. I promise." He enfolded her in his arms and held her tight for long moments as they comforted each other.

~

Bears paused before entering the Merc, as a man stepped in front of him. "Excuse me," he murmured and then frowned as the man blocked his movement.

"You should be begging my pardon," the man in dirty miner's clothing said, stepping closer until they were nearly chest to chest.

Bears shook his head at the man. "By your clothes, you're a miner. I have no quarrel with anyone from the mines."

"Then you are as dumb as they say. I'm Asa Schuman, and you interfered with my courtship of Miss Fidelia Evans." He pushed at Bears, forcing him back a pace. "How dare you believe you have the right to touch such a beautiful woman."

Bears's gaze glinted with anger, but he smiled in a self-deprecating manner. "I can understand your confusion, Mr. Schuman. I was just as astounded that such a discerning, intelligent woman would choose me."

Asa's gaze flit over Bears, and he shook his head in disgust. "No woman would choose a half-breed over a man like me. Did you appeal to her baser nature, as is her natural tendency, to entrap her?"

Bears stood taller, and his voice lowered with his rage. "You would do well to remember that you're disparaging the woman who will be my wife." He took a step forward, forcing Asa back. He nodded as the man seemed to recognize the veiled strength and threat in Bears's words and actions. "You will never speak of Miss Evans in such a disrespectful manner again."

The miner snorted. "It's not as though everyone in the area don't know what sort of woman she was."

Bears gripped Asa's neckcloth with lightning speed, dragging him up to his toes. "Yes, a respectable woman forced into a life she hated by horrible circumstances. If you want to have success with a woman who interests you in the future, I suggest you respect her, not insult her." He released Asa, who collapsed to his knees, gasping for air. "Don't bother us again, miner."

Bears stepped around Asa and entered the Merc, meeting Tobias's inquisitive stare. Tobias stood near the door with a broom in one hand. "Tobias," Bears said with a nod.

Tobias nodded and set aside his broom. "For a moment there, I wasn't sure who I'd use the broom on."

Bears snorted and shook his head. "It's not like you to show compassion to my intended. I'm surprised you didn't join the miner in his abuse of her."

Tobias straightened his shoulders and walked with stiff formality behind the counter. "I may have been incorrect in my assessment of her." He met Bears's incredulous stare. "Although I refuse to admit I was wrong."

Bears smiled. "You will." He let out a deep sigh as he looked at the section reserved for women's clothes. "I need a red hair ribbon."

"Red?" Tobias asked. He walked to the area and pulled out a tray that held the ribbons. "If it's for your daughter, I'd suggest this pink."

Bears fingered it, a dark pink that glimmered in the light. He nodded as he set down his coin. "Thank you." After picking up the small wrapped parcel, he stared at Tobias for a long moment. "You could have more than this, if you apologized."

Tobias shook his head. "Some things are unforgiveable. I know what I've done. So do my nephews."

Bears watched him with no rancor. "You've never approved of me working in the livery. You've always seen my presence as reprehensible." His eyes lit with anger for a moment, and then he calmed. "You've shown, over and over, your disapproval of Fidelia. What has changed?"

Tobias straightened, staring out the door, as though awaiting another customer. After a long moment, he whispered, "I've come to understand the price of acting dishonorably. I've always resented those who've had the ability to act with honor, even under duress." His gaze glinted with envy. "I will have a grandniece or grandnephew soon, who will never know me. Who will be raised to consider me an enemy."

Bears watched him in astonishment. "You envy us because of the bonds we have forged?" he whispered.

Tobias's eyes shone with resentment. "Why should one such as Fidelia be welcomed back into the bosom of her family after all she did, and yet I remain a pariah?"

Bears leaned forward, until he was nose to nose with Tobias. "She regretted every day she spent in that place, even though she had no alternative. But she forgave herself." He watched as Tobias jerked, as though Bears had just run him through. "It didn't matter what her sister thought. Or what I thought. All that mattered was that Fidelia learned to forgive herself." He nodded as Tobias stood in stunned silence. "Think about that, Tobias." Bears nodded again and spun on his heel to leave the Mercantile.

"Bears?" Tobias called out. "I wish you well in your marriage."

Bears looked over his shoulder and met Tobias's devastated gaze. "Thank you. No one will make the first move, Tobias. Not until you do."

Nearly two weeks later, near the end of October, Fidelia worked in the bakery on the day before her wedding to Bears. They had hoped for a small wedding ceremony, followed by an intimate party with close family and friends. However, the townsfolk wanted to be invited to the ceremony, since they had witnessed the declaration of their love at the Harvest Dance. So all who wished were welcome to the reception. Annabelle had made three large cakes and more cookies and breads than Fidelia had known were possible to bake. Annabelle had closed the bakery for two days in preparation of her sister's wedding.

Now, rather than return to the room she had lived in since her escape from the Boudoir, Fidelia lingered in the bakery. She dried pots and pans. She swiped the counter clean for the third time. When Annabelle tried to shoo her sister home, Fidelia shook her head. "No, I don't want to go there."

"Why not?" her sister asked, collapsing on a stool. The small back room had tables along every wall crammed full of treats for the following day.

"Will I still be able to work here after I marry?" Fidelia asked as she cleaned an imaginary smudge.

"Of course you will. But only if you want to." Her sister watched her in confusion. "I don't understand. What's the matter, Dee?"

Her sister shrugged. "I worry he'll come to regret his choice in me." She bit her lip as she blurted out her fear.

Annabelle nodded. "I think that is a common fear. I didn't marry Cailean for love. I never thought I'd love him. But I always worried he'd regret marrying me, when he could have chosen someone else. In the end, I came to realize I had to trust in him, as he had to trust in me."

"I think love is easier than trust," she whispered.

Annabelle propped her chin on her hand. "They're both fragile but in different ways." She looked at her sister. "Do you remember when I was first ill? When I lost my first baby?" Her eyes clouded with grief as Fidelia nodded. "I never thought I could regain my trust in Cailean. But I did." When Fidelia remained quiet, Annabelle whispered, "Has Bears done something to cause you to lose faith in him?"

"No," Fidelia said rapidly, shaking her head emphatically. "No." She flushed as she looked at her sister. "It's ..." She closed her eyes. "I'm being foolish."

"What is it, Dee?"

Fidelia pulled out a stool and sat next to her sister. "I've missed this. Being sisters." She smiled at Annabelle. "I'm afraid I'll shock you, and I don't want to embarrass you."

Annabelle shrugged. "I'm a married woman, and I'm tougher than I look." Her smile broadened as Fidelia nodded in agreement.

"I have this fear that he believes I'm more skilled in the bedroom than I am. Aaron never found me particularly exciting, and, at the Boudoir, I just had to lay there." She flushed beet red. "I don't want to disappoint Bears."

"Oh my," her sister said as she fought a matching blush. "I can't say I understand because I don't. I went to my wedding ignorant. However, Cailean and I spoke through most of it. Laughing and teasing and saying what we liked." She speared her sister with a glare. "Don't you dare tell anyone I told you that."

Fidelia giggled and nodded, and Annabelle smiled.

Annabelle shrugged. "I think, if you're honest, you'll be much better off than if you try to act like you're something or someone you're not. He wants *you*, Dee. Not some dream of you."

"I think that is even more frightening than anything else. What if I'm me and I disappoint him?"

Her sister watched her with patient, loving eyes. "That's what trust and faith are about. You must trust him."

Fidelia nodded and rose. "I feel better. But I must speak with Bears before tomorrow." She spun around and pulled Annabelle close. "Thank you."

Fidelia slipped from the bakery and walked the short distance to the livery. When she entered, she found Bears in the tack room. "What are you doing?" she asked.

"Arranging and polishing tack that doesn't need anything done to it," he said with a shy smile. He watched her with a curious gaze. "I thought I wasn't to see you today."

She wrung her hands and bit her lip. "I found I needed to speak with you." She jumped as she heard Alistair and Cailean in a stall.

Bears's gaze sobered, and he nodded. "Come. I want privacy for what you must say." He frowned as she became skittish when he reached for her hand and so dropped his hand to his side. He waited for her to follow him and led her from the livery to his home. "Mildred is with Hortence. She'll spend the next few days with Alistair. If need be."

Fidelia frowned as she watched him pace his small living area. "I don't understand. What do you mean, *if need be?*"

"Why are you here, Fidelia? Why don't you want me to touch you?" His intense gaze bore into hers and noted her acknowledgment of him not using her nickname. "Do you want to call off the wedding?"

"No!" she gasped, then moved toward him. She cupped his cheeks and shook her head frantically. "No, my love." She stood on her toes and kissed him. She sighed as his arms banded around her and held her close. After a few more kisses, she rested her head on his shoulder. She relaxed as he caressed her back.

"Why did you need to see me then before we wed?" he whispered into her neck.

"I worry you will find me a disappointment," she breathed. She backed away as he froze. "I'm … I'm not as skilled as I fear you think I am."

He tilted his head to one side and shook his head subtly as though attempting to decipher exactly what she had said. "You're worried that I will find you lacking in the bedroom? That because you used to work at the Boudoir, I will have the expectation that you are more knowledgeable than you really are?"

She nodded and began wringing her hands again.

He reached forward and grabbed her hands, stilling her nervous movement. A slow, sensual smile spread. "Did it ever occur to you that I'm worried you'd find me lacking?"

She frowned as she looked at him and shook her head. "Never."

"Why is that?" he murmured as he tamed a strand of hair and then threaded his fingers into her long, silky locks.

"Because I've felt more pleasure with you than I've ever felt with anyone in my entire life. I know that you will only ever bring me joy."

His brilliant smile made her breath catch, and he leaned forward to kiss her. "Did you ever think it's the same for me? That I've never felt this way either?" He bracketed her head with his strong palms. "I've known passion. I've known love. But I've never known what I feel with you, Stitch." He took a deep breath. "I know I ask the impossible. But my hope is that, when we marry, we are the only two in our marriage bed."

She looked at him, tears filling her eyes. "I hope that too. I don't know if I will be successful, but I will try."

He rested his forehead against hers. "That is all I can ask." He released her and backed up a step. "Come. You should go. According to Alistair, I shouldn't see you, or it's bad luck."

"It would have been worse luck if we had not spoken," she said as she met his kiss. "I love you. I can't wait to marry you tomorrow."

He smiled. "I can't wait for you either."

She paused at the doorway. "May I ask you a favor? It might seem presumptuous." She waited until he nodded. "I want to marry you, Bears. You know I do." She took a deep breath. "But I also want to be a mother to Mildred. To Bright Fawn." She saw his eyes flash with a deep emotion. "Think of a way to have her be a part of our ceremony, for what we do tomorrow affects her too."

He nodded, and she slipped from the room.

CHAPTER 9

The following morning, the MacKinnon men were at Bears's house to help him prepare. He shook his head at their arrival but allowed them into his small home. "I don't know why you're here. I can dress myself."

"'Tis tradition," Ewan said. "The women fuss over the bride, an' we commiserate with the groom."

"I don't need you to commiserate. I want to marry Fidelia," Bears said as he moved to his daughter's room to don his clothes.

"Aye, but ye're still givin' up yer freedom," Ewan said with a wink to his brothers. "That which is lost must be mourned."

Bears poked his head out, his long black hair falling around his shoulders. "If you think I'm mourning, you're a fool, carpenter."

Alistair rolled his eyes. "Ye ken Fidelia is as anxious to marry ye as ye are her?"

Bears emerged from the back room in a black suit with white shirt. He wore a beaded belt made of three colors: cream, turquoise, and red.

"Where did ye get that?" Alistair asked, staring at it in wonder. "'Tis beautiful." He reached out and waited until Bears nodded before he touched it.

"My mother gave it to me. It was her grandfather's. She gave it to me, and I rarely wear it."

"No better day than today," Cailean said with a broad smile.

Bears nodded and smoothed down his hair, flowing freely along his back.

"Are ye intentionally tryin' to rile the preacher?" Ewan asked with a raised eyebrow. "Ye ken we had a hard-enough time convincin' the man to marry ye in the church."

Bears grinned. "And now I'm arriving as though I'm part of a war party looking for scalps?" He rolled his eyes. "My people are peaceful. And this is part of my heritage. What is it that Alistair was spouting yesterday? Honoring traditions?"

Alistair shrugged.

"Something old, something new?" Bears said. He patted at the suit. "This is new. And this"—he touched the beaded belt—"is old."

"That's for the bride. The groom is only expected to show up with a ring," Cailean said with exasperation.

Bears shrugged with a shake of his head, as though he would never fully understand these traditions and that he didn't particularly care if he got them right. "Thank you, Alistair, for watching Mildred for a few days," he murmured.

"Aye, 'tis no bother, an' Hortence is delighted to have her stay with us. I fear Mildred will return home no' havin' slept a wink the entire time she's been away."

"I—We'll be back before school starts. I want to be here for her first day."

Alistair smiled. "Hortence canna wait for school this year because of Mildred."

"She canna wait because she loves school. She takes after her mother," Ewan said.

Alistair tilted his head in agreement and continued to smile.

"Come. Let's get you to church. We don't want the townsfolk to think you are anything less than eager to marry your bride," Cailean said as he slapped Bears on the shoulder.

"Aye, they've had enough drama watchin' the two of us marry,"

Ewan said with a laugh, pointing to Alistair. Ewan's wedding had been interrupted by the arrival of his soon-to-be father-in-law, protesting the marriage.

Alistair groaned and shook his head as he considered his first attempt at marrying Leticia, which was interrupted by the arrival of her first husband who, unbeknownst to Alistair, was still alive. "Let's hope ye are blessed with a quiet ceremony, like Cailean and Anna's," Alistair said. They walked from Bears's small cabin toward the church, telling jokes and teasing Bears the entire way.

F idelia stood at the rear of the church and took a calming breath. Annabelle was about to walk up the aisle as her only bridesmaid, and Cailean would escort Fidelia. She ran a hand over her cream-colored dress with lace at the hem and wrists. The simple cut of the dress enhanced her curves but was modest with a small bustle and buttons running down her back. She clutched a bouquet of dried pussy willows, since no wildflowers were in bloom this time of year, and tried not to fidget.

"Are you all right, Fidelia?" Cailean asked. "Do you still want to marry Bears?"

She met his worried gaze and laughed. "Of course I do. I just wish it were in front of the family instead of the townsfolk." She saw him grimace.

Rather than the small intimate wedding before their family and friends, the townsfolk had filled the pews, ignoring how their invitation was only to the reception afterward. The MacKinnon brothers and Warren had decided it was better to allow them to stay and to witness the wedding rather than start a small riot by forcing the uninvited guests to leave. A few townsfolk had protested the marriage of a former Boudoir Beauty marrying in the church, but they had been enticed to the Stumble-Out with the promise of as much whiskey as they could drink for the day by Ewan.

"You won't have anyone doubting the legitimacy of your marriage," her sister murmured. "Not like what happened to Sorcha or Helen. Everyone who wants to witness it will be here, and it is blessed by the pastor."

"The unwilling pastor," Fidelia muttered. Her ears still rung from the uncharitable words he'd shouted at her when she had requested he marry her. To her surprise, the pastor's wife had championed Fidelia's marriage and had talked him round. "I'm ready, Anna."

Her sister squeezed her arm and took a step into the aisle. Fidelia watched Anna walk down the aisle with measured steps, and she knew her sister would smile at everyone who looked at her. "I don't deserve her," Fidelia whispered.

"Aye, you do," Cailean said. "You deserve all of us. And you deserve a man like Bears." He held his elbow out and winked at her, as she slipped her hand through it.

He turned her so they walked down the aisle. His firm hold on her hand prevented her from dashing down the aisle toward her betrothed when she caught sight of Bears waiting for her. "Dinna fash. Dinna rush," Cailean whispered, his accent thickened with strong emotion. "Enjoy."

She nodded, and then her eyes filled as she saw Mildred standing beside Bears. Fidelia beamed at both of them and ignored the towns-folk, who watched her with fascination.

When she stopped in front of the altar, Bears whispered, "Will you have both of us, Stitch?"

"Yes." She nodded and reached out a hand to stroke a finger over Mildred's head. "Will you hold my flowers?" She held out her bouquet, and Mildred's eyes widened. Fidelia urged her closer, to stand beside Annabelle. When Mildred joined Annabelle, Fidelia saw her sister grab the young girl's hand and give it a gentle squeeze.

Soon the pastor began to speak, and Fidelia attempted to pay attention to the ceremony. However, her focus was on Bears. On her urge to grip his hand. On his subtle scent of musk and horse and cologne. She sniffed and thought it was bay rum. She finally gave into her urge and reached out, her fingers teasing his.

She felt him give a small jolt, and then his hand clasped hers. She nearly missed the pastor asking her to repeat her vows, and she focused on the words she needed to say. When Bears slipped a ring on her finger, she couldn't stop a tear from slipping down her cheek.

Her eyes avowed her love, and soon she leaned in for his kiss. They pulled away sooner than she would have liked, and she clung to his arm as they made the walk down the aisle. She flushed at the smiles and shouts of congratulations from the townsfolk who had witnessed their marriage.

"They seem genuinely happy for us," she whispered.

"Those who are here are," he said. "The rest don't matter." He shook his brother-in-law's hand and was pulled into embraces by all of the MacKinnon women.

"Finally we are truly the family we always knew we were," Annabelle said.

"Bears!" Sorcha yelled as she pulled him close and kissed him on his cheek. "I canna tell ye how happy I am for ye." She turned to Fidelia and held her in a long embrace. "Be happy," she whispered in her ear.

Fidelia smiled and saw her holding her belly. "How are you feeling?"

"I already feel as big as a house, an' I have months to go." She shook her head in consternation and then leaned into the strong arms of her husband, Frederick Tompkins. "I ken I need to be patient ..."

"But that's never been one of her strong traits," her husband teased. His adoring gaze met her disgruntled one, and a slight breeze ruffled his black hair. She raised a hand to brush it back in place.

"Ye think ye want to be understood, but then ye realize a little mystery is no' always a bad thing," she grumbled and then giggled when he whispered something in her ear.

Fidelia shared a look with Bears and smiled. She looked for Mildred and held her hand out for her. "Come, Millie. Walk with us, as we are family now." She shared a smile with Bears as Mildred walked between them, holding each of their hands. They made the short stroll to the nearby Odd Fellows Hall, and Fidelia stopped short when she stepped inside. Rather than the usual streamers strung from the rafters, white orbs dangled from strings that twirled with any breeze. Vases of pussy willows were on the tables, and the dessert table overflowed with Annabelle's treats.

Another table quickly filled up with main dishes as the townsfolk arrived. Fidelia rubbed her stomach when it growled. She flushed as she met Bears's knowing smile. "I didn't have much of an appetite this morning, and now I'm starving."

Her sister approached and shook her head ruefully. "I'm afraid you won't have much time to eat," she said. "At my wedding, I was supposed to mingle."

"Or hide on the other side of the room from your groom," Cailean grumbled. "We were not a convincing couple in love at our reception."

Annabelle smiled at her husband. "Because we weren't. Love came later." She kissed him and then gave a small squeal of delight at the arrival of Skye with Jessamine and Ewan. "Thank you for watching her this morning." She kissed her daughter's cheek and then let her down as she wriggled to get to the floor.

"She's more energy than ten adults," Jessamine said with a shake of her head. "How is that fair?"

Jessamine and Ewan congratulated the newlyweds, and soon Fidelia and Bears were busy greeting and chatting with all the townsfolk. After a while, the music began, and they danced a waltz together, alone on the dance floor.

"I hate having them all watch," Fidelia murmured.

"I don't. I want them all to see my beautiful bride in my arms."

When the dance ended, she whispered in his ear, "Dance with Mildred." She nodded when he seemed unsure, and then she pushed him in his daughter's direction. When another waltz began, he approached his daughter and led her to the dance floor. Rather than the smooth dance he'd shared with his wife, they tripped over each other's feet, ran into other couples, and nearly fell to the floor twice. However, through it all, they laughed and teased each other.

When they emerged from the dance floor, Mildred remained by her father's side. "Will you teach me how to dance properly, Father?" she asked. "I want to dance like you and Fidelia do."

He nodded. "Yes, although I won't want you dancing with anyone but me for many years to come."

She giggled at his statement—as though it were a foolish notion, her dancing with another man—and then raced off to be with Hortence.

Bears turned to face his wife and saw her watching him with a deep tenderness. "Thank you," he whispered. At her inquisitive stare, he said, "Thank you for insisting I have a moment with my daughter today. I should have realized she'd need one as much as I did."

She squeezed his hand. "Thank you for finding a way for her to be a part of our ceremony. I'm sure the pastor was not pleased."

He shook his head. "No, I think he was. He seemed to understand the need to include her." He nodded to Annabelle. "Your sister wants you."

Fidelia looked across the room and shook her head. "No, she wants us both. We need to cut the cake." They walked hand in hand toward the cake, where Annabelle handed them a knife. She stood next to them, beside a stack of plates. Soon Leticia and Jessamine were there too, to help with the cake cutting.

Fidelia held her hands on the knife and motioned for Bears to put his hands over hers. "We cut the cake together," she whispered.

"Another one of those traditions?" he asked with humor in his gaze.

She nodded and then lowered the knife into the cake. Although it had a white frosting, it was a chocolate cake. Fidelia smiled at Annabelle in thanks, although she couldn't hide a hint of disappointment. Annabelle nodded as though in acknowledgment and then busied herself with serving the cake to the townsfolk, who could never get enough of her sweets.

"Chocolate is my favorite," Bears said, although he watched his wife intently. "I wish she'd made your favorite."

Fidelia donned a bright smile. "I love chocolate too."

He shook his head and stroked a finger down her cheek. "No need to fake your joy. Not with me." He sighed when they were interrupted by the Tompkinses' arrival. He shook Harold's and Irene's hands, although he kept a firm hold on the large slab of cake Annabelle had cut for him.

"About time you showed sense," Harold said. He winced as his wife elbowed him in his side.

"The good things in life shouldn't be rushed," she said with a broad smile. "I hope you will be very happy."

Harold nodded and watched as Irene led Fidelia away to speak with other women of the town. "Your life will be much happier once you rid it of a certain malcontent."

Bears continued to eat his cake and made a noncommittal noise. "I promised the MacKinnons I'd do nothing violent."

"Sometimes a promise must be broken for those we cherish," Harold said. "I fear that man will make you break every promise you hold dear, or you will lose more than you thought possible." He met Bears's worried gaze. "I've heard rumors that his anger is only growing toward you and Fidelia. He can't abide her marrying you."

Bears shrugged. "I imagine he thinks she is debasing herself, marrying a half-breed." He grunted as Harold hit him on his healed but still tender shoulder.

"Let the fools of this town speak poorly about you. No need to do it for them," he muttered. "I think Walter would react in a similar way to any man she chose. He can't stand the thought of her with anyone but him." Harold's gaze was filled with warning. "While she remained single, he let her be. Now that she's with you, he considers her fair game again. I'm not sayin' his logic has merit, but it's how he thinks."

Bears nodded. "It's similar to how his cousin acted and thought."

Harold shrugged. "I shouldn't speak ill of the dead, but I will say that I'm glad they had a sturdy rope." He gave a decisive nod at the thought of Bertrand March hanging for the deaths of the women he had murdered in Helena.

"The *second* time," Bears muttered, as he remembered what he had read in the paper. The first time Bertrand had been strung up, the rope had broken. Bertrand had tried to convince those present that it was an act of God and that he should be set free. However, one of the victim's relatives had come forward with another rope, and he had soon died for his misdeeds.

"Well, we don't always get it right the first time." Harold shrugged again. "Congratulations on marrying Fidelia. She's a fine woman, and she'll bring you much joy." He slapped Bears on his good shoulder this time and moved away to join his wife.

Bears stood aside, watching as Fidelia mingled with the townsfolk. Before today, she had always remained at the periphery of any event she was forced to attend. Even after their impromptu announcement of their engagement, she had clung to him and had attempted to remain out of the limelight. However, today she laughed and spoke with confidence, and his chest tightened with happiness to see her as she always should have been. A woman respected by those around her with little to fear and everything to look forward to. He hoped she'd never have a reason to regret her choice in him.

Bears helped Fidelia down from the wagon and smiled at her gasp of surprise. "Where are we?" she asked.

"Cailean has a friend who has this cabin. He's away mining most of the time, and he doesn't mind if we use it. This is where Cailean and Annabelle came for their honeymoon too." He frowned as he saw her bite her lip. "I hope that doesn't bother you, but I wanted to find a secret place outside of town."

She shook her head. "No, I remember Anna came home very happy after her honeymoon." She looked around, noting a small barn in the distance with a privy not too far from the cabin. "How long can we stay?"

"A few days. A week." He shrugged. "Less than a month." He laughed as she batted him on his arm. "I suspect we'll leave when we run out of food."

She looked at the baskets of food in the back of the wagon and smiled. "Then I think we'll be here for some time." She grabbed his hand. "Come, husband. Explore this place with me."

He watched her childish enthusiasm as she pulled up the long hem of her wedding dress and walked toward the door. He allowed her to tow him along behind her and tugged her close when she stopped suddenly. "It's even smaller than my cabin."

"Yes, but we don't have to worry about anyone interrupting us here," she murmured as she spun to kiss him. The kiss deepened as he groaned, and he sank his fingers in her hair.

He stilled his movements when he felt her grimace. "Stitch?"

"I have too many pins holding my hair back," she complained. As she reached to pluck out a pin, her stomach grumbled.

"And you're hungry." He kissed her again and then marched to the wagon to pull out a few baskets of food. He returned inside and marveled that the icebox had been stocked with ice. "Our food will last longer."

"Good," she said. She set the table and sighed with appreciation as he pulled out fried chicken and mashed potatoes. "I never got to eat with everyone congratulating us."

He smiled. "Neither did I, but I won't complain. It made me proud to stand beside you as the townsfolk congratulated you."

She shared a tender smile with him. "They were just as pleased for you." She groaned as she ate her fill.

After washing the dishes, he peeked into a box and frowned. "I wonder what this is?"

She watched as he opened the box and pulled out a cake. Fidelia paled as she saw the small yellow lemon peel at the center of the cake. "It's a lemon cake," she whispered. A tear tracked down her cheek.

"Why should a lemon cake make you cry?" Bears swiped at her cheek.

"It's my favorite from when I was a child. Anna told me that she hasn't made one since I left home." She covered her mouth and stared at it as another tear slipped down her cheek.

"She wanted to surprise you, my love," Bears said as he watched her tenderly. "Do you want to try it?"

"Yes! I've waited years to eat her lemon cake again." She smiled as he gave her a knife and set two plates beside the small cake. She cut generous pieces and then waited for him to take a bite. When he shrugged after he ate his bite, she frowned. She took a bite and closed her eyes as the lemon flavor hit her taste buds. "Heaven," she whispered.

He smiled. "It is quite good, but I prefer her chocolate cake." He smiled. "I'm like Cailean."

Fidelia ate the rest of her slice and then replaced the cake in the box to save for the following day. After everything was cleaned up, and Bears had returned from stabling the horse, she clasped her hands together on her lap. "Now what?"

He fought a chuckle and shook his head. "Now we can do what we want. Read. Tell stories. Sing. Sleep." He shrugged. "It's up to you."

Her frown intensified with each option. "I thought you'd want to …" She broke off and met his patient stare. "I thought you'd want to make love."

He nodded. "I do. I have for some time, Stitch. But I won't rush you. We have our whole lives to live together."

She studied him. "So … it's like the kiss? It's up to me?"

He nodded again.

"For now, will you hold me, like you did that night we spent together?" she whispered. "I know it's not what you dreamed your wedding night would be like but …" She stopped speaking when he pressed his fingers to her lips.

"Knowing that you are my wife and that you don't have to sneak away before dawn to preserve your reputation is more than I ever hoped for," he said. He rose and held out his hand. "Come."

She stood, and he helped free her from her wedding-day finery. When she was in her shift, he backed away from her and tugged off his jacket. The beaded belt was tied around his waist, and he pulled it off, setting it aside on top of his coat. He kicked off his boots and left on his dress shirt and pants.

"You can take off your shirt and pants and leave on your under-things," she whispered.

He stared at her and shook his head. "No, love, it's better like this."

She flushed and climbed under the sheets. When he pulled her against his chest, she relaxed, forming small circles on his arm. "I love you, Bears."

"And I you, my Fidelia."

~

Bears woke with a grunt as he was kicked in his leg and then bashed on his head by a flying fist. Fidelia thrashed beside him, and he grabbed her to still her erratic movements.

"No, let me go!" she screamed. "I will not bend! I will not!"

"Fidelia," he whispered as he released her arms. "Stitch," he said. "It's Bears, and I will not hurt you. I'll never hurt you."

She began to whimper and shake, and she curled into herself, still lost to her nightmare. He stroked her back and whispered soft words to her, until she calmed into a deep asleep again. He lay awake beside her for long hours, watching dawn as it lit the sky.

He slipped from bed and went outside first to the privy, then to check on the horse. When he had fed and watered Lightning, he reentered the cabin to find Fidelia awake and watching for him.

"Why weren't you in bed?" Her eyes rounded as she saw a bruise near his temple. "What happened to you, Bears?"

He let out a deep breath and pulled over a chair from the small kitchen table to sit beside the bed. "You had a dream last night. A nightmare. And you kicked and hit me." He closed his eyes for a moment. "I didn't know how to help you."

She flushed with shame. "I have them sometimes. They don't mean anything."

He studied her. "Don't they? You seemed to fear having your will broken."

She sat up in bed until she was on her knees and faced him. "Every man I've known, until you, has wanted to break my spirit in some way. To control me. To change me. To make me into what he envisioned I should be. You aren't like that, Bears. I know that." She shook her head in dismay. "Some fears are deep and only come out when I am vulnerable."

152

"Do you trust me?"

"Yes. I'd never sleep with you if I didn't."

He frowned at her answer but didn't pressure her for more. "I don't know what more I could have done last night, love. You cried yourself to sleep, but I was terrified to touch you. I worried I would make what you were imagining worse."

She shook her head. "Next time, shake me until I wake up. Don't let me stay in those bad dreams. Show me that I'm with you. The fears will lessen as I learn that I have nothing to fear now."

He sighed and lowered his head.

She moved forward to kiss the top of his head. "I do fear, Bears, and I'm tired of it," she whispered, and she backed away so he could look at her. "I want to make love with my husband. Please tell me that I haven't ruined your desire for me."

He gave her a rueful smile. "I'm terrified that whatever I do will make your night terrors worse."

She traced one of his eyebrows and shook her head. "No, you chase them away. Please?"

He leaned forward, kissing her softly. When she wrapped her arms around his neck and arched into his kiss, he ran his fingers over her scantily clad body. When she gasped as he touched her breast, he groaned. "God, I want you, my love. But I only want you to know pleasure."

"With you, that's all there is," she sighed. "Come, husband," she coaxed, as she backed onto the bed, tugging him to follow her. "Come to bed with me."

He continued to kiss her as he lay beside her. His hands stroked over her body, eager to show her the joys to be found in their time together. "Tell me what you like. What you don't. What brings back fears." He paused to look into her eyes.

She nodded and pushed at him. He fell to his back and sighed as she tugged at his shirt, and he lifted so she could pull it over his head.

"I love how strong you are," she whispered as she ran her hands over his chest and shoulders. She massaged his shoulder that had been injured, earning a sigh of pleasure.

"God, that feels good," he moaned as he arched into her touch. "I rub at it, but nothing has ever felt as good as your touch."

"I want you to feel as good as you make me feel." She blushed as she looked at him but then smiled at the agreement she saw in his eyes.

"It's not fair that I'm half naked, and you aren't," he teased.

Her hands reflexively tightened on the hem of her shift, like an innocent girl's would, and she bit her lip as though uncertain. She took a deep breath and moved to lift it over her head. When she dropped the shift to the floor, she hunched her shoulders forward, as though attempting to hide herself.

"You're beautiful," he whispered as he raised a hand to her cheek. He watched as she battled shyness and indecisiveness. He tangled his fingers in her unkempt hair and waited for her to meet his gaze.

After a moment she sat tall and looked deeply into his eyes. "I want to be brave for you."

He shook his head. "Be brave for yourself alone, love. I don't need you to be anything other than what you are."

She took his hand and kissed it before placing it low over her belly, where her skin had been stretched loose and had silvery lines.

He nodded in understanding. "This only proves you sheltered your baby," he whispered.

Her eyes flashed with deep emotion. "Yes." She took a deep breath. "Until this moment, I've never wanted anyone to see. I've thought it a sign of my greatest shame."

He shook his head. "No, my love. It is the sign of your greatest love." He opened his arms as she fell forward and cried in his arms.

"Only you, Bears, could turn my shame into love," she whispered after many moments. She kissed him with a passionate intensity, her hands stroking his bared chest, while her legs moved over his pant-clothed limbs. "Love me. Show me how it can be."

"Always."

Afterward they lay tangled together, their arms and legs wrapped around each other, as though afraid to lose the connection they had forged while making love. His hands stroked her back, while hers played with his long silky hair.

"Thank you," she whispered.

He gave a grunt of displeasure and moved away enough to see her eyes. "For what?"

"For showing me how it should be. For never making me think of my time at the Boudoir. For ridding me of the fear I had." She settled her head on his chest again, his arms tightened around her.

"I can't erase what happened, Stitch. But I hope the time between us will be good enough that you will soon rarely think about what your life was like before."

She chuckled. "Our life will be better than *good enough*, Bears. It will be wonderful."

He tensed. "I can be a hard man to live with. I have moods, and I can be stubborn. I will do things to unintentionally hurt you." He waited as she lay quietly in his arms.

"Of course you will," she whispered after a long pause. "And I'll do the same to you. Do you think Annabelle and Cailean don't fight? I've heard screaming matches I thought would lead to the end of their marriage. But I've come to understand that not all anger leads to violence and not all temper leads to the destruction of what you hold dear."

"I drove Sara away," he whispered.

Fidelia moved her head to lay on the same pillow as Bears, so she could stare into his eyes. "What do you mean?" She stroked a finger over his chin. "You've never spoken to me about her."

He closed his eyes a moment. "I want you to know the type of man I was. The type of man I could become. I don't want to lose you too."

She kissed him, her heart aching at the remorse and pain in his voice. "I'm not Sara, and you won't lose me."

He watched her a long moment and then whispered, "She was the daughter of one of my father's trapper friends. We saw each other as often as trappers meet, and I always thought we'd marry. My father warned me that my feelings might be stronger than hers and to not exaggerate the affections of a young woman into some kind of permanent love, but I wanted her. And I thought she wanted me."

He sighed. "I could tell after the passion waned that she was restless. That she desired more than a life living in a cabin in the woods as the wife of a simple man who lived off the land."

She growled in disagreement, made a face, and shook her head in disgust. "You are not—and I'm sure you never were—a simple man."

He half smiled at her loyalty. "I was then. I was content to help my father. To trap, to hunt, to work with horses, and to love Sara." His smile faded, and his gaze filled with loathing. "And then *he* came. Bertrand March. With his tales of the big city and his plans for what he'd do after he had success as a trapper."

Bears shook his head and took a deep breath. "I disliked him from the first, but I think it was mainly because I saw how he watched Sara. And how she watched him," he admitted. "She looked at him in a way she'd never looked at me. As though he were fascinating and a man she felt honored to know."

"What did you do?" Fidelia stroked a hand over his tense shoulder muscles.

"I acted a fool. I showed Bertrand up every chance I got in an attempt to prove I was the better man. Instead, it only made her feel sorry for him. Made her mad that I wasn't more charitable to him. And, in the end, she said I was a half-breed with no ambition and that she wanted more from life than to live it stuck in a cabin in the backwoods."

Fidelia sucked in a breath, leaned on an elbow and stared at him with wide eyes. "She never ..."

His eyes were laden with pain as he nodded. "Yes." He waited, but Fidelia only studied him, as though sensing there was more. "She said she wished she'd never met me, as no woman with sense would desire a man who knew nothing about pleasure and cared more for his animals than he did his wife."

Fidelia's hand shook as she stroked his cheek, her eyes lit with fury. "If she weren't already dead, I'd find her and …" She bit her lip when he smiled at her and shook his head.

"She paid for her folly. And she made our daughter suffer for it too." He watched Fidelia with cautious hope.

His wife clasped his face between her small hands and looked deeply into his eyes. "She lied. You are kind and patient to all, not just to your animals. Do you think I feigned my pleasure?"

He shook his head and smiled. "No, love. No."

"Then that's another doubt you can rid yourself of." She kissed him. "In fact, I find myself in need of your attentions again."

Fidelia tugged on Bears's hand as he led her through the forest. She gasped from climbing up a steep mountainside, and she swiped at a trickle of sweat down the side of her face. "I'm not in as good a shape as you," she rasped. They shared a smile as she caught her breath. "How do you know where we're going?"

He shrugged. "If you look closely, we've been following a trail." He waited for her to discern the path, and, when she shook her head in frustration, he grinned. "There." He pointed to a part of the forest not quite as thick with shrubs.

"How do you know that's a trail?" she asked.

"If you spend enough time in the forest, you know what to look for. They're not always man-made trails, but animals will make their own paths through the forest. We can follow them."

Fidelia tilted her head back and closed her eyes, breathing deeply. She smiled with contentment. "I never thought being in the middle of a forest could bring such peace. Although I'd hate to be here alone."

He nodded. "You aren't. The *tap-tap-tap* is a woodpecker busy at work. That high-pitched call is a chipmunk, angry with us for intruding on his territory. Deer have recently passed through this area." He pointed to a hoof print. "You're never alone in the forest."

She gripped his hand. "You know I meant that I didn't want to be alone without you or someone competent."

He smiled and pulled her forward. "Come. It's still a little ways until we reach my surprise." He chuckled at her grumbling and led her along the path, holding branches aside for her and slowing his pace.

When they neared the crest of a ridge, she paused. "Why does it smell like rotten eggs?"

He chuckled. "Come, love." He tugged on her hand, and they emerged into a small area with steam rising off the water. Small pools fed into one large pool, which slowly drained into a creek that headed down the mountain. A granite cliff face with snowcapped peaks framed the area, giving it a sense of a hidden oasis. "Let's head over there, upwind."

"I don't understand," Fidelia whispered as she followed Bears.

"These are hot springs." He grinned as she gasped in delight. "Only trappers know about this one."

"Which means only you," she said. She laughed as he shrugged.

"Most likely a few more know about it, but hardly anyone comes here." He tugged his shirt over his head. "I thought you'd enjoy soaking in the warm water."

"Is it like taking a bath?" she asked as she dipped her hand in. "Ouch!" She shook her hand at the hot water temperature.

"Each pool will be a different temperature. You can find one you like. Or sit for a few minutes in a hot one and then go to a cooler one." He nodded to one. "I like that one. I find it not too hot or too cold, and the rocks in there are comfortable to sit on." He led her to it, and she bent to dip her hand in.

"Oh, that's lovely," she breathed. She flushed as she watched him kick off his boots and shuck his pants. He set the rifle he carried on top of his clothes. "I ... I couldn't go in without clothes on."

Bears looked around and shrugged. "I don't see why not. It's not as though someone will join us." He winked at her and waited as she slipped from her clothes. He held out his hand to help her in, as she eased into the warm water.

"Oh, heaven," she sighed, sinking into the water up to her ears. "I could stay here all day."

He chuckled. "You'd never make it back to the cabin if you did." He sat on one of the rocks and watched her with joy while she relaxed in the hot water.

"Are there any hot springs closer to Bear Grass Springs?" she asked.

He shook his head. "I haven't found them, and, if there were, they wouldn't be private like this." He stilled and tugged her to him. When she began to speak, he shook his head for her to quiet. He glanced toward the far end of the pools and relaxed.

"What is it?" Fidelia asked.

"A mountain goat," he murmured. "Isn't he beautiful?"

His white pelt shimmered in the sunlight, with its small black horns a stark contrast. It walked easily over uneven terrain before scaling the rocky cliff face.

Fidelia stared in wonder as the goat disappeared as quickly as it had appeared. "How does it do that?"

"Climb the rocks?" Bears asked. At her nod, he shrugged. "It has special hooves, and it was made for that life."

She sighed and relaxed into the warm water, snuggling into his embrace. "Thank you for bringing me here. You didn't have to."

He looked at her with love and pride. "Of course I did. I want to share my favorite places with you. And I wanted you to relax in the soothing waters."

She kissed his shoulder. "By sharing the places that are special to you, you are allowing me to know you, Bears. Thank you."

He nodded and wrapped an arm around her. "Yes. I hope you're never disappointed."

She shook her head as she smoothed a hand over his head and then tangled her fingers in his long, silky black hair. "Never. No matter what, I'll always love you."

He groaned and pulled her close as they floated in their private hideaway for many more minutes.

~

Two days later, their food supply ran low, and they knew they'd have to return to town the following day. Fidelia walked hand in hand with Bears beside a creek that ran from the mountains near the cabin. He paused as they found an area by the creek with a bed of grass. "Come. Sit with me," he urged. Large cottonwoods that stood nearby provided shade, and the tall grass blew in the gentle breeze. He dropped the blanket he carried over one shoulder and then settled so she could sit between his legs and lean against his chest. He rested his head alongside hers and sighed. "Heaven."

"Yes, heaven," she murmured. "What do you see when you look at me?"

He smiled into her neck. "I see a woman who fits perfectly against me."

She turned until she rested her arms on his chest. "No, Bears. I see you watching me, as though waiting for something to happen. Something bad. What is it you are looking for? What have I done?"

He frowned at the anxiety in her voice and shook his head. He stroked a hand over her hair, playing havoc with the loose braid she'd tied. "I look at you and wonder how long you'll be satisfied with me. How long until you're restless too."

She frowned as she stared at him. She shook her head to silence him, and then she glared at him. "You think I'll be like her. Like Sara. That, when the passion fades, I'll be discontented too."

He nodded with fear in his gaze.

She closed her eyes as though in defeat and then squared her shoulders. "I don't know what more I can do, Bears. We've just married. We've just begun to know each other as husband and wife. But I hope and pray every night that what we have doesn't fade. That we fight to keep what we have alive." She stroked his cheek. "I never believed in love. I never believed that it could last. But I've been proven wrong as I've lived with my sister and seen how all the brothers are. I've seen that it can last. I want that too."

He nodded. "As do I."

"I know we had friendship and a regard for each other long before we ever had passion." She watched him in confusion as he shook his head in disbelief.

"If you think I didn't want you from the moment I saw you at the MacKinnon house, you're a fool. I just never thought you'd return the sentiment." He stroked a hand over her cheek. "We had love before we married too."

She nodded. "Yes, and that's more than most marriages have." She took a deep breath. "What I've learned is that we must always talk, even if it's painful or embarrassing. We must have honesty between us." She gripped his shoulders. "That might be hard for me, since I learned how to hide what I really felt and thought, but I promise you I will try to speak the truth."

He caressed her back. "You've always been honest with me, my love. I promise you the same."

"When you are afraid, share it with me. I can't ease your fears if I don't know what they are. And I hate not knowing what I'm battling."

He smiled. "I agree." He pulled her close. "I hate that we have to leave tomorrow."

"Me too," she whispered. "But I miss Mildred."

His arms tightened reflexively on her waist. "Thank you for caring for my girl."

She smiled as she turned to settle her back against his front. "She's *our* girl now."

CHAPTER 10

They returned from the miner's cabin the following day, four days after the wedding, arriving home on a sunny day in early November. Bears left the wagon at the livery and walked with Fidelia to the cabin. He opened the door to his two-room home and stood stock-still when he stared inside. He felt Fidelia push at his back, but he remained in front of the doorway, unmoving.

"Bears?" she asked. "What's wrong?"

"Nothing's here," he said. "The cabin's empty."

"What?" She pushed him aside and marched inside. Everything was gone. The table, chairs, cups, and dishes. The small lace doilies she had tatted him. The curtain he'd kept pushed to one side that she'd hung when he had first moved in. The stove. "Who would do such a thing? Who would take everything we own?"

He shook his head. "I thought the townsfolk liked us."

"They do. Dinna fash," Ewan said from the doorway with a sly grin. "Ye dinna live here anymore."

"What?" Bears asked. He shook his head. "I can't afford to buy a new home, Ewan."

"An' ye dinna need to. This is yer weddin' present. From the MacKinnons. Come." He motioned for them to follow him and took off at a brisk walk. They walked behind Cailean's house and down the small alley that ran parallel to the main road through town. Soon they approached Warren and Helen's home and stopped before a brand-new residence a few houses before the lawyer's home.

"You've been working on this for a few months," Fidelia said, staring at the large home with an inviting front porch and windows on either side of the front door.

"Aye, an' the man who was to buy it decided he'd rather live in a place called Deer Lodge." Ewan shrugged. "I dinna ken why, but it left me with an empty house. I was goin' to leave it to finish the inside this winter, but then I kent ye were to marry." He looked at them and shook his head. "Ye need more privacy than that wee cabin will afford ye, with yer daughter livin' there too." He laughed as Fidelia blushed.

"We can't accept this," Bears said.

"Aye, of course ye can. Ye're family now officially," Ewan said with joy. "That means we have even more right to give our advice than we did in the past. An' ye ken we love to meddle."

Bears groaned.

"You'll get used to it," Fidelia whispered to her husband. She looked at Ewan. "May we go in?"

"Aye," he said with a smile. He led them across the porch and opened the door. Annabelle waited for them inside, and Fidelia ignored the home and ran to her sister, pulling her in a tight embrace.

"Dee," Annabelle murmured, holding her close. "Are you well?" She pulled back and stared into her sister's watery eyes.

"Yes. Thank you for the lemon cake." She saw a flash of under-standing in her sister's gaze. "I ... I was so sad at the wedding when the cake was chocolate. I thought it meant you'd never fully forgive me."

Annabelle shook her head. "I feared, if I made you a lemon cake for the reception, that your emotions would overcome you. I wanted you to celebrate your future, not think about the past." She squeezed her sister's hand. "I'll only make lemon cake for you, Dee."

Fidelia shook her head. "No, you should make them for everyone. It was even more delicious than I remembered."

Her sister smiled, and Fidelia looked around her. She saw Bears waiting by the doorway to explore their new house together. She smiled at her sister one more time before joining her husband. On the left side of the door was the kitchen with its large stove and a round dining room table in the middle of the space. On the other side of the door was a small living area. Through a doorway, they walked down a hallway with two small bedrooms on the right and a larger bedroom on the left. In the large bedroom, the stove from the cabin was set on bricks with a pipe leading outside.

"In the winter, ye'll have to leave all the bedroom doors open to try to heat them back here," Ewan said.

"Or Mildred can sleep on a pallet on the floor," Bears said. He shook his head as he looked at his furnishings in this new home. "The cabin seemed large to me."

Ewan smiled. "It's not just ye now, Bears. Ye have yer wife and daughter to consider."

"And it will be good for you to not live right at the livery. You need to spend more time away from where you work," Annabelle said to Bears. "You're still close to the bakery, Dee. And it will be good for you to not be so close to me."

Fidelia shook her head. "I've needed to be close to you, Anna. And I'm only a few houses away."

Annabelle gave her a hug and then turned to leave. "Alistair and Leticia are delighted for Mildred to spend another night. And your larder is stocked. Cailean will be furious if you return to the livery today. Enjoy another day free of work."

Bears shook his head. "I must return and care for my horse."

Ewan chuckled. "I ken my brothers, and I ken they've already seen to Lightning. Enjoy your time alone together. Soon ye'll dream of this." He winked at them and then walked out with Annabelle.

Fidelia returned to the kitchen area and stoked the fire in the large oven. She watched Bears pace around the room but remained quiet. She set a kettle on to boil water for coffee and then sat at the dining room table. She saw him fingering the fabric of the settee, and then he settled into his well-used rocking chair.

"Why would they do this?" he whispered. "Don't they understand I've already adapted to enough change this year?"

Fidelia flinched. "Am I what you've had to adapt to?"

He gave her a warning glance. "Don't turn my words around on me, Stitch." He frowned at the hurt in her gaze. "I'd dreamed of our simple cabin. Of watching you teach Mildred to cook and to sew at our table together." He frowned. "But ... I hadn't yet determined how we'd make love with her so close by."

"This home is big, Bears. It might be too big." She sniffed. "I fear they ensured we had three bedrooms because they believe we'll have another child."

"You don't believe Ewan's story about the man moving to Deer Lodge?"

"Oh, I'm sure a man moved away. I'm just not certain it was this nice a home he was building. Ewan would always give us the best home. We are family, and he cherishes family." Fidelia shrugged. "I can still do all those things you envisioned here, Bears. With the curtains drawn and the stove lit, this will be a comfortable home."

He shook his head in frustration. "I wanted to provide for you."

She smiled. "And you do. I know many things about you. I will never be hungry. I will never be cold. And I will never be unloved." She nodded at the hope in his gaze. "It doesn't matter where we live, my love. All that matters is that we are together."

He stood and approached her. "It will take me some time to realize this is our home."

She rose and wrapped her arms around his neck. "Dance with me."

"You call it dancing now?" he teased as he kissed her. He sighed as she hummed, and they twirled around their small living room together. He bumped into the rocking chair and tripped, heaving them onto the settee.

She gasped as he fell on top of her, and her eyes rounded with momentary fright. However, she focused on Bears, and any fear was replaced by humor and then passion. "I think that's enough dancing, my darling. Why don't we see how comfortable our bed is?"

He chuckled. "A fine idea." He rose and held out a hand to her, his smile bright as he beheld the joy and wonder in her gaze.

~

When they lay tangled in bed, he kissed her head. "I'll be home soon," he whispered.

She grabbed his hand. "Bring her home, Bears. I miss her too." She met his smile and kissed him. "But give me time to wash up."

"I'll talk to Alistair a little while. Will thirty minutes be enough time?" When she nodded, he kissed her forehead, whispered his love, and rose to dress.

He slipped from his new home and walked across the main street of town to the row of houses behind the café, bakery, and bank. He knocked on Alistair's door and smiled as his friend opened it.

"I did no' think ye'd wait until tomorrow, no matter what Ewan said," Alistair said with a slap to Bears's shoulder. "How was the honeymoon?"

Bears merely smiled, and Alistair nodded.

"Good. Mildred's been waiting for ye. Hoping ye'd come, even though she's put on a show she's fine waiting until tomorrow."

Bears entered the kitchen area to find Mildred and Hortence drawing. "Hello, little one." At his voice, Mildred looked up, dropped her pencil, and ran to him. He held her close and kissed her head. "I missed you."

She kept her arms wrapped around his waist for a long moment, only easing away when he tickled her. At her giggle, he smiled at her.

"Did you have a good time with your cousin?" He stroked a hand over her hair and frowned at the tears clinging to her eyelashes.

"Yes! We swam in the creek and hunted for lost treasure and ..."

"Ran around like wild young ladies," Leticia said with a wry smile. "Hello, Bears." She opened her arms as she hugged Mildred and kissed her head. "We'll miss you. Know you're always welcome, Millie."

Mildred hugged Leticia and ran to Hortence to give her a hug and to whisper something in her ear. While his daughter was distracted for a few moments, Bears motioned for Alistair to stand near him.

"What is it?" Alistair asked, as he watched his daughter and Mildred together.

"Now that I'm married, I think it would be appropriate for me to take over the inheritance left me from my father. I want to ensure Fidelia and Mildred never want for anything."

Alistair nodded. "Aye, 'tis reasonable. An' few in town dinna like ye." He smiled. "I'll speak with Cailean, an' then we can talk with Warren." He tousled Mildred's hair after she raced back to Bears.

"Bye, Hortence! I'll see you tomorrow!" Mildred yelled as she stood beside her father. She grimaced as she heard Angus give a soft cry. "Sorry."

Leticia smiled. "He needs to adjust to a noisy house."

Bears nodded to Leticia and Alistair and walked home with his daughter hand in hand. "Let's hope Fidelia isn't upset we're arriving too soon. She asked for thirty minutes to wash and change, but I didn't feel like lingering at Alistair's."

"I want to go home, Father," she said. She swung their joined arms and laughed when he twirled her around him as though dancing with her. "I thought you could only dance the waltz."

He grinned at her. "I can't do more than this." As they crossed the main street toward their new home, he studied her. "Did you help decorate the new house?"

She jumped up and down. "Yes! Don't you love what Uncle Ewan did? I love it!"

"Did you pick out your room?"

She bit her lip and nodded. "Do you mind? I loved the back corner room with two windows."

He shook his head and squeezed her shoulder. "I want you to feel as at home in our new house as in our cabin. I wish I'd been here to share moving with you."

"But then it wouldn't have been a surprise!" Her brown eyes were lit with youthful logic. He nodded in acknowledgment.

When he opened the door to their home, he paused at the sight of

Fidelia in the kitchen, heating water and singing. His breath caught as she spun to them with a bright smile and held her arms open to Mildred.

"You're finally here!" she said as Mildred ran to her. "Oh, how I've missed you."

Mildred hugged her and then backed away. "Do you like the house, Fidelia?"

Fidelia nodded, her smile bright. "I do. I love it. I saw the room you picked out. May I sew you something for your room?"

Mildred's eyes grew round. "You'd do that for me? I know how expensive your items are."

"Of course I would. You're my daughter." She flushed as she corrected herself. "My stepdaughter." She motioned for Mildred to join her in the kitchen. "Come. Help me with dinner." She talked her through the preparation of chicken potpie, sharing innocent stories of her honeymoon and listening to Mildred's adventures during her absence. Through it all, she shared contented stares with Bears as their house turned into a home.

∼

A week later in early November, school had started, and Fidelia was adjusting to her new life. At home, Fidelia fought against her mothering instincts and attempted to accept her role as step-mother. The more time she spent with Mildred, the more she considered Mildred her daughter. Fidelia continued her work at the bakery, but most days only she and Annabelle were at the bakery. Leena remained at home with her baby, Mette, and Leticia was at home with her children.

Annabelle sighed and scrubbed the counter clean. "I think we need more help. Leticia enjoys her time at home." She shared a look with her sister. "I suspect she would rather be there than here."

"Will you hire another baker?" Fidelia asked.

Annabelle shook her head. "No. It's a lot of work right now, but I hope that Leena will return at some point. Even if only one or two days a week." She sighed and sat on a stool. "But we need someone to run the front. Leticia will soon be away for months after the birth of her new baby. As it is, she's gone more than she's here right now as she prepares for the baby and spends time with Angus and Hortence. You can't do everything while I'm baking. It isn't fair."

"You know I've never complained," Fidelia protested.

Her sister smiled. "No, but I'm complaining for you. You shouldn't have to work as hard as you are. Not when you have a family of your own and your own work." She looked around the enlarged bakery. "Maybe I was a fool to expand the bakery."

Fidelia rolled her eyes. "Never. Your baked goods are even more popular here than they were in Maine."

Annabelle nodded and shrugged. "Yes, but part of the reason for the expansion was for you to sell your lace and for Sorcha to sell her wool. You're so busy here, you have little time to tat lace, and, with Sorcha on the ranch, it's impossible to remain stocked with her beautiful wool."

Fidelia shrugged. "It just means that, when we do have products to sell, they are that much more valuable." She wrapped an arm around her sister's shoulders. "I think you're tired. Skye must still keep you up at night. Everything will look better after you get some sleep."

Annabelle dropped her head onto the countertop. "I am exhausted, but it's not just from Skye." She looked around her again. "I worry about our business." She frowned as Fidelia's eyes filled with tears. "What did I say?"

"You called this *ours*," she whispered. "*You* made this dream a reality, Anna. I know it's yours."

Annabelle stood and pulled Fidelia into a hug. "It wouldn't mean nearly as much to me if you weren't here every day to share my frustrations with and to gossip with. I'll always consider it ours, Dee."

Fidelia sniffled. "Thank you, Anna." She swiped at her cheeks and looked at the basket waiting to be delivered. "I must get that to the café, before Irene sends out a search party." Annabelle laughed, and Fidelia left with a spring in her step as she headed down the back street to the nearby café.

"Don't dawdle outside in the cold. Come in for a visit," Irene admonished when Fidelia arrived. The stove pumped out heat on this cool fall day, and Irene sat at the table.

Fidelia smiled at Harold as he set a glass of water in front of her and watched as he returned to the main room of the café to gossip with customers. "I can't remain here long. I still need to make a delivery to the hotel."

Irene hushed her concern and encouraged her to sit back and relax. "I can only imagine how hard you sisters are working now that most of your help is away. Hopefully that Johansen girl will come back, since I enjoy some of her treats. But, if she doesn't, we'll be all right."

"She had a baby, Irene. She'll come back to work when she can," Fidelia said. "Annabelle won't want her to work until she is ready."

"Didn't stop your sister from working sooner than she should have after she had Skye," Irene said. "But that's how Annabelle is. Now I want to know what's put that shadow in your eyes. Has that man been pestering you again?"

Fidelia shook her head in denial at anything bothering her but then slumped her shoulders. "You miss nothing." At Irene's shrug, she said, "I haven't seen Walter since my announcement at the Harvest Dance."

Irene watched her shrewdly. "Don't let his absence make you feel safe. He's biding his time, Fidelia. A man like that doesn't give up easily when he feels as though he's been wronged."

"*He's* been wronged?" she asked in outrage. "I'm the one with scars from his attentions." She flushed from the admission.

Irene nodded. "I always wondered if that wasn't how it was." She smiled at her friend. "But now you've married a good man. A man who will treat you well." Irene continued to study her. "If it's not your husband and not that man, then I don't know what could be bothering you. Unless it's his daughter."

Fidelia shook her head in wonder. "You miss little, Irene."

"Is it that you have no desire to be a mother? Some women aren't meant for it." At the sorrow in Fidelia's eyes, she gave a *tsk*. "No, that's not it. What's happened, Fidelia?"

"The night Bears and I arrived home, we made sure Mildred was with us. We missed her. She seemed delighted to be with us. But, sometime since then, she's been distant. Wants little to do with me. Calls me *stepmother*."

"And that hurts," Irene said. "When you'd rather be her mother."

"Or like her mother. I can never take her mother's place. I can't be Sara." Fidelia rubbed at her head. "I don't know what to do."

Irene frowned. "When did everything change? Was it after she started school?"

Fidelia furrowed her brows and then nodded.

"I've heard rumblings. The schoolteacher can't control the children, and the young'uns say horrible things. I wonder what they're saying about Mildred?"

Fidelia shared a long look with Irene and then rose. "If you excuse me, I must find my daughter."

Irene nodded at her. "Good luck."

Fidelia returned to the bakery, informed Annabelle that she had to find Mildred, and then walked toward the school. Rather than march in and demand to know what was happening, she stood near the church, hidden in the shadows, and watched the children on the playground. She grimaced as she heard one boy taunt Mildred for wearing a hand-me-down dress. When another called Mildred an "ignorant half-breed with a whore for a mother," Fidelia stepped from the shadows and marched into the playground.

"How dare you speak about my daughter in such a manner?" she demanded. She grabbed him by the ear and dragged him inside, ignoring his pleas for mercy and that he had done nothing wrong. Hortence and Millie followed them.

The school door banged open as she pulled along the unwilling child. The small entryway's pegs were empty, as the children were outside with their coats on. In the main schoolroom, a potbellied stove sat at the rear of the large room, while four rows of neat desks faced the teacher's large desk in front. Behind the teacher's desk was a large chalkboard, while windows allowed in bright light on either side of the room.

The teacher, Mr. Danforth, looked up from preparing a lesson to stare as Fidelia marched down the central row of desks, towing one of his students in her wake. He rose and frowned at her. "I'm certain you have no right to act in such a manner," he said in a disapproving voice. He pushed his glasses up his nose.

"Why aren't you outside ensuring there are no fights during recess?"

"I'm certain you have no right to criticize me. I am the teacher, not you."

"And I'm certain that you should have a better control of your students. Why aren't you outside during recess, watching over the children and keeping them safe? You should know the vile things they are saying about my daughter." She repeated what Tommy Whitlock had said and saw the teacher pale. "Do you approve of such abuse?"

"Of course not, but there's little I can do, Miss … Mrs. …" His words trailed away.

"Mrs. Renfrew," she said in a hardened tone. "I am Mildred's mother. And I refuse to believe you have no ability to rein in your students."

He looked at her in a patronizing manner. "It's unfortunate, but everyone knows what you were."

Her gaze hardened. "Yes, and they know what I am now too. A respected married woman with a successful business. Tell me. What punishment do you plan for Tommy?" She kept a firm hold on the boy, while Mildred stood next to her. Hortence stood in solidarity next to Mildred.

"It is not my place to punish," he said. "I do not believe in corporal punishment."

"You do not have to believe in corporal punishment to maintain control of your students." Fidelia's eyes flashed with anger. "I highly doubt your predecessor utilized such methods, but she was respected by students and parents alike."

He stared at her with a haughty disdain. "I refuse to be chastised by a woman such as you."

Fidelia let out a disgusted sound and released Tommy's ear. "Then my daughter will no longer attend your school. And you are no longer welcome at my sister's bakery. Not until you learn how to control your students."

She turned to face Mildred, held out her hand, and walked out of the school with her head held high, Mildred walking beside her. Hortence remained with them and left school too. Rather than return home, Fidelia walked with the girls to the nearby livery.

She entered to find Bears and Alistair exchanging stories and laughing. Bears looked at her and then at Mildred and Hortence, setting aside his pitchfork. "Stitch?" he asked as he approached her and kissed her forehead. Then he did the same to Mildred. "What brings you to the livery?" He stared at Mildred, who continued to study her shoes. "Why aren't the girls at school?"

Alistair approached and held out his arms as Hortence ran into them. "What happened?"

Fidelia kept a hand on Mildred's shoulder and looked at Bears. "I spoke with Irene today. I've been worried about Mildred. About the fact she's seemed distant." She flushed at his gaze as he frowned at her admission. "I didn't tell you because I thought I should feel happy enough to be called her stepmother. But I want more." She looked down at Mildred, who stared at her with wonder. "I thought you did too."

"I do. I did."

Fidelia looked at her. "Until school started." When Mildred nodded and lowered her gaze again, Fidelia pulled her tightly against her side. "I went to the school today to speak with the teacher. I arrived during recess. I heard the boys taunting Mildred. Calling her names."

She paused, and Mildred spoke up. "She marched up to Tommy and took him by the ear and dragged him up to Mr. Danforth and demanded he punish Tommy for his bad words."

Bears looked at his daughter and smiled at her. She was more animated in the last minute than she'd been in the last week. "And what did Mr. Danforth say?"

Mildred flushed. "He said he was not there to punish the children."

Bears's jaw ticked, and Alistair swore under his breath. "What did your mother do?"

Mildred smiled. "Mama told him that, until he learned how to control the children, I wouldn't attend school there and that he wasn't welcome at Aunt Annabelle's bakery." She looked up at Fidelia and frowned as she saw her fighting tears. "Isn't that right?"

"Yes, darling daughter, it is right." She stroked a hand over Mildred's head. "I should have discussed it with you before I made such a rash decision, but I don't want Mildred treated in such a manner."

Bears nodded. "I agree with you, Stitch." He turned to look at Alistair. "What do you think?"

"I wonder if Leticia would be willin' to teach a few students, so they dinna fall behind," Alistair said.

Fidelia smiled at Alistair for his support. The girls jumped up and down and gave each other a hug, but Bears shook his head. "That does not mean you will have days to run wild, girls. You must study and learn."

"I know, Father, but Aunt Leticia is such a good teacher. It will be fun," Mildred said. She gave her father a hug.

He watched as the girls raced off to find their uncle Cailean and to tell him about their day's adventure.

"What more happened?" Bears asked as Alistair left to continue working.

Before she could answer, Tom Whitlock the elder burst into the barn. "You!" he called out as he approached them. His focus was on Bears. "You need to learn how to control your woman."

Bears watched him as though he were part of a circus act. "I have no need to control her. She is her own person."

Tom Whitlock leaned forward, quivering with rage at Bears's answer. "How dare you allow her to run wild in this town! Do you know how she treated my son?"

Bears shook his head. "Whatever she did was warranted. Your boy is a bully."

"How dare you, half-breed!" Tom seethed as he pushed at Bears.

Bears stood tall and shook his head. "I know what I am. It's no wonder your boy acts as he does with you as an example, peddler." He saw his jab at Whitlock's inability to hold down steady employment hit its mark.

"She has no right to touch my son." He looked at Fidelia with derisiveness.

"What did your son say about my daughter?" Bears asked.

"Nothing that isn't true." Whitlock jutted out his chin. When Bears stared at him for a long moment, Whitlock muttered defiantly, "That your daughter is a half-breed, the daughter of a whore, who shouldn't mix with those of pure race."

Bears glared at him. "Get out. Now. You are never again welcome in my livery."

"How dare you deny me access to the livery?" Whitlock stopped short of further insulting Bears when he took a warning step closer. Whitlock glared at Bears and looked behind him to see Cailean and Alistair in agreement with Bears's statement. Both girls watched with wide eyes.

Whitlock turned on his heel and stormed out of the livery.

"What did you do to his son?" Bears asked her.

"I tugged him into the school by holding onto his ear. Nothing else happened to him, and he obviously won't be punished at home or at school." She ran a soothing hand over her husband's arm.

He moved toward her and held her face between his palms. "Thank you," he whispered. He backed away as a customer entered the livery. "I'll see you at home tonight."

She smiled at him and called out for Mildred, saying goodbye to Hortence. They waved at the men as they left, leaving the livery hand in hand. When Fidelia and Mildred arrived home, Fidelia pointed to the rocking chair. She'd noticed that Mildred enjoyed sitting in it when her father wasn't home. "I'm not upset with you, Mildred,"

Fidelia said, when she saw her daughter tense. "I want to know what else has happened during the first week of school."

Mildred shrugged. "More of the same. I thought it would be fun at school. Hortence is there. But it's just like at Mrs. Marday's. Except it's the boys who pick on me and the girls who laugh."

Fidelia sighed. "Why didn't you tell us?"

"I wanted you to be proud of me. To see that I could be as strong as you and Father are. I didn't want you to think I was a failure by running to you complaining." She sat with stooped shoulders as she fought tears. "I didn't think you'd believe me."

"I will believe you because you've never given me any reason not to. I trust you, Mildred." She met Mildred's gaze, happy to see dawning hope in them. "You were being belittled and bullied, dearest. I would never consider you a failure because you wanted to be treated fairly." She looked at her with remorse. "I won't lie and say that I wasn't treated poorly too when I was a girl. I think everyone has someone in their past they wish they'd never met."

"What did your parents do?" Mildred asked.

"They told me to quit complaining and turned a blind eye when I was abused by the older girls at school. I learned I couldn't rely on my parents." She leaned forward, her elbows resting on her knees as she looked intently at the girl she considered her daughter. "I don't want you to ever feel that way about me, Mildred."

"I don't, Mama," she whispered through her tears. "Do you know how proud I was when you towed him away? I wanted to yell out that you're my mama!"

Fidelia blinked away tears and nodded. "I'm so glad. I consider you my daughter. I never want you to think I'm trying to take the place of your mother. I'm not. But I'd be honored to be your mama."

Mildred threw herself in Fidelia's arms, crying a little, but mainly seeking comfort. After a few minutes, she whispered, "Can we bake cookies?"

Fidelia burst out laughing. "Yes, why not? Let's bake something special for your father." She rose and moved to the kitchen with

Mildred. Soon they worked side by side, exchanging stories and laughing together.

When Bears arrived home, he paused to sniff at the air. "It smells like the bakery." He breathed in deeply again.

"Mama and I wanted to bake you cookies," Mildred said as she jumped up and down in her excitement. "Here, Papa, try one!" She handed him an oatmeal raisin cookie and waited expectantly. When he groaned, she looked at Fidelia in confusion.

"That means he likes it," she said with a wink to her daughter.

"Yay!" Mildred exclaimed.

Bears smiled. "I can see you enjoyed your afternoon free from school. However, Leticia came by the livery because she heard about the ruckus at the schoolhouse. She's happy to help teach the girls, although she's worried about what it will mean for the bakery."

Fidelia rubbed at her forehead. "I think it means Annabelle needs more help. We already spoke about it today, and I'll talk with her again tomorrow about hiring someone. Should Mildred go to their house tomorrow for her lessons?"

Bears nodded. Mildred went to her room for a while, and he waited until he heard her door close. "Now will you tell me what happened?"

She sighed. "It's silly, and I should be used to it. But Mr. Danforth implied that punishing Tommy wasn't part of his job because I had no right to complain. He said that everyone knew what I had been." She saw her husband's eyes glint with anger. "I hate having my past thrown at me when I've worked so hard to get that behind me, Bears," she whispered.

"I'm sorry, my love. I can't change their prejudices. I can't make him be a better teacher." He rubbed at his head. "But ... I have heard rumblings that an impromptu meeting of the town's Improvement Committee has been called. It seems two of the three members are dissatisfied with the teacher."

Her eyes widened at his statement. "How can that be?"

He smiled. "The teacher should have known better than to anger the MacKinnons. They hold more sway than many realize, and you are a MacKinnon by marriage."

She shook her head. "I don't want anyone to lose his job because of me."

"Then you are more generous than I am. I want Danforth to suffer for what he allowed to happen to Mildred. I know children can be cruel, but, as the teacher, he should punish those who are caught saying cruel things."

"There's no guarantee the next teacher will be any better," Fidelia argued.

"I doubt he or she could be worse." He pulled Fidelia close and held her. He ran soothing hands over her, frowning into her hair as he realized she was shaking. "*Shh*, love. They aren't worth your concern."

She kissed his neck. "Did you hear Mildred?" she whispered. "Did you hear her call me *Mama*?" She backed away, and her eyes were lit with an incandescent joy. "I never hoped that she'd feel that way about me."

"You've accepted her from the first, Stitch. Even when you weren't sure what would happen between us, you treated her well, if at arm's length. Can you imagine what she felt, having you defend her at school before the teacher and the bully, when she's always felt powerless and alone? You showed her that she is loved and valued and worth fighting for." His eyes shone with love and gratitude.

"I love her, Bears, as much as I would my own child." She gasped as he swept forward and kissed her passionately.

"Thank you," he whispered. "Thank you for being as brave as I knew you were." He stepped away and moved to the kitchen a moment before Mildred emerged from her bedroom. He winked at his wife and then listened to them talk about their afternoon together.

CHAPTER 11

Wanted: A competent, resourceful assistant to work in Annabelle's Sweet Shop. Interested applicants should come to the bakery between 2:00 p.m. and 4:00 p.m. by Friday, November 18.

When the chime over the door sounded, Fidelia moved to the front of the bakery. She paused as she saw Mrs. Jameson, Walter's mother, standing in front of the cases. "How may I help you?" she asked.

"You could start by showing respect to your elders. To your betters in town," Mrs. Jameson snapped. She quickly closed her mouth and attempted a smile. However, it appeared as more of a grimace, as though she had a toothache on one side of her jaw.

"Are you all right?" Fidelia's gaze examined the middle-aged woman, who had needled every woman who had worked at the bakery. Mrs. Jameson detested every MacKinnon bride because they had denied her daughter, Helen, the opportunity of marrying a MacKinnon. Then Mrs. Jameson detested them because they'd shown charity to Fidelia. Now, though, Mrs. Jameson attempted to look meek in her navy-blue dress, which was a change from her stark black dress that always made her look as though she were a female undertaker. She wore her corset as tight as ever and stood ramrod straight.

"I am here about the position," Mrs. Jameson said. She held out the flyer that Jessamine had printed the previous day.

"I beg your pardon?" Fidelia asked, looking from the flyer to Mrs. Jameson and then back to the flyer.

"I read that you are in need of help. I am here to offer you my incomparable aid." She stood as tall as her five-foot frame allowed and attempted another smile.

"I … I fear you are not acceptable for the position," Fidelia stammered, shaking her head in stupefaction.

"How dare you deny me out of hand! I have every right to inquire about the position!" Mrs. Jameson slammed her hand onto the glass-topped display case, marring the polished surface.

"Yes, you do. Just as I have every right to deny you your request, Mrs. Jameson. My sister and I decided yesterday that we would not agree to hire anyone who either of us did not like." Fidelia's tone cooled. "I do not like you. I refuse to work with you. You will never work in the bakery."

"You would deny me?"

Fidelia smiled. "I would. And I do not have to explain or justify my reasons to *you*."

Her nemesis's mother leaned toward Fidelia, hatred glinting in her gaze. "You think you're so high and mighty now because your sister has accepted you and you've married that man no one else wanted. You might believe the townsfolk accepted you when they celebrated your wedding. They were really there for the free cake."

Fidelia let out a deep breath. "I might have believed your horrible words before, Mrs. Jameson, but I realize now that you are the one who is isolated. You are the one no one likes. Not me. Please leave."

She stared at Mrs. Jameson and waited for her to leave. She grimaced as the older woman slammed the door so hard that she nearly broke the glass in the door.

"What was that?" Annabelle called out from the back. She had been tending Skye in the rear room, when Mrs. Jameson entered.

Fidelia flipped the sign to Closed and locked the front door. They had nearly sold out, and, what they hadn't sold, they could bring home to their families. "I'm tired, and I've closed the bakery for the day," she said as she walked to the back. "Mrs. Jameson came to apply for the position as our helper."

Annabelle's mouth dropped open, and then she pealed with laughter. Skye stared at her mother in confusion and then began to laugh too. She clapped her hands, as though a trick had been played. "Yes, darling, it was a wonderful joke. Oh, how marvelous it must have felt to turn her down," Annabelle said as she swiped at her eyes. She ran a hand over her daughter's black hair, tidying her ribbon, since Skye had just woken from a nap.

Fidelia shared a grin with her. "It did. But I think we must find someone soon, or we'll have people we don't want hounding us."

Annabelle shrugged. "We can't be forced to hire just anyone." She yawned. "And I've been thinking. Do you want to talk to Warren about writing up a formal contract? You and I don't need one because we are family. But I think we should have one for the person we hire. I'd like to have something written in it about a trial period."

"Why can't you just fire someone if they're no good?" Fidelia asked as she picked up Skye and held her against her shoulder, sighing with pleasure to hold her niece.

"We can, but I don't want anyone to ever threaten our bakery," she said with a smile.

Bears stood with his arms slung over the paddock rail, watching as Brutus pranced around inside. "Hello, Harold," he said as Brutus's owner joined him.

"Have you found something other than carrots or my pantaloons' bottoms that he likes as a reward?" Harold asked as he stared at his horse.

Bears shook his head. "I can't find a way to tame him."

Harold sighed. "I should have listened to Irene and not trusted that drifter." He studied the chestnut-colored horse. "But I liked Brutus's spirit and thought to surprise Frederick."

Bears snorted. "Frederick would never have thanked you for gifting him such an animal." He rubbed at his forehead. "What do you want me to do with him?"

Harold shrugged. "Keep him for now. I'll think of something."

Bears shrugged. "Maybe you should let him run free. Some horses were never meant to be tamed." He stared at Brutus, who eyed Harold with malicious intent. "Come, old man. I fear Brutus will attempt to break down the paddock to get to you." He led Harold into the barn, and they sat on the stools that faced the paddock. They left the door open, although Brutus ignored them now that they were out of his immediate eyesight.

After a few moments, where Harold remained quiet, Bears frowned. "What is it?"

Harold looked at him with anger in his gaze, and Bears froze. "You know I try to never gossip about what I hear at the café. That I consider what I hear to be like a sacred trust between me and my customers." When Bears nodded, Harold still glowered. "But I have to break that now."

"What did you hear?" Bears whispered.

"Vicious talk about you and Mildred. Talk that you have such little value for her that you refused to pay the orphanage for having cared for her for all the time she was there." He paused as he watched Bears's cheeks flush with anger. "That you were shamed into taking Mildred, how that orphanage marm had to threaten throwing Mildred onto the streets before you agreed to take her."

"That vicious harpy," Bears rasped as he stood and paced. "The judge warned me that she'd act out when I refused to pay her a generous *bribe* for Mildred." He paused and stared at Harold. "What else?"

"That you never planned to keep her and that, by marrying the woman you did, you intended to prepare Mildred for a life at the Boudoir."

Bears froze, and the flush faded as he paled. "Never. Dear God, never."

Harold rose and walked toward his devastated friend. "I know you, and I know it all to be a lie. But your womenfolk might believe it, even for a moment. Talk with them before they hear these rumors. Or you may lose what is most precious to you."

Bears gripped Harold's arm and then called out to Cailean, who poked his head from inside the office. "I have to see Fidelia." When Cailean nodded, Bears took off at a near run for the bakery.

Fidelia left the bakery for the day with a basket over her arm and a spring to her step. Annabelle would hire more help, Fidelia's relationship with Mildred and Bears grew stronger every day, and the sun was shining. "I couldn't ask for anything more," she whispered to herself, turning her face up to the sun for a moment as she neared her house.

She gasped in pain as a hand gripped her arm. Although she tried to wrench her arm free, she only succeeded in digging the fingers deeper into her flesh. "Let me go!" she said. as she met the smug smile of Walter Jameson.

"I have no intention of letting you go. Now that you are a married woman, I imagine you are less reserved in bed. Although I always liked you docile. You seemed to like it that way." He laughed as Fidelia tried to kick him in his shins. Her shoes were no match for his thick boots and caused him little discomfort.

"You have no right to speak with me. To touch me." She tugged on her arm again, but he refused to let her go. Instead, he backed her up until she was in the shadows against the rear wall of one of the buildings that faced Main Street.

"Oh, I have every right to speak with you, Charity." His smile deepened when he noted how his voice and his use of her Boudoir name affected her. "I fear you've missed me and my attentions. You've gone soft."

She shook her head. "I *never* missed you." She tilted her head up in defiance. "I have Bears now. I have a family."

His mocking laugh provoked another shudder. "You always were naive. Why do you think that half-breed married you? He hopes you'll teach that girl your wiles so he can sell her to the Madam. It's what any man with sense would do with a girl like that."

Fidelia shook her head. "No, Bears wouldn't do that."

"Why wouldn't he?" Walter stroked a finger down her cheek. "Wouldn't your father have done that to you?"

She screamed in anger and butted him hard in the chest with her head, knocking the air out of him. He loosened his hold on her, and she wrenched herself free. "Not all men are cruel like you. Never touch me again." She turned on her heel and ran for home, slamming and locking the door behind her.

When she had secured the door, she fell to the floor, shaking and crying as she relived the scene over and over. When the door handle turned, she stifled a scream and pulled her legs tightly against her chest. Pressing with all her weight against the door, she muttered, "I will not let you in."

"Stitch!" Bears called out as he pounded on the door. "Stitch, let me in!"

"Bears," she breathed. She moved to her hands and feet and flipped the latch and then grunted as the door hit her in her thigh. "Ouch."

He poked his head in and frowned. "Back up a little." When she had, he eased inside and knelt on the floor across from her. "Stitch?" he asked in a hesitant voice.

Fidelia gave a small sob and threw herself into his arms. "Oh, Bears, I was so afraid. But I got away. I got away on my own." She continued to sob as she clung to him, and he murmured soft words into her ear.

When her crying abated, he whispered, "Tell me." His hands swiped her cheeks, clearing away her tears, although fresh ones continued to cascade down.

"I was happy as I left the bakery. Content with my work and with my family." She saw the question in his gaze and stroked a hand over his face. "With you and Mildred. I let my guard down." She sniffled. "And then Walter was there. Telling me that I must have missed his attentions." She shuddered.

When she paused and looked down, he murmured, "Tell me. Share it with me. Let me help take away his words' power over you."

She bit her quivering lip. "He called me Charity again, and I hated it. I hated the memories it evoked." Then she snorted. "And he spun a monstrous tale about you only marrying me because you wanted me to train Mildred for the Boudoir."

He closed his eyes and sighed.

"Bears?"

He ran his fingers through her hair and then rested his hand on her shoulder. "Harold just told me that rumor." His eyes lit with fire. "The woman who ran the orphanage in Helena has begun spreading horrible lies."

Fidelia shook her head in confusion. "Why?"

"She remains angry that I never paid her what she considered her due for her care of Mildred." He paused as he looked at Fidelia. "Did you ... Did you ever doubt?"

She looked at him in confusion a moment and then shook her head. "Never!" She cupped his cheek. "I know you, Bears. I know how much you love your daughter. Our daughter." She took a deep breath. "I know how much you love me. You'd never want that for any woman."

He smiled and pulled her close. "I worried your memories and fear would momentarily override what you knew to be true."

She shook her head and leaned into him. "Never. All I wanted, once I was safe at home, was your arms around me." She smiled at him. "And now they are." After many moments in his arms, she whispered, "Why didn't you pay her what she wanted?"

"I knew, if I paid her, she would continue to come back for more. She's a greedy, unscrupulous woman." He shrugged. "Besides, Mildred is my daughter. Why should I have to pay for her?"

Fidelia traced a finger over his back. "Would you pay her now for her to cease her lies?"

Bears moved so that he leaned against the door, and Fidelia leaned against him in his arms. "No, although I'll put some of my father's money to good use by hiring Warren to threaten the woman so she ceases her lies." He rested his cheek on top of her head.

She traced a hand over his chest. "Hire Warren, Bears." She paused as she thought a bit more. "What about the judge in Helena who Warren had you meet? Helen told the family about him on one of her visits with us while you were away."

Bears nodded. "Yes, I'll write him too. He was a friend of my father's, and he's the one who signed the adoption decree." He sighed and relaxed. "I love holding you like this."

She snuggled into his embrace. "I love being held by you," she whispered. "If need be, use any and all of the money left to me by my father. Mildred is more important than anything."

His arms tightened around her, and they sat for many minutes in contented silence.

CHAPTER 12

In late November, Annabelle and Fidelia continued to work at the bakery alone. Winter weather had struck, with temperatures plummeting, and the first snowstorm of the year arriving the day before Thanksgiving. However, compared to the previous year, it was not nearly as harsh. Fidelia continued to hope it would be a normal Montana winter, rather than another horrible winter like last year.

Annabelle's advertisement in Jessamine's newspaper had inspired great interest, but few qualified or dedicated applicants had applied. They remained uncertain if another advertisement would be worthwhile. Leticia was now at home every day, teaching the girls before the birth of her babe. "How hard can it be to smile to patrons and to sell them goods?" Fidelia grumbled to herself, as she pasted on a smile and bantered with the latest round of townsfolk visiting the bakery. When she reached the final customer, she was relaxed and enjoying herself.

"Any chance Mrs. Johansen will be back in time to bake us some of her *pepperkake?*" the barber asked, taking an appreciative sniff of the cinnamon roll Fidelia had just placed in a bag for him. Leena's Norwegian gingerbread had been a huge hit with the townsfolk the previous Christmas season.

Fidelia shrugged. "We are hopeful she will surprise us during the holidays, but we can make no promises." She winked at him. "If she does bake *pepperkake*, I'll save you a piece."

He beamed at her. "Save me two, missus." He gave her a deferential nod. "Say howdy to your husband for me." He left with a wave, shutting the door behind him.

Fidelia returned to the kitchen sink to wash the mounting pile of dishes.

Annabelle watched her with curiosity. "I think you should work the front. You enjoy it, when you overcome your shyness. Whenever we hire help, the new hire can wash and hide out here in the back with me."

"I do not hide!" Fidelia protested and then laughed as Annabelle watched her with amusement in her gaze. "Well, I have hidden since I left the Boudoir. But, with Leticia so busy teaching the girls, I've done much better."

Annabelle nodded. "Yes, you have. You never were shy when we were girls. I was the one hiding behind you, not the other way around."

Fidelia shrugged. "Life can be a hard teacher." When the front door jingled, she sighed and dried her hands. Her step hitched a moment before she continued to the front.

The woman standing on the other side of the glass counter looked as if she'd last eaten a month ago, and she eyed the baked goods as though they were a particular form of torture.

"How may I help you?"

The woman, who appeared to be in her early twenties, clung to a cloth bundle tied together at the top with a rope. Her threadbare coat did little to keep out the cold wind howling on this late November day, and her shoes were one mile short of falling apart at the seams. "I heard you needed help."

Fidelia nodded. "Why do you think you could help us?"

The stranger refused to respond, turning immediately for the front door.

Fidelia moved with alacrity to grab the young woman's arm,

preventing her from fleeing. "We do need help, but I want to hear from you why you believe you could help us."

The woman thrust her chin back. "I'm a hard worker. I'll do whatever you tell me to do."

Fidelia nodded as she released the woman's arm. "Excellent. Please follow me. I'm Fidelia, and my sister Annabelle is the baker." Fidelia led the woman into the kitchen area and watched as Annabelle hid her surprise at the woman's appearance.

"Please, have a seat," Annabelle said as she motioned to the opposite side of the counter, where she had finished baking the final batch of cookies for the day. "I'd enjoy your opinion on this cookie. I've just started selling them, and I believe they are a particular treat this time of year." She poured a cup of milk and set a plate of three cookies in front of the woman.

The woman stared at the plate, then at Annabelle and Fidelia, but kept her hands on her lap. "Why would you want my opinion?"

Annabelle laughed. "If you are to work with me, you will have to accustom yourself to me asking for your advice. Frequently. I like to experiment." She frowned as the young woman continued to stare at her. "Do you not like sweets? I'm afraid you have to like sweets if you are to work here."

"You won't call the sheriff because I've eaten this cookie?" the woman asked.

Annabelle shook her head and made a noise of disgust in her throat that rivaled anything her Scottish husband made when offended. "No. I offered them to you. And I gave you a cup of milk." She turned to the oven and pulled out the last batch of cookies. She watched as the woman nibbled at one of the cookies. "So, what do you think?"

"They have a funny taste," she blurted out and then flushed.

"Bad or good?" Annabelle asked.

"Good." She closed her eyes, as though thinking hard. "It makes the chocolate more chocolaty."

Annabelle smiled at Fidelia, and the sisters shared a grin. "Exactly. I put in a touch of mint extract, and I find it makes all the difference."

The woman frowned. "Mint is for when you're ill."

Fidelia laughed. "I'm glad you'll tell us what you think." She snagged one of the cooling cookies. "You already know that I'm Fidelia, and she's Annabelle. Who are you?"

The woman's eyes rounded. "I'm Jane. Jane Keith." She took a sip of milk and then another bite of cookie. "I would never have thought I'd be good enough to work in the bakery with one of the MacKinnons."

Annabelle choked on a laugh. "I'm not royalty. And neither is my husband." She watched the young woman. "Where are you coming from, Jane?"

Jane's shoulders hunched. "I don't care what you think about me, but I ain't going back. You can't make me!"

Fidelia made a soothing noise. "If you know anything about me, then you understand that I won't ever pass judgment on how a woman has lived her life."

Jane looked at her and nodded. "Sometimes those who have reformed are the most zealous against those they believe need reforming."

Fidelia chuckled. "That is true. But I'm not one of those people. We won't force you to share more than what you're willing to. But I would like to know if an angry man will arrive, demanding you return to him."

Jane shook her head as a tear slipped out. "No. Horatio decided I was a useless woman and threw me out." She clung to her bag. "I've little more than my clothes and this bag."

"Has he found another?" Annabelle asked in a gentle voice.

Jane nodded as another tear tracked down her cheek. "Yes. She's prettier and more biddable than me." She pushed at her limp reddish brown hair. "I feared I'd go to the Boudoir, but I don't want that life." She looked at them, expecting censure. "My mama was one of those women, and I escaped that life when I was ten."

"Or so you'd hoped," Fidelia murmured. "How old are you, Jane?"

"Twenty-two," she whispered. "I don't want to work for the Madam. She treats her girls mean."

Fidelia nodded. "Believe me. I know." She looked at her sister, and Annabelle nodded.

"Jane, we can't pay you much, but you'll always have food. Always have a place to stay. And you'll have friendship." Annabelle looked at her. "In return, I expect you to work hard and to be loyal. Do you think you can do that?"

Jane looked from one sister and then to the other and nodded. "Yes. Of course."

Annabelle smiled. "Good. For now, I want you to sit and relax, while we finish the day's work. Then you can come home with me tonight and meet my husband and our daughter. Other than bread and sweets, there's no food here, and I want you to have a good supper. You need your strength to work well." She paused, as though remembering something. "Just one moment," she said, stepping into the small room that now served as a nursery and her office. She grabbed some paperwork and returned, handing it to Jane. "If the employment I'm offering you is acceptable, we can finalize our arrangement. Warren, the town lawyer, wrote a basic contract for any employee I eventually hired, and I think you will see he is always fair."

Jane looked over the contract and shook her head in confusion. "I don't understand why you need a contract."

Annabelle smiled. "I like to protect what Fidelia and I have. And I sense you have secrets yet to be learned." When Jane jerked, as though stuck by a pin, Annabelle gripped Jane's hand. "We all have secrets. We all have episodes in our pasts we'd rather forget." She waited for Jane to meet her gaze and to finally nod. "This is merely precautionary." She tapped at part of the contract. "And I believe you'll find that it protects you too. It states that I can't fire you without just cause."

Jane took a deep breath. "I do have secrets, but I promise they will not harm you."

Annabelle smiled. "You'll learn that we are understanding, Jane." She smiled as Jane accepted the pen and signed her name with a flourish to the bottom of the contract. Annabelle signed it, as did Fidelia as a witness.

After Annabelle tucked away the signed piece of paper, Jane asked,

"Will I live with you?" She ate another cookie. She took a sip of milk and closed her eyes as though in ecstasy. "I love milk and cookies."

Annabelle grinned. "Who doesn't? But to answer your question, no, you won't live with me. That small room behind you would be mostly yours. Many days my daughter is with me, and she takes a nap and plays in there."

"Why are you taking a chance on me?" Jane asked. "You have no reason to."

Fidelia waited for Annabelle to speak, but, when her sister remained quiet, Fidelia said, "You remind me of myself at one point in my life. I was offered a different sort of help."

Two days later, Jane worked in the back, washing dishes. She talked little, although she had begun to laugh at the stories Annabelle and Fidelia told. Jane eagerly tried every sample Annabelle offered her, giving her honest opinion. She loved the oatmeal raisin cookies, the cheese rolls, and the chocolate mint cookies. She thought the snickerdoodles were bland and the gingerbread a waste of good baking materials.

Annabelle laughed at that last pronouncement. "If Leena were here, she'd make you her famous *pepperkake*, and you'd realize why we love it so much. I don't have her recipe, so I'm improvising this year for the townsfolk. I fear they will be disappointed at my feeble attempt."

Fidelia returned from the front and snagged a sample of Annabelle's gingerbread. She tilted her head from side to side and then shrugged. "It's all right, but it's missing something. I'm not sure what."

Annabelle frowned. "Should we even bother selling it?"

"Call it gingerbread and sell it for a little less than Leena's special item. That way, when Leena is back, you can charge more, and people will be willing to pay for it," Jane said. She flushed as Annabelle and Fidelia stared at her.

"A sound plan," Fidelia said, now snagging a piece of snickerdoodle. "Something's off with this too."

Annabelle grabbed a bite of it and shook her head. "No, it tastes like it always has. And I agree with Jane's plan for the gingerbread. The snickerdoodle should be the usual price."

Fidelia nodded and brought out the trays of cookies to the front. The door opened, and her smile dimmed as their customer entered. "Hello, Mrs. Jameson. What would you like today?"

Mrs. Jameson approached the counter, eyeing the goods. "A piece of gingerbread," she said.

Fidelia nodded. "This is Annabelle's special gingerbread, and you're fortunate you visited when you did. She won't make it every day, and she's offering it at a special price today, as a way to thank her loyal customers for their patronage this year."

"If she wanted to thank us, she'd give it to us for free," Mrs. Jameson snapped as she slapped her coin onto the counter. She took a bite of the gingerbread and sighed with delight. "Excellent. Much better than that foreign concoction we were forced to eat last year. The simplicity is in the spices."

Fidelia nodded, ignoring Mrs. Jameson's criticism of Leena's baking, and looked at the door as she waited for Mrs. Jameson to leave.

"I heard you hired a kindred spirit, Mrs. Renfrew," Mrs. Jameson said.

"I'm certain I do not understand," Fidelia said, any friendliness in her voice replaced with an icy disdain. "We hired a competent young woman to work with us."

Mrs. Jameson snickered. "If she were competent, you wouldn't force the townsfolk to suffer your presence out front. You'd remain in the back, hidden away, washing dishes." She shook her head and *tsk*ed. "No, I've heard she's just like you. Ashamed of who she is and what she's done. It just proves this establishment is becoming more indecent every day."

Fidelia took a deep breath and gripped her hands into fists at her side as she attempted to rein in her temper. "The last time I checked,

Mrs. Jameson, the running of our business was none of your affair. You applied for the position, and we found you lacking. I wish you a good day."

"I would have been a much better worker than that strumpet in the back. Selling her wares at night to all who come calling."

"Get out," Fidelia hissed. "And don't bother to come back."

She stood ramrod straight, her aging corset creaking as she stood even straighter than usual. "You'd deny me entrance? One such as I, whose good opinion grants your bakery legitimacy in town?"

"If we depended on your good opinion, we'd have shuttered our doors years ago. Get out. Now." Fidelia glared at the older woman and watched as she grabbed up her slab of gingerbread and departed.

After a long moment with a lull in customers, Fidelia returned to the kitchen. "Mrs. Jameson was as charming as ever," she muttered. She looked at Jane for a long moment and then asked, "Jane, why would Mrs. Jameson say you are having men visit you at night after-hours?"

A clatter sounded in the sink, as Jane dropped a metal measuring cup.

Annabelle ceased her gentle singing and stared at Jane with shocked concern. "Jane?"

Jane looked from one sister to the next. "It's not what you think." Her gaze pleaded with them to understand.

"It rarely is when the news comes from Mrs. Jameson. Please, help us to understand," Fidelia said.

Jane grabbed a dish towel and dried her hands, holding onto the towel even after her hands were dried. "I have a brother. He's seven years younger than me. Can't find proper work. And I didn't like the life of a miner for him." She flit a furtive glance at the sisters, and her shoulders relaxed when she saw no condemnation in their expressions. "He comes here at night and sleeps."

"And he leaves before we arrive," Annabelle said. She nodded as though something just made sense to her. "It's why I smelled aftershave yesterday."

Jane's eyes rounded with surprise. "Yes. He'd visited the barber. He was so proud he finally needed a shave." Her eyes filled. "I … I can't lose him."

Annabelle watched the young woman. "We'd like to meet him."

"He's the reason you're not gaining weight. He's eating all your food," Fidelia said, studying the skinny woman.

Jane flushed. "Neither of us are starving any longer."

Annabelle gave a snort of disgust. "But you're still hungry." She tapped at the countertop. "You're a hard worker, and I appreciate your blunt talk about my experiments. Others are too kind to me." She winked at her sister. "I need to know if you have any other surprises for us." She met Jane's wary stare. "A child? An irate mother? Anything?"

Jane shook her head. "No, the man I was with doesn't want me anymore, and we were never properly married. And I have no one else besides my brother."

Annabelle nodded. "Fine. Have him live here with you. We'll find another bed. And the MacKinnons always have work. He'll be busy soon."

Jane stood in shock as she stared at Annabelle and Fidelia. "You're not firing me?"

Fidelia frowned. "Why would we fire you? If there's one thing we admire, it's loyalty to family, Jane. You'll learn that about us. Now, where does your brother spend his days?"

Jane shuddered. "He's made a sort of lean-to in the woods. It's getting very cold there for him."

"Go fetch him," Annabelle said. "That way we can meet him, and he'll understand he's welcome here too."

Fidelia watched as Jane pulled on a secondhand coat, given to her by Jessamine, and rushed out the rear door. After she left, Fidelia looked at her sister. "I'm sorry if you regret hiring her now."

Annabelle shook her head. "I never regret being kind, Dee." She smiled at her sister. "I have a feeling those siblings have rarely been shown much consideration or kindness. Besides, Ewan or Frederick can always use help."

Fidelia let out a deep breath. "Thank you, Anna. We don't know Jane well, but I feel as though we do."

Annabelle nodded. "She reminds you of yourself, Dee. I'm thankful she's proven worthy of your concern. So far." She nodded as her sister shrugged at her subtle warning.

As the back door opened, allowing cold air into the warm bakery, Fidelia and Annabelle smiled in welcome. Jane tugged on the arm of a tall gangly teenager with unruly auburn hair. Fidelia fought a smile as he had no whiskers, and she envisioned the barber's amusement at shaving the young man.

"Hello," Annabelle said with a smile. "Welcome to our bakery. Would you like a cookie?"

His amber eyes lit up at the word "cookie," and he lost a little of his reticence. "If you don't mind." His sister hit him in his middle. "Thank you, missus," he said, bowing his head deferentially.

"I'm Fidelia, and the kind woman offering you cookies is my sister, Annabelle." She paused as he wolfed down two snickerdoodle cookies.

Jane flushed. "This is Duncan. He's forgotten his manners."

Annabelle shook her head. "No, he's a growing young man and hungry. Please go to the café, Jane and Duncan, and have a hot meal. Eat your fill. Fidelia and I can manage here for an hour or so."

Jane shook her head. "But we couldn't. That wouldn't be proper."

"Of course it is," Fidelia said. " Besides, Irene and Harold want to meet you."

The sisters shared a smile as the siblings departed for the café. "There's a pair who could use the wisdom and care of the Tompkinses," Fidelia murmured.

Annabelle nodded. "Thankfully, Irene and Harold relish being honorary grandparents." They laughed and continued the day's work.

Annabelle plumped up a pillow and then sat in a rocking chair. She listened for voices as she heard a wagon halt near the livery. Smiling, she heard Sorcha call out to her brother, and then

Frederick admonishing her to be careful. "I bet she's impatient and trying to get out of the wagon on her own."

"Don't peek out the window," Fidelia whispered. "That would ruin the surprise!" She glanced around the two rooms that had been Bears's home and grinned. "It's not the comforts of the ranch house she's used to, but I think she'll enjoy being near family."

"And still having her own private space," Annabelle said. "At least Frederick will be relieved." They heard footsteps and Sorcha arguing with Ewan.

"I canna understand why I must go to Bears's old house," Sorcha said outside. "I ken ye like to meddle, Ewan, but I want to rest after that wagon ride."

Ewan made a soothing noise. "A fat piece of cake waits for ye in the kitchen, *after* ye've looked at the piece of furniture I made ye in there."

Sorcha grumbled, "I'd rather a feather bed at the moment." She thrust open the door and stumbled when she saw Annabelle and Fidelia waiting for her. "Did ye want to see the cradle too?"

Annabelle giggled and pulled her pregnant sister-in-law into her arms. "No. *This* is the surprise, Sorcha. This will be your home while you're in town." She spread her arms wide, as Sorcha took in the room with new curtains, a polished stove, and a large bed in the corner. As promised, a cradle sat at the foot of the bed. A tacked-on blanket covered the doorway to the back bedroom.

Fidelia moved forward to hug Sorcha. "We thought you'd want to be near family but not living with family."

Sorcha swiped at her tears. "Oh, how perfect." She sniffled when she looked at the small touches around the room. She looked over her shoulder and beamed at her husband. "Look, Frederick."

He wrapped his arms around her waist and pulled her tight against him. "Our home away from home," he murmured into her ear. "Your quilt will look beautiful on that bed."

Sorcha rested her hands over her husband's. "Ye ken I would have been happy in a bedroom at Cailean's?"

Annabelle smiled. "I know. But I also know stairs become more difficult as your pregnancy progresses. And Skye has taken to singing in the middle of the night. It's not conducive to a good night's rest." Her gaze was filled with understanding as she looked at her sister-in-law. "You should sleep as much as you can now."

"I dinna think that's possible," Sorcha said, fighting a yawn. "Seems I'm always tired." Sorcha smiled at Fidelia and Annabelle. "An' I ken this has nothin' to do with wee Skye an' her singin'. Ye kent we'd miss havin' our own place."

"Thank you," Frederick said. "This is perfect."

CHAPTER 13

NEWS & NOTEWORTHY

It has come to this reporter's attention that certain townsfolk believe the lies trickling in from a bitter, greedy woman in Helena. Dear reader, it is time you learned to discern truth from lies and to discern when you are being played for a fool. For, if you believed these lies spread by those who yearn to sow dissension, you are a gullible goat.

If you doubted for one moment that an upstanding member of our town stole a child from an orphanage, you are a brainless bat. A judge's decree granted that fine man the right to adopt his own daughter. The daughter he had been denied knowing. The daughter who is cherished and flourishing in our town. Don't allow your prejudices to blind you to the truth.

If you believe the woman who runs that orphanage, then you believe that her comfort comes before the care of the girls she has been charged to protect and to shelter. Remember this, dear reader. No one should prosper off the misfortune of others. A lesson I'd hope you'd remember this holiday season.

"I t's time!" Mildred yelled as she burst into their bedroom. She launched herself onto their bed and squirmed until she rested between the two of them. She giggled as Fidelia and Bears wrapped an arm around her. "Saint Nicholas came in the middle of the night, just like you said he would, Mama."

Fidelia brushed at Mildred's tangled black hair. "Are there presents under the stockings?"

Mildred squirmed until she was free of their hold and then bounced on the bed on her knees. "Yes!" She frowned as they remained in bed. "How can you just lie there?"

Bears watched her with wonder. "How can you have this much energy so early in the morning?"

"It's Christmas, Father!" She launched herself into his arms and hugged him tight. After kissing his cheek, she jumped from the bed and raced away.

"I knew it was too much to hope for a peaceful morning," Fidelia said in a humor-laden voice. "Merry Christmas, my love." She traced Bears's cheek as he propped himself on one elbow and kissed her.

"Merry Christmas, Stitch." His eyes shone with love and devotion. "I never knew I could be this happy."

Her eyes filled, and she arched up to kiss him again. "Come. If Mildred finds us kissing, she'll be disappointed."

He chuckled and followed her from the bed. After donning clothes and warm socks, they ventured into the cool living area. Bears stoked the stove, and Fidelia made coffee, while Mildred sat by the stockings hung by the stove. She traced the wrapping paper and looked at the presents with awe.

While the coffee brewed, Fidelia pulled a blanket around herself and sat beside Mildred. "What was Christmas like with your mother?"

Mildred shook her head. "Never like this. We didn't have presents." She looked at her father to see if he took offense at her talking about her mother and then relaxed as he watched her with curiosity and concern but no censure. "He said we weren't worth celebrating."

Bears gave a grunt and dropped to his knees so he knelt beside his daughter. "I hope by now you know he lied. You deserve everything good in this life, dearest daughter." He looked at the small pile of presents. "I hope you aren't disappointed by what you receive today."

She beamed at him and threw herself into his arms. "Opening a present will be fun. I love surprises. But I already have the best gift." She looked from Fidelia to Bears. "A home with you and Mama. When I woke this morning and realized it wasn't a dream, that was the best present."

Fidelia stroked a hand over her head. "Do you still wake many mornings, wondering if this was all a dream?"

Mildred nodded and shrugged. "Not as many as before. But I crept out here this morning, and there were presents with my name on them!"

Fidelia looked at the small mound of gifts. "Are they all for you?"

Mildred giggled. "Of course not! Some are for you and Father." She reached forward and snagged one that had Fidelia's name on it. "See?"

Fidelia looked at the tag and then at Bears, since it was written in his handwriting. He smiled at her and nodded for her to open it. She carefully untaped the red paper. "We can reuse it," she murmured as she set it aside. Her eyes widened as she saw the fine silk thread that would be perfect for tatting high-quality lace. "I've never had such fine thread."

Bears smiled at her. "I hoped you would like it."

She reached out a hand to him and pulled him to her. "Thank you," she whispered as she kissed his cheek.

"My turn!" Mildred yelled. She pulled out a box and gave it a little shake. When nothing rattled, she frowned. Rather than following Fidelia's example, Mildred ripped open the paper and yanked off the lid. "Oh," she breathed, as she beheld a red velvet dress with white lace at the sleeves. Her hand shook as she reached forward to stroke the soft fabric.

"Do you like it?" Fidelia asked in a gentle voice.

"I … I've never had such a beautiful dress." She bit her lip and stared at it. "It's really mine?"

Fidelia smiled. "Of course. I don't know any other girl in town it would fit." She laughed as Mildred threw herself in her arms.

"Thank you, Mama," she whispered as she fought tears. "I love you."

"Oh, darling, I love you too."

Mildred looked back at her dress and stood. She pulled it from the box and held it up to her. "I want to wear it today!"

Bears nodded. "I hope you will. You'll be the most beautiful person at Uncle Cailean's party."

"Except for Mama," Mildred said loyally. She scampered over to the presents and pulled out one for her father. "This one's for you."

Bears fought a smile at the irregular wrapping job. He winked at his daughter and ripped it open with equal abandon as she had. "Neither of us has the restraint your mama has." He stilled when he saw a beautiful horse brush with a silver plate with his name on it. "Mildred?" he asked as he traced his name.

"Mama helped me," she said with a shy smile.

He held his arms open. "Thank you, my little love." He cradled her for a minute and kissed her head. "I'll use it every day and treasure it."

Mildred pulled out a box and shook it, smiling as it rattled. She looked to her father, who watched her with fond amusement. "This is from you, Father." He smiled and nodded, encouraging her to open the gift.

She took her time and stared at the brown box after she had removed the decorative paper. She bit her lip and lifted the lid and let out an "Oh" as she looked inside. "You remembered," she whispered.

"Of course, my little darling." He tugged her to him, so she sat on his lap, the box filled with drawing supplies in her hands. "I can't wait to see what you'll sketch now that you have more than a stick."

She threw her arms around his neck. "Thank you, Father." He held her tight a moment, before she wriggled away to hand out the rest of the presents.

After they finished opening their presents, which included a scarf for Bears, a book for Mildred, and warm socks for Fidelia, they ate a light breakfast. "We shouldn't eat too much, since Aunt Annabelle is preparing a feast."

"I hope she made cake," Mildred said.

Fidelia shook her head. "I think she's making pies for today."

Mildred gave a sigh of contentment. "Pies. I've never eaten pie."

Bears fought a frown at all his daughter had been denied. "Well, you're in for a treat. Nothing is better than your aunt's pies."

Bears led Fidelia and Mildred into Cailean's living room. A small tree stood in one corner, decorated with homemade ribbons. Red and green velvet garlands were strung over the window sashes, and pine boughs were on the tables. "Oh, this is even prettier than last year," Fidelia said as she hugged her sister.

Annabelle smiled. "Thank you." She held her sister close for a moment. "Skye helped me decorate this year." Her gaze was filled with love as she looked at her twenty-two-month-old daughter.

"You are fortunate to have such a wonderful helper," Bears said, smiling at Skye, who held her arms out to Fidelia to be lifted up.

Annabelle lifted a brow as she looked at her niece. "What a beautiful dress, Mildred."

Mildred jumped up and down once and then spun around. "Isn't it beautiful? Mama made it for me!"

Annabelle hugged her close. "How wonderful." She smiled at her sister, and her eyes filled as she saw how contented Fidelia was with her family. "You and Hortence will be the most beautiful girls here." When she saw Mildred brighten at Hortence's name and then race off to be with her cousin, she grinned at her sister.

Annabelle and Fidelia moved to the settee, where Leticia sat with her two-week-old daughter, Catriona. "How are you, Leticia?" Fidelia asked as she sat beside her and cooed at the baby in Leticia's arms.

Leticia smiled at the women she considered sisters. "I've never been happier. But I'm so tired," she whispered. "I never realized how much work it would be to have a newborn *and* little Angus." She attempted a smile and then leaned her head against Annabelle's shoulder.

"We'll do all we can to help," Annabelle soothed.

"I know. How do women do this without support?" She looked across the room to Hortence playing with Mildred. "I have no idea how I raised her alone for so many years."

Fidelia squeezed her arm. "You do what you must at the time. Thankfully, this time, you aren't alone."

~

When Fidelia settled in with Leticia, Annabelle, and the girls, Bears approached Jessamine and let out a deep breath. "I appreciate what you tried to do, Jessamine, but I fear you'll only make the situation worse for Mildred and me."

Jessamine smiled at him. "Call her Bright Fawn, Bears. The family is used to hearing you call her that." She smiled as he flushed. "I won't apologize for pointing out the hypocrisy in the townsfolk's actions. They were willing to believe a woman they've never met and the words of inveterate gossips who thrive on creating strife. They should have doubted everything they heard simply because they knew you and saw how your daughter has bloomed since she arrived in town."

Bears shrugged. "There will always be those who believe that I should have had to pay some sort of token reverence to a white woman for having cared for my daughter."

She scowled. "Then they're worse than fools. The orphanage had benefactors." She placed a comforting hand on his arm. "I never meant to make things worse for you, Bears. But I couldn't stand by and do nothing. Not when I have a printing press. Not when I have a voice."

He smiled. "I understand, Jessamine." He looked across the room to Fidelia and Mildred, sitting side by side on the settee. "And I refuse to allow the concerns of the past to ruin today."

"Good," she said as she turned into her husband's embrace. "What have you been up to, Ewan?"

"Why do ye always suspect me of mischief?" he asked with a twinkle in his eyes. "Happy Christmas, Bears."

"Merry Christmas, Ewan," Bears said and slipped away as the

couple continued to banter. He walked toward his wife and daughter but was waylaid by Warren. "Lawyer," Bears said as they shook hands.

Warren nodded and smiled, watching his wife interacting with the extended MacKinnon clan. "I hoped for a private word, but I have a feeling this is as private as it will be today." He took a sip of the punch and choked. "Don't let Mildred drink this. Ewan spiked it."

Bears looked at his friend Ewan, who continued to play innocent with his wife, and smiled. "I wonder when she'll discover what he did?" He lowered his voice. "What was the news you had to impart? Is it about Walter?"

Warren shook his head. "No. The matter in Helena." He saw Bears frown and nodded. "I know you sent a letter to Judge Hammond, and I did the same. Seems he took a keen interest in the situation at the orphanage. After her favorite judge, Judge Carlisle, had an unfortunate hunting incident, another judge was assigned to the orphanage." He waited, but Bears was patient and remained silent. "Judge Hammond began to work with Mrs. Marday and was appalled to find the graft worse than you had detailed. She is now on a train to California as we speak."

Bears gaped at Warren. "What?"

"The scandal hit Helena a few days ago and will be slow to dribble in to Bear Grass Springs, but Mrs. Marday was found to be placing her orphans in particular homes for personal profit. She favored those who transferred their adoptees to places similar to the Boudoir. Few who left that particular orphanage went to a good situation. Thankfully it was the smallest orphanage in Helena. The main orphanage is quite respectable."

"Why is she allowed to escape punishment?" Bears asked.

Warren shrugged. "She slipped out of town when she realized the sheriff was coming for her. Unfortunately few will take out a bounty for orphan girls, so I fear Mrs. Marday will go free and will reinvent herself somewhere in California."

Bears's horrified gaze found Mildred, and a portion of his horror abated at finding her laughing with Hortence. "She was saved due to her youth."

Warren nodded. "Yes, and, because of Mrs. Marday's horrible treatment, Mildred was so skinny, few could see her beauty waiting to shine through." Warren raised his doctored punch to Bears. "The children of that orphanage have you to thank for having a new, kinder headmistress."

"And you," Bears whispered. "You also spoke to the judge."

Warren shrugged, as though it were of no matter. "It helps to have more than one voice informing authorities what is occurring." He watched as Mildred sidled up to Fidelia. "You have been very blessed this year."

Bears's gaze glowed with love and contentment as he looked at his wife and daughter. "I am truly blessed. Last year I never could have imagined I'd have a daughter and a wife." He grunted as Sorcha threw herself into his arms. "Sorcha."

"Bears!" she said as she rammed him with her full belly. "Finally ye are no' hidin' in the corners, yearnin' after yer Fidelia. Finally ye are together."

Bears smiled. "The same could be said of you and Frederick."

She glowed as she cradled her belly. "I could. I canna believe I'll be a mother any day now."

He looked at her and sobered as he discerned her unstated fear. "You will be a wonderful mother. Devoted and loving."

Her eyes filled with tears. "I worry I'll be like, … like my mother," she whispered.

He shook his head. "I would look to those you love and who love you." He nodded to Cailean and Alistair, who played with their children. "Look to your brothers. They haven't been limited by their upbringing. Have faith. You won't be either."

She clung to him a moment, grunting with frustration that her belly got in the way of her embracing him. "Thank ye, Bears."

He nodded. "Never doubt the family you have will support you through whatever you need." He shrugged in a self-deprecating way. "I've learned my lesson."

"Good," she said. "For ye are family, Bears. Ye always have been."

CHAPTER 14

NEWS & NOTEWORTHY

If you are anything like this reporter, you have spent the holiday season dreaming of the delicious Norwegian treats Leena Johansen shared with us last year. Although at home due to the birth of her daughter, Mette, Leena's absence has been keenly felt by all the residents of Bear Grass Springs. Even though Annabelle's gingerbread is delicious, it does not rival Leena's pepperkake.

Pay attention, dear reader. Rather than spend your New Year's Eve at home, spinning yarns in front of your fire, I urge you to attend the Third Annual Bear Grass Springs' New Year's Eve Dance. Yes, you will have a chance to dance with your sweetheart and to gossip with your friends. Yes, you will again have the opportunity to support the town's Improvement Committee in its important work. But, more important, I'd suggest bringing pocket money, as I heard a rumor that Leena will sell pepperkake *for that one night only in support of the school fund. Her husband, Karl, will again make his delicious* glogg. *I believe it will be money well spent as we ring in the New Year.*

Bears ushered Fidelia and Mildred into the Odd Fellows Hall for the New Year's Eve Dance. He smiled at the sight of pine boughs strung over the windows and red-ribbon streamers hanging across the ceiling. "They decorated differently tonight," he murmured to Fidelia. She laughed and nodded.

"Leena!" she squealed as she saw her friend near the table where treats were to be sold in support of Bear Grass Springs' town Improvement Committee. "Oh, I had hoped the rumors were true." She pulled Leena close. "You look wonderful."

Leena laughed as she stepped away from Fidelia. "*Ja*, I feel wonderful. Mette is growing and not waking so much at night now. I have more energy." She glanced over her shoulder to her husband, Karl, who held young Mette in his arms. "I can't believe she is already five months old."

Fidelia tickled Mette's stomach and laughed as Mette giggled. Leena kissed her daughter's head. "She just began to giggle for us, and it's wonderful." She looked at her friends. "Will Leticia be here tonight?"

Annabelle shook her head. "I doubt it. She will have a quiet evening at home with her two young children, plus Millie is staying overnight with Hortence." She smiled. "I think Alistair wanted time for just them on this New Year's Eve."

Leena frowned. "I'll have to bring her *pepperkake*." She grinned at her friends and dropped her voice to a barely discernible whisper. "I have some set aside for all of you."

Fidelia fought a delighted squeal and squeezed Leena's hand. "Oh, how wonderful." She flushed as she looked at her sister with a guilty expression. "Anna has made gingerbread, but it's not quite the same."

Leena grinned. "I should hope not." She kissed Mette's head. "Come, Karl. I must say hello to the townsfolk."

They watched her leave, so she could mingle with the townsfolk, her husband beside her and Mette snuggled in her arms. Fidelia and Annabelle moved to one side of the Hall, where Sorcha sat on a chair. "How are you feeling, Sorcha?" Fidelia asked.

"Like I could burst any minute," Sorcha said as she ran a hand over her large belly. "I dinna understand how Leticia did no' look like a ripe pumpkin, unlike me." She sighed with frustration.

"Every woman's pregnancy is different," Annabelle soothed.

"Aye, that's what Helen tells me," Sorcha mumbled with a disgruntled frown. She smiled at Frederick, who kept an eye on her from the circle of men who conversed nearby. "He watches me, like a hawk."

"You should be thankful," Fidelia said, taking the vacant chair next to Sorcha. "Many women would be grateful for such a solicitous husband."

Sorcha rolled her eyes. "He doesna believe I can make it to the privy on my own."

Annabelle stifled a giggle. "Can you?"

"Nae, but that is no' the point," Sorcha said, even while she fought a smile. She elbowed Fidelia as she giggled next to her. "I tripped last week, an', since then, he willna let me walk outside alone."

"Oh, you married a fine man," Annabelle said.

Fidelia looked at their men, standing nearby. "We all did." She met their appreciative smiles, before beginning to gossip.

Bears looked at Fidelia, seated beside Sorcha, and fought a momentary annoyance that Stitch was not circulating and mingling with the townsfolk. However, when she burst into laughter at something Sorcha said, any annoyance fled at the evidence of her joy.

"We are fortunate men," Cailean said, standing beside Bears, sipping at a glass of whiskey smuggled in from the Stumble-Out Saloon. He focused on Warren. "When is the town committee meeting again?"

Warren shrugged. "It's hard to say. I had hoped we'd meet sometime during the past few weeks, but, with the arrival of little Catriona, Alistair has been distracted."

"Sleep-deprived," Ewan muttered with a smile. "What do ye want to meet for?"

Warren looked around, but they were a small isolated group, and no one listened in on their conversation. The townsfolk were used to them being a tight-knit group and had grown bored of their conversations about family and work. "There is growing concern about the teacher, Mr. Danforth."

Bears nodded. "I've heard little that would recommend him."

Warren sighed. "Not only does he have little-to-no control over his students but he is also insistent that he only has to follow the minimum requirements as a schoolteacher."

"I dinna ken what that means, Warren. Can ye explain in nonlawyer talk?" Ewan asked. He took a small sip of his whiskey as he focused on Warren. "Jessamine's written about it, and we've discussed it, but I dinna understand why ye canna force the man to teach more. Leticia did."

"According to the most recent Montana Territory laws concerning schools, they must be open only twelve weeks a year, with six weeks of continuous instruction." He saw the men glower. "Leticia had the school open for twice as long for the same pay, but that was her choice and a sign of her dedication. Our town's current teacher, estimable though he may be"—he met the men's dubious gazes as his voice dripped with sarcasm—"insists that he be paid the same amount as Leticia but for half the work. That he's not breaking any laws by teaching the minimum amount required by law."

"That's preposterous!" Cailean stammered. "The children deserve to learn more than that."

Warren nodded. "I'm inclined to believe that, but then many in this town believe I received too much education. Many are hopeful their children will learn the basics of reading and arithmetic and consider that sufficient for what life will bring."

Bears shook his head. "No matter what you do in life, a good education will help you."

Warren nodded. "Yes, and those of us on the town's Improvement Committee believe that, if we have a strong school, then more settlers will move to this area, and our town will thrive. To accomplish that goal, we need a teacher dedicated to the students and to teaching for longer than the minimum required by law."

Frederick tapped a finger against the side of his glass. "What are you suggesting, Warren?"

He smiled. "I wrote the contract, so Mr. Danforth is only guaranteed a posting through this school year. If Leena's gingerbread sells well tonight, along with the proceeds from the Harvest Dance, we will be in a solid position to hire a better teacher."

Bears glowered at the man in question. Mr. Danforth stood across the room, speaking with Mr. Atkins, the hotel proprietor. "Now that Leticia has had her babe, Mildred is out of school. I do not like her to miss out on an education."

Warren followed Bears's gaze and stared impassively at the teacher, who watched them like a frightened hare. "I understand. However, it must be clarified that the decision considered by the town's committee is not solely for one MacKinnon relation. It must be for the good of all schoolchildren."

"Have a town gathering to discuss your concerns," Bears said. "You're a lawyer. You can persuade the majority of the townsfolk to your way of thinking."

Warren flushed as Ewan and Cailean chuckled.

"A sound plan," Cailean said. When the musicians began to play a slow song, he looked at his wife. "As interesting as worrying about the school is, I want to dance with my wife." He slapped Bears on the shoulder and approached Annabelle. Skye was passed to Sorcha, and soon all the men had approached their wives for a dance, except Frederick, who sat beside Sorcha with an arm over her shoulder as he gently rocked them to and fro to the strains of the soft music.

Jane swiped her hands down the altered hand-me-down evergreen wool dress. Standing on the periphery of the MacKinnon clan gathering, she watched as they laughed and joked with each other, silently berating herself for the envy coursing through her. She watched as townsfolk stood in line to buy glasses of the spiced warm punch called *glogg* and the exotic-smelling *pepperkake* gingerbread. She gripped her hands in front of her to prevent them from running through her hair, tied back in a simple green ribbon. Her brother, Duncan, mingled with the townsfolk, and she smiled as he coaxed a young woman onto the dance floor. "Incorrigible," she whispered to herself.

She jolted with surprise as a man stood in front of her, blocking her view of her brother. She frowned as she recognized the tall, lanky man with black hair and dark brown eyes. "Mr. Metcalf?" she asked hesitantly.

He smiled, revealing a dimple in his left cheek. "Hello, Miss Keith. Happy New Year."

She gripped her hands together and looked down. "And to you, sir."

He cleared his throat, and she looked up, meeting his amused gaze. "I noticed you had yet to try Karl's *glogg* or Leena's *pepperkake*." He held out a mug and a piece of bread. "I thought you might like to try them."

"Oh, that is very ... kind of you, sir. But I couldn't." She kept her hands firmly clasped in front of her.

He frowned as he studied her, still holding his offering out to her. "You couldn't? Why ever not?"

"It wouldn't be proper," she whispered, casting a furtive glance around to see who was watching them. She flushed when Ewan MacKinnon winked at her.

"You are an associate of Annabelle's, and I work with Ewan. We are ... associated in a way. Please." He held them out again toward her.

She let out a breath and watched him with a mixture of trepidation and resentment. "Fine." She accepted both and stared at him, as though expecting him to leave her alone. However, he waited, and she let out another sigh. She took a sip of the *glogg*, and her eyes closed at the mixture of spices in the drink. "Oh, that's heavenly."

He chuckled, and she opened her eyes to meet his amused gaze. "It is. It's one of the reasons the dance is so well attended this year."

"One?" she asked.

He pointed to the bread she'd yet to try. "That's the other reason. Annabelle says you have a discerning sense of taste. Tell me what you think of that."

She frowned at his subtle order before nibbling at the bread. Her eyes widened. "Oh my," she whispered. "Annabelle's gingerbread was good, but this is delicious." She took another bite before looking at the table with longing. "I can see why there is such a long line for it."

Ben smiled. "Leena's a talented baker, and the townsfolk have missed her while she has been at home with her new baby." He glanced to the small group of MacKinnons. "I have a feeling she'll return soon."

"Why?" Jane asked, then took another sip of the *glogg*.

"She's being reminded tonight of the tremendous kinship she felt while working with Annabelle and Fidelia. She'll want that again, even though she has a daughter and her husband."

"Why would her husband want her out of the house?" Jane asked. "Her place is at home."

Ben let out a huff of air, as though trying to hide a laugh. "I fear the MacKinnon women and their associates don't believe much in 'places,' Miss Keith. They believe in what makes them happy, as long as it doesn't harm another."

Jane frowned and was about to say more, but her brother, Duncan, approached her at that moment. He grabbed the mug of *glogg* she'd been savoring and swallowed the remainder of it in two gulps before snagging the rest of her *pepperkake* and eating it in three bites.

"Wow, that's delicious. Can you buy me more, sis?" he asked. He looked curiously at Ben, who glared at him.

"I didn't buy it," Jane said as she flushed with embarrassment. "Mr. Metcalf wanted to ensure I tried it, and I was ..."

"Savoring it," Ben said in a low, disgruntled voice. "You should ask before you steal what isn't yours."

Duncan shrugged in an unrepentant manner. "Jane always shares what's hers with me. She's never minded." He looked at his sister and frowned when she seemed upset. "Right, sis?"

She sighed. "Right, Duncan. I'd already tried it. I'm glad you had the opportunity to taste it too."

Ben flushed with indignation but held his tongue. "You should buy your own treats," he said to the young man.

Duncan flushed and ran a hand through his auburn hair. "Ah, I would, except I'm not currently working." He shrugged and stood tall, as though to ease his embarrassment.

Ben looked between the siblings, from Duncan's mild embarrassment to Jane's defiant protectiveness. "I see. Is it that you don't like to work or that you haven't found work?"

The young man cleared his throat. "I work hard, sir."

"Duncan's adjusting to life in town," Jane said as she attempted to diffuse any tension between the men. "Annabelle has said that she will speak with the MacKinnons about finding Duncan a job when he is ready."

"*Ready*?" Ben asked. "So, for now, you live off your sister's hard labor?" He shook his head in disgust. "Do you know one end of a hammer or saw from the other?"

Duncan flushed a brighter red but met Ben's challenging stare. "I am a quick learner."

Ben's gaze flit to Jane. "I see. Well, I'm foreman for Ewan MacKinnon's construction business, and we're always looking for strong hardworking men. I'll speak with Ewan." Ben looked at Jane, and his gaze softened. "I wish you the happiest of New Years, Miss Keith." He nodded and stepped away.

When Ben departed, Jane let out a deep breath and fought the desire to fan her flaming cheeks. "How nice of him," she murmured to her brother.

"Seems like a pompous jerk," Duncan said. He jolted when she hit him on his arm.

"If he's to be your boss, you'd better be more respectful," she said. "We owe the MacKinnons quite a bit already, and we'll owe them more if you get a job."

Duncan sighed and turned so only Jane could see him speak. "What will they do when they realize you've deceived them?"

She fought tears. "I have no idea." She pasted on a smile as Annabelle approached, and soon she and Duncan were pulled into the larger MacKinnon circle.

∾

L ate that evening, Fidelia rested in Bears's arms in bed, as the stove in their bedroom pumped out heat. The hand-stitched quilt and wool blankets also helped keep them warm on this cold evening. Although impractical, Fidelia had insisted on leaving the curtains open, so the moonlight could brighten their room as they welcomed the New Year.

"Happy New Year, my love," she whispered. She kissed his chest and squeezed her arms around him.

"Stitch, you'll never know how happy you've made me," he whispered. "This has been the best New Year of my life."

She traced a finger over his shoulder and flushed as she blurted out, "Even better than the ones you spent with Sara?"

He gripped her fingers and raised them to his lips. "Yes. For you know me, all of me, and still love me." He looked deeply into her eyes. "You don't shy away from the parts of me I'm not proud of."

"You are worth loving, Bears," she whispered.

He kissed her head. "As are you. I couldn't be prouder than I am right now to call you my wife. I couldn't love you more than I do. Yet somehow tomorrow I will be even prouder and will love you more than I imagined. You and Bright Fawn both." He cupped Fidelia's cheek, watched her expression change, and asked in a low voice, "What is it?"

"Why don't you care about my time at the Boudoir?" she asked as she stared into his eyes and saw regret flash through his gaze.

"I care, Stitch. I care that those men hurt you. I care that they left scars on your soul. I care that you still suffer nightmares for what you lived through there." He ran a hand over her shoulder and down her arm. "But I see more than the woman who spent years at such a place."

"What do you see?" she whispered.

"I see a woman who used to be invisible." His intense gaze bore into hers. "But now you have the courage to step into the light, and you are blossoming. You are beautiful and witty and draw people to you because of your kindness. Not due to any costume or attempt at being a coquette." He shook his head as she frowned. "Your courage inspires me, as it does our daughter."

"I'm not brave, Bears," she protested, running a finger over his lips, frowning, as though she couldn't fully comprehend what he said.

He chuckled. "But you are. You interact with those who would degrade you because of what you were, and you never fail to treat them with respect. You are honorable and decent and good."

Her eyes filled as she shook her head. "I did what I must."

He kissed her. "I know, Stitch. I lived in the shadows too. Spurning friendships and the offer to be a part of that marvelous family." His fingers caressed her cheeks. "Even when I hid in the barn, you saw me, and you never thought I was lacking."

She shook her head. "How could I possibly think that?" She traced one of his eyebrows. "You're the most extraordinary man I've ever met."

"Most everyone else believes I am lacking. I'm neither Indian nor a white man. I don't fully belong anywhere. And I thought I'd be alone forever. When I saw you, when you looked at me and saw me, I had hope for the first time since Sara." He swallowed. "For the first time since my father died, I had hope that I wouldn't have to spend the rest of my life alone."

"Oh, Bears," she whispered as she kissed him. "Anyone who doesn't see you as you truly are is a fool."

He smiled and nodded. "And, as old man Tompkins likes to say, the town is filled with them."

A few days after New Year's when the bakery remained closed, Fidelia visited Sorcha. Before her move into town, she had given up trying to spin yarn as her large belly prevented her from reaching around the loom and made everything too awkward. Instead, she sat in a comfortable chair in Bears's former cabin and sewed quilt pieces together.

Fidelia warmed by the stove a moment and then sat beside Sorcha, pulling out her silk thread to tat lace.

"I dinna have the chance to speak with the new hire at the bakery at the Christmas celebration. She was as quiet as a church mouse, an' then she disappeared afore Cailean's blessing," Sorcha said. She put the needle between her lips as her fingers nimbly worked with the cloth and thread.

Fidelia sighed as she focused on an intricate pattern. "She's shy and has trouble believing that we welcome her into our group."

Sorcha shook her head. "I think she dinna like Ben."

Fidelia paused in her work and stared at Sorcha. "Ben? He's always been friendly and kind."

"Aye. We ken that, an' he's helped Ewan grow his business an' is a great partner for Ewan. But we dinna see him as a man we'd be interested in a romance with, do we? We already have our men." She shrugged. "Jane seemed afraid of him showin' her too much interest."

Fidelia shrugged. "Well, I think that's smart on her part. From what she told Annabelle and me, she was in an abusive relationship. I think she needs time to heal."

Sorcha shrugged. "Aye, but she should no' take too long. At times we should stew in our own memories an' fears, but no' for long, or then we lose the opportunities of the present. Besides, Ben is a good man. She could do worse."

"Not all women are looking to marry," Fidelia argued as she rolled her eyes. "Just because you and I are finally happy doesn't mean everyone we meet should be encouraged to marry."

Sorcha grinned at her friend. "I ken. But, if she could find a good man like my Frederick or yer Bears an' be happy, then why should I no' hope for that for her?"

Fidelia smiled as she thought about Bears. "I agree."

Setting aside her sewing, Sorcha settled her hands over her belly. "'Tis good to see ye so contented, Dee. Ye used to have that lost look in yer gaze that Jane has now." She frowned as Fidelia blushed and looked away. "'Tis no' a criticism. 'Tis an observation."

"I know." Fidelia cleared her throat. "Anna believes the reason I was willing to help Jane, to hire her when she has no real skill, was because she reminded me of the time I lived on the streets in Albany. Before I met the Madam." Fidelia met Sorcha's compassionate gaze. "When Jane first entered our bakery, I looked at Jane and saw what I must have looked like when I had nothing—a bedraggled, desperate woman, clinging to her pride as she prayed someone would help her."

Fidelia closed her eyes. "In my case, the Madam rescued me from my dire circumstances." She opened her eyes, and a flinty determination lit her gaze. "I refused to allow Jane to turn to that life. Not when Anna and I could help her."

Sorcha nodded. "Well, ye made a good choice, as she seems loyal to ye an' Anna. I hope ye never have a reason to second-guess yer kindness toward her."

Fidelia nodded. "Nor do I."

~

Fidelia knocked on Sorcha and Frederick's cabin a few days later in the first week of January, frowning when she didn't hear Sorcha calling out for her to enter. She knocked again and heard a chair move, but Sorcha still did not call out to her. "Sorcha?" Frowning, Fidelia pushed open the door. "Oh no," she breathed. Sorcha was on her hands and knees, panting through a contraction. Fidelia rushed to her friend and swiped away the sweat from her brows. After Sorcha's pain eased, Fidelia asked, "How long have you been like this?"

"I dinna ken. The pains knocked me off my feet, an' I couldna make it to Frederick." She took a deep breath as she relaxed between the contractions.

Fidelia squeezed her friend's shoulder and rose. "I'll be back in a minute." She raced out the door, ran past the paddock and burst into the livery.

Alistair looked up from one of the stalls. "Fidelia?"

"It's Sorcha. Get Helen." She saw Frederick poke his head out of the tack room at the mention of his wife's name. "Get home, Frederick. It's time." She spun on her heel and ran back to her friend. When she arrived, Sorcha screamed in pain, just before the contraction ebbed. Fidelia dropped next to her friend, then moved aside when Frederick hurtled through the door.

"My darling," he whispered as he ran a hand over her back and forehead, "why don't you rest on your back?"

Sorcha allowed him to help her to her side and then to her back, while Fidelia put water on to boil and pulled out the sheets and cloths for Helen. "Give her your love, and then you should go, Frederick," Fidelia murmured, blinking away tears as she watched him cradle Sorcha in his arms.

"Nae," Sorcha breathed, arching into another contraction. "I want ye to stay." She gripped his hand as she writhed with pain.

"I don't know what to do for you," he whispered as he held her, kissing her head and murmuring his love and encouragement as she struggled to breathe throughout the pain.

When she could relax against him once more, Sorcha spoke. "Just be here. Please dinna leave me." Her anxiety at him leaving her abated when he soothed her.

Helen arrived, setting aside her bag. She hung up her coat and quickly washed her hands. Helen crouched in front of Sorcha. "When did your pains start? How long ago?" Helen asked as she rested a hand on Sorcha's leg.

Sorcha shook her head. "I dinna ken. 'Twas so sudden. One moment I had a backache, an' the next I could barely breathe."

Helen frowned and then smiled. "It seems your child is as restless as you are, Sorcha."

"God help you," Fidelia muttered with a smile. Soon Fidelia focused on aiding Helen during her examination of Sorcha and then helped her through each contraction. Fidelia kept a basin of water warming on the stove, another near boiling, and a ready supply of cloths and rags. Sorcha was as comfortable as she could be, where she sat resting on the floor, and resisted being moved.

"One more big push," Helen murmured, while Sorcha writhed and screamed. Frederick clenched his jaw as he held onto her shoulders, whispering his love like a mantra.

"That's it. Here comes your baby," Helen said with a broad smile, as she eased one shoulder and then the next out. "Oh, a fine baby boy," she said after Sorcha's next contraction. She smiled at Fidelia, who handed her a clean blanket to wrap the baby in. "Aren't you a handsome boy?"

"A boy?" Sorcha gasped, tears pouring down her cheeks. Her hand shook as she reached out to touch him, and then she arched again. "Oh, God, 'tis startin' again."

Helen frowned and passed the baby to Fidelia, who cradled him to her chest.

"Helen?" Frederick asked, terrified, as his wife shuddered through another contraction. "What is happening?"

Helen placed her palms on Sorcha's belly and let out a deep sigh. She looked at the parents with amusement. "Seems you'll have a larger family than you expected. You're about to have your second child."

When Frederick let out a surprised laugh, Sorcha hit his arm. "'Tis no' funny," she gasped and then let out another howl. "Oh, make it stop. I canna do this again," she pleaded, tears continuing to pour down her cheeks.

Fidelia looked at her friend and said, "But you can, Sorcha. You're strong and capable, and soon you'll have two babies to spoil. Find that inner strength."

Sorcha shook her head and then took a deep breath. When the next contraction came, she bore down, groaning from the pain and pressure.

"One more, Sorcha. One more and we'll see if you have twin boys," Helen urged.

"Oh, God couldna be that cruel," she murmured and then smiled at her friends, before grunting with another contraction.

Helen sighed as the second baby slipped out. "Oh, how marvelous," she whispered, a tear tracking down her cheek. "You have a daughter. A son *and* a daughter."

Sorcha sobbed, collapsing into her husband's arms. "Frederick," she cried out, as he cradled her.

Helen swaddled the baby girl and handed her to Sorcha, while Fidelia handed the baby boy to Frederick. "We'll give you a moment."

Helen and Fidelia turned away to wash their hands and to tidy the room as much as possible. Fidelia looked at Helen and asked, "Is it all right if I leave to tell the family? They are all concerned."

Helen nodded. "We should be fine. Frederick is here. Although come back when you can. With two babies, there's always more than twice the work."

Fidelia laughed. "I'm sure I'll return with Annabelle and Leticia." She dried her hands and grabbed her coat. She walked the short distance, marveling that she had lived so close to Bears for so long, and yet they had been separated as though by a chasm. She gave silent thanks that she had overcome her reticence. She opened Cailean and Annabelle's kitchen door and paused to see Cailean pacing, Ewan with his head in his hands, and Alistair staring out a window. Annabelle rocked Skye.

Cailean spun to face her. "Well? How is she? We could hear her screams from here."

Fidelia beamed. "You have a niece." Her smile broadened as they exclaimed for joy. "*And* a nephew."

"What?" Ewan sputtered. "Sorcha had twin bairns?" His smile faded. "How is she?"

Fidelia gave them a reassuring nod. "She's well, although exhausted. Frederick remained with her the entire time and was a tremendous support to her. After she and the babes are cleaned up, we'll have you meet your niece and nephew."

Annabelle handed Skye to Cailean. "I'll help," she said. "Leticia went home with the girls and Angus. They were frightened when they heard Sorcha's screams."

The women left to return to Bears's old cabin, amid promises to return for the men as soon as possible. When they arrived at the cabin, Sorcha was *coo*ing to her children. One was at a breast, while the other was in Frederick's arms.

"Congratulations, Sorcha," Annabelle said with a broad smile as she watched her sister-in-law with her children. "I wish you health and happiness."

Sorcha smiled. "Aye, an' a little sleep, but I ken that is no' goin' to occur." She smiled at the young babe, who fell asleep on her breast. and switched babies with Frederick. When she had finished breast-feeding, she groaned as she stood.

"Let us help bathe you," Helen said. She looked at Frederick. "Go see the men. Have them pound on your back and congratulate you. Give us a little time to tend to Sorcha, and then you can return."

He saw Sorcha's agreement with the plan and kissed her forehead. "I love you, darling. Thank you for being so strong." He kissed her again and slipped from the room.

Sorcha smiled at her womenfolk. "Thank ye, for always supportin' me. For insistin' I be in town for the birthin'. I dinna ken what I would have done with twins on the ranch."

Annabelle wrapped an arm around her shoulders. "You would have done well. But now you have all of us to support you, so you can focus solely on your babies."

"As you should," Fidelia said with a watery smile. She hugged her friend too. "Congratulations, Sorcha."

Later that evening, both twins slept, and Sorcha lay in Frederick's arms in their bed. She kissed his chest and sighed with contentment to be held close. "Thank ye for no' leavin' me today when they said ye should go."

He smiled against her head. "If you want me here, I will never leave you. Propriety be damned." He chuckled. "I don't think Helen truly minded. I understand she's been in plenty of situations where her only attendant has been the husband."

"Thank God ye had sense to convince me to come to town. I dinna ken what I would do without family around us," she whispered. "Tomorrow we'll see the grandparents, aye?"

He nodded. "Aye. They'll be astonished to see we have a boy and a girl." He traced a finger over her forehead. "What would you like to name them?"

She shrugged. "I like Scottish names, but I ken ye must have names ye like."

He smiled and shook his head. "No, I've never much thought about what I would name a child. I only prayed that our child would live." He smiled. "I thought we'd name her Mairi."

Her eyes filled. "Truly?"

He nodded. "Yes. Your mother, your real mother, should be remembered. It seems a wonderful way to honor her."

Sorcha kissed him. "Thank ye, Frederick. Just when I think I canna love ye more, I realize my love for ye is an infinite pool inside me." She sniffled and turned her head into his palm as he swiped away her tears.

"As is my love for you, Sorcha."

She met his gaze. "Then let us name our son after yer grandfather, Harold."

He nodded. "Yes. Harold and Mairi. Our beautiful children."

"They'll ken what it is to be cherished. To be loved and wanted," Sorcha said as she kissed him. She smiled as she felt his rumble of agreement under her ear. "I feel I could sleep for days."

"I fear you have an hour at most," he whispered. "Sleep, my love. I'm here with you." He held her as she tumbled into a restful slumber.

CHAPTER 15

In late January, during a break in the freezing winter temperatures, Hortence and Mildred ventured outside to build a snowman. Alistair, Bears, and the uncles were busy at work, while the aunts were busy at the bakery, the newspaper, or tending babies. Hortence tugged on Mildred's arm as they clattered down the steps at Mildred's house. "Come on. Let's do something fun. If I'm at home, I'll have to tend Angus." She ran ahead of Mildred as they approached an open field behind Mildred's house.

"Isn't this the perfect place to build a snowman?" Hortence asked, twirling around in glee.

Mildred giggled and shook her head. "No, over here. That way I can see it from my bedroom."

Soon the girls were on the ground, pushing around pieces of snow that were slowly built into the size of small boulders. Hortence's was so big that she could barely push it. "I think this should be the bottom."

Mildred looked at it and laughed. "It's lopsided."

Hortence shrugged. "He has a potbelly, like Mr. Stubbens." The girls giggled at the thought, and soon the snowman was done.

After resting a moment and admiring their fine creation, Mildred jumped up. "Come. Let's make snow angels." She moved a short distance away from the snowman, closer to the tree line, and fell backward, landing with a *thud* and a giggle. She moved her arms and legs around and then crawled out. "A beautiful angel."

Hortence followed suit, and soon she was covered in a fine layer of snow too. "Do you think the aunts will have cocoa and cookies for us?" she asked as she shivered.

"No, let's go to the café," Mildred said. "Irene said we could always visit, and she won't make us work on such a beautiful day."

They gave a *whoop* at their brilliance in evading their responsibilities and moved to race away from their snow angels and the snowman. Mildred slid to a stop, with Hortence skidding into her back, when a man stepped out from behind their snowman. "What are you doing here?" Mildred asked with feigned bravura she had learned from her aunt Sorcha.

"I wanted to see what the town brats were doing on such a day." Walter Jameson stepped toward them, and they backed up a pace. His long greasy hair fell over his brows, and he swiped it away to better peer at them from alcohol-dulled eyes. "Seems wrong to me that illegitimacy is accepted, when one, such as I am, is shunned."

He made a stealthy grab and latched onto Mildred's arm. She howled in protest and kicked and struggled as he hauled her toward him. "You little witch, cooperate," he slurred.

"Never!" Mildred screamed as she was lifted in the air.

"Let her go!" Hortence bellowed as she beat at him with her tiny fists. He swiped at her, hitting her hard against her cheek. She careened to the ground, and her head hit a newly exposed rock with a *crack*.

"You hurt Hortence!" Mildred's foot connected with his thigh and then with his midsection, provoking an *oof* from him as he spun in pain and toppled them both into the newly constructed snowman. She continued to kick him, and his hands released their hold on her.

The minute she was free, she ran to Hortence and pulled at her friend to get her to stand. "Come on, Hortence." When Hortence lost her balance, they stumbled and then trotted as fast as they could away from their field. Mildred cast furtive glances over her shoulder, but no one followed them.

Mildred whimpered when the livery came into sight, and she urged Hortence to keep moving. "Almost there," she said. When she got to the door, her hands shook, and she was so tired that she had trouble working the latch on the door. Hortence leaned on her friend with more of her weight, so Mildred kicked on the livery door and waited for someone to answer. After a moment, she kicked again.

"Do you think the livery is full service and includes having the door opened for you?" Cailean grumbled. His smile and good cheer faded as she saw the girls. "Alistair! Bears!" He eased Hortence from Mildred's hold and pulled her into his arms to carry her inside. "Mildred, you did well, little one."

He walked down the main aisle of the livery, pausing as Alistair threw down his pitchfork at the sight of an injured Hortence in his brother's arms.

"Hortence!" Alistair bellowed. "What's happened to ye, my little love?" He knelt with Cailean and ran his hands over her, his eyes wild with fear.

Bears had knelt and pulled his quivering daughter into his arms. "What happened, Bright Fawn?" he murmured as he brushed hair away from her forehead and eyes. He ran a hand down her arm and frowned when he saw her grimace at his light touch. "Who did this to you?"

"The bad man. The man who hurts Mama," she sobbed. as she pushed herself into her father's arms.

He pulled her close, his gaze meeting first Alistair's and then Cailean's. "Walter," he said in a lethal tone. "He is a dead man."

Mildred pushed away, swiping at her tears to look beseechingly at her uncles. "We didn't mean any mischief. We played near the house, like you asked." She swiped at her runny nose with her arm. "The snow was perfect today. We made a snowman, so I could see it from my bedroom. And then snow angels. We were going to visit Grandma Irene for cocoa and cookies." Her tears began again, and she shuddered.

"You're safe, little one. You are here with us now," Bears said, running his hands over her head and shoulders.

"The bad man grabbed me. Hortence hit him to make him let me go, and he hit her hard. She fell and hit a rock." She looked at her friend and clung to her father. "Is she going to die?"

Alistair shook his head. "No, she's no'. Are ye, wee Hortence?"

"No," Hortence said. "I hurt my head, Mildred. But we'll have more adventures soon." She kept her eyes closed and grimaced. "Can we go home, Papa?"

Alistair kissed her head softly. "Of course. Your mother will fuss over you, as will your aunt Helen." He rose, picking her up in his strong arms, and looked at Bears and Cailean. In a whisper-soft voice, he said, "I'll see ye at Warren's within the hour."

The men nodded and watched Alistair depart with Hortence cradled in his arms.

"She's almost too big for him to carry," Cailean said.

Mildred clung to her father. "I want to stay with you today, Father. Please?"

He nodded. "There's nowhere else I'd want you to be, little one."

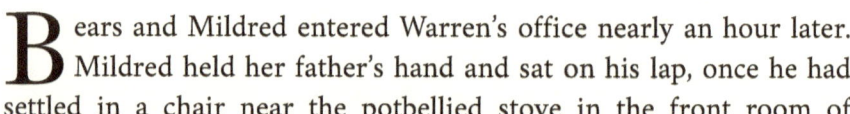

B ears and Mildred entered Warren's office nearly an hour later. Mildred held her father's hand and sat on his lap, once he had settled in a chair near the potbellied stove in the front room of Warren's office.

Warren emerged from the back room with a pot of coffee and a handful of cups. "I imagine this will be a gathering of the clan," he muttered. He smiled at Mildred and shared a long look with Bears. "You've warned Fidelia?"

Bears shook his head in frustration. "Annabelle said Stitch was off on deliveries. She wasn't at the café, but Irene said she had just left for the hotel, and she'll return to the bakery after the delivery. Annabelle will tell her what happened."

Warren nodded. "Good." He looked at Mildred, who continued to cling to her father, and then back at Bears. "I understand you didn't want to wander the town today with Mildred."

Bears nodded, hugging his daughter close.

Ewan entered, letting in a burst of cold air. "If I ken anythin' about Montana weather, it'll start snowin' soon," he said as he took off his warm coat. He moved to the stove to warm his hands and then crouched to look at Mildred. "How are ye, little darlin'?"

"I'm all right. Hortence is the one who was hurt," she said as she fought tears.

"Dinna cry," he said. "I just visited wee Hortence, an' she's doin' well. Helen saw her an' believes she'll have braggin' rights for a few days for the goose egg on her head but otherwise will be fine."

"He left bruises on Mildred's arms," Bears said in a near growl.

Ewan nodded and ran a hand over Mildred's silky black hair. "I'm sorry he scared ye. I dinna ken what we can do to ensure he doesna scare ye again but ken yer father and uncles will do all they can, aye?" He smiled as she snuggled deeper into her father's embrace.

Soon Alistair and Cailean had joined them, although Cailean said he would only be here a short time, since he didn't like leaving the livery unattended. Warren looked at the door as Frederick stumbled inside. "Are you all right?" Warren asked.

Frederick shivered as he took off his coat and yawned hugely. "Why are two babies four times the work?" he asked, then collapsed into a chair. His black hair was disheveled, and he had black circles under his eyes.

"'Tis the mystery of life," Ewan said, giggling when Frederick belted him on an arm.

Warren sighed and rolled his eyes at their antics. "You know why we are here." When he saw Frederick's confusion, he said, "Mildred and Hortence were approached and hurt by Walter today. Mildred has bruises on her arms as he attempted to grab her and take her away, while Hortence has a goose egg on her head from where she hit her head on a rock when he tossed her down."

"She fell after he hit her. She was trying to get him to let me go," Mildred said in a small voice.

"Bastard." Ewan flushed and apologized to Mildred. "What can we do to prevent him from approaching our children and wives?"

Warren pinched the bridge of his nose. "There is no law, no precedent that says a man has no right to speak with whom he chooses. As for the physical injuries today, Walter can be brought up on charges of abuse, but I fear no one but the children saw it, and it would be hard to prove it was Walter."

Alistair's eyes gleamed with righteous anger. "Are ye tellin' me there is no' one thing I can do to help keep my daughter safe? My wife safe? What about my two youngest bairns?"

Warren sighed. "Increased vigilance ..."

He was interrupted by Cailean. "So that man can wander our town, free to do what he pleases to whomever he pleases, and we must keep our children and wives locked up or under our constant care to ensure they're safe? Doesn't seem right to me, Warren."

Warren shrugged. "I'm not saying it's right or just, but that is the reality."

Bears stared at the lawyer. as he let a squirming Mildred out of his arms. He watched as she roamed the room, and then Bears focused on Warren. "Do you ever worry about Helen as she wanders the town and surrounding areas? Do you worry that he'll attack her too?"

Warren nodded. "Of course. And every day that I come home to find her well, I am thankful. But I can't prevent her from doing the work that brings her joy. Not due to fear. That would slowly ruin what we have."

Bears watched him closely, absently noting that Mildred slipped into Warren's back room. "How do you protect what you have but not smother it?"

Ewan made an *aah* sound as though he understood. "Ye ken, with a man like Walter, it is no' possible to be rational?"

Bears nodded. "I know what you want, Ewan. You want Walter dead. As I think we all do." He looked at the men in the room and saw the grim agreement on all their faces. "But I refuse to prove right those in this town who believe I am little more than a savage."

Ewan made a noise of disagreement. "It proves ye are a man, like any of them. That ye protect those ye love."

Bears shook his head. "No, Ewan, they would believe that of you because you are a white man. They wouldn't believe that of me. I would never be given the benefit of that doubt. Not by all. And not by enough of the townsfolk. I would hang, if I dared harm Walter."

Warren nodded. "Unfortunately I agree with Bears. We outsmarted Bertrand without resorting to violence. We should do the same to his cousin."

Alistair grunted in disgust. "Ye're a lawyer, Warren. Ye love to talk an' find ways to trap people with their words. That's no' goin' to keep my daughter safe. Or Mildred and Fidelia safe. Walter respects no one, an' he'll no' respect yer laws, Warren."

Warren rubbed at his head. "I want us to agree that no one will harm Walter. No matter what." He looked at the defiant men sitting in front of him. "I have no desire to be a defense attorney, convincing a judge as to why any of you shouldn't hang."

Bears shook his head. "I can't make such a promise, lawyer. If my daughter or wife are in danger, I will aid them." Bears remained deep in thought as the conversation continued around them, declining the offer to visit the sheriff with the MacKinnon brothers. "No, the sheriff will heed your words more if I'm not there." He watched through the window as the brothers walked down the boardwalk in the direction of the jail.

"I fear the sheriff won't be swayed by what they say," Warren said with a sigh.

Bears nodded. "They know that. But I understand their need to do something. If I weren't..." He cut off his words and shared a frustrated smile with Warren. "I'll find a way to protect those I care about."

That afternoon, Fidelia finished her deliveries early and walked to the livery in search of Bears. "I must tell him," she muttered to herself. She had had a long visit with Irene and then had haggled over the payment of an outstanding bill with the hotel owner, Mr. Atkins. As she approached the livery, she tugged her cloak around her, shivering as the winter weather had hit hard again this year, and the short break in the weather had been replaced by cold winds and the threat of more snow. "I hope it's not as bad a winter as last year," she muttered. After pushing open the livery door and shutting it behind her, she sighed with pleasure at the relative warmth that pervaded the space. She walked down the main aisle, not seeing her husband in any of the stalls.

"Bears?" she called out as she approached the tack room. When she found that empty, she poked her head into the office and frowned as that was empty too. "Why would the livery be unattended during the day?" she asked aloud, staring at one of the horses.

When she walked past the darkened area that led to the closed door and the paddock outside, a hand reached out from the shadows and grabbed her. "It's because they're looking for me."

She froze at the sound of Walter Jameson's voice. "Let me go at once," she said in as strong a tone as she could muster.

"Do you think you're a match for me?" he asked. "Do you think I have to do anything you say?"

She tugged at her arm. "Let me go!"

"No, you're coming with me. Where you've always belonged." His eyes shone with a desperate purpose. "To where you've been sorely missed."

"No!" she screamed. "I'm not returning to the Boudoir." His evil laughter evoked memories of the abuse she'd suffered at his hands when he was at the Boudoir, giving her added strength. "Never." She kicked at his shins, earning a grunt of discomfort and momentarily taking him off guard. She wrenched her arm free and raced away. She shrieked as he grabbed her cloak. It tightened around her neck, cutting off her air. With shaking hands, she pulled at the button until she ripped it free, releasing herself from his hold once again.

She glanced to the livery door, thinking it had opened, but it remained closed. She knew she'd never make it to the exit and raced to a stall, jerking open the door, backing into it before shutting the

UNBRIDLED MONTANA PASSION

stall door. She heard a wild stomp behind her and turned at the ominous sound. Her eyes widened as she realized she'd entered Brutus's stall. She spun to leave, but Walter approached her, his belt in hand. She whimpered as she plastered herself to one side of the stall, praying for a quick death.

⁓

"Father!" Mildred screamed as she pushed open the front door to Warren's office. The three remaining men now stood near the stove, discussing the problem of Walter Jameson and theorizing how to finally rid him from the town. Frederick looked at Mildred but continued to speak. Bears shook his head and pushed past Frederick to his gasping daughter.

"What is it, Bright Fawn?" Bears asked, crouched in front of her. He took a gentle hold of his daughter's shoulders. "How did you come to be outside? I thought you were in the back room."

"He's with her. In the livery. And he's going to hurt her."

"Stay here!" Bears released his hold on her, and she gasped and fell to the floor, as her father raced from the room.

"Bears!" Warren yelled and followed him down the boardwalk with Frederick on his heels.

Bears ran as fast as he could, but he knew that every second Fidelia was with Walter was a second too long. He reached the livery and tore open the door. He paused when he heard a maniacal laugh and a whimper coming from a stall. He searched for a weapon but found none as he ran toward the stall.

He flung open the stall door to see Walter looming over his wife, with his belt raised and his boot lifted, as though he were about to kick her. In that moment, Bears heard the horse whinny and rear, and he looked up, realizing they were in Brutus's stall. "Walter, the horse!"

Walter spun to glare at him. "Do you think I'm stupid enough to fall for that trick? You train even the wildest of animals."

Brutus landed on all fours without harming anyone, but he was far from calm.

RAMONA FLIGHTNER

"Look what you've done to Charity, making her think she's a fine woman of this town. But I know better. I know what she really is." He spun toward Fidelia, intent on kicking her, and Bears launched himself at Walter.

"You will not hurt her again!" Bears roared. "Stitch, get out of the stall!" He punched Walter, and they rolled over the ground a few times until Bears was pinned down by Walter.

At that moment, Brutus reared again, dropped down, and slammed his two front hooves onto Walter's back, earning a howl of agony.

Bears gasped, losing his breath at the force of the horse's blow.

Frederick arrived, jumping into the neighboring stall, waving his arms about and distracting Brutus. Warren dragged Walter from the stall, and Bears crawled out, remaining on his hands and knees, gasping for breath.

He looked at Walter, who remained unconscious. "What happened to him?" Bears asked, clutching his chest as he took a shallow breath. "The last thing I remember is Brutus rearing up."

"It seems Brutus trampled him," Warren said with a shake of his head. "I don't know the extent of his injuries. I'll go for Helen. For now, don't move him." Warren raced away.

Bears groaned as he rose, his arms cradling his chest, and approached his shaking wife. "Stitch, are you all right?" He turned at Mildred's call as she entered the livery.

"Father!" she screamed as she barreled toward him. She looked at Fidelia. "Mama," she whispered. "I tried. I promise, I tried."

Fidelia reached out an arm, and Mildred flung herself into her arm. "Thank you, daughter. Thank you for getting your father."

Bears looked at his wife, holding his daughter, and he fought a deep emotion. He moved to pull them both into his embrace, sheltering them as he had been unable to do before. "My love, are you all right?"

"I think so. He scared me, and I ran from him. He only hit me a few times." Her lips trembled. "I'll have to speak with Helen."

He nodded. "I'll be with you the whole time."

"No!" She shook her head emphatically. "I ... I want to be alone."

236

He jerked as though Brutus had just hit him with a hoof. "I … If that is what you want." He released her and rose as Helen entered the livery.

He watched as Helen paled at the sight of her brother, laying prostrate on the floor, each breath shallower than the last. She knelt beside Walter, lifting his shirt to inspect his chest, then tilting him to lift his shirt to see his back. A tear slipped down her cheek. Her hands traced over large bruises on his chest and back, swallowing a small sob as her soft touch elicited a shudder of pain. "It appears Brutus crushed his ribs," she whispered. "I think they could have punctured his lungs or damaged his heart." She swiped at her cheeks. "There's nothing I can do. Even if the doc were here, there's nothing that could be done. Not fast enough." She traced a hand over her brother's ashen cheek. "I can't save him."

"You always were useless," her brother rasped, and Helen recoiled at the hatred in his gaze as he gasped for air.

"No, you are the worthless one," Warren growled, glaring down at Walter. "You're a bully and a brute who only excelled at terrorizing those you thought were weaker than you." He knelt beside Helen and pulled her into his arms.

"Let me see him!" a woman shrieked in a loud voice from the livery doorway. Mrs. Jameson tripped and ran down the aisle, until she fell on her knees beside her son. "Oh, my boy. How they have abused you! I always knew they'd do something to kill you."

She glared at Warren. "Now you have no excuse. You must bring charges against these MacKinnons and all their associates for how they treated my poor boy."

Warren shook his head. "That's the sheriff's job, ma'am. And, if there's any need for a defense, I will work on behalf of the MacKinnons and Bears. Never you."

"You are my family!" she shrieked. "How dare you disrespect me in such a manner?"

Warren shook his head. "Your daughter is my family. As are the MacKinnons. You, ma'am, are nothing to me." He watched impassively as she threw herself over her son, inadvertently knocking air from his lungs.

"Mama," Helen murmured, "you're hurting him."

"Don't you dare tell me what to do! You lost any right to have an opinion when you abandoned us to marry this charlatan." Mrs. Jameson's cheeks were streaked with tears, but she no longer lay over her son. She gripped his shoulders as though willing him to stay alive. However, each breath Walter took was more labored than the previous one.

"Say goodbye to Walter, Mama," Helen whispered as a tear streaked down her cheek.

"Do something!" her mother screamed at her. "I thought you were supposed to be a healer! Heal!"

Helen shook her head. "I can't help him. The horse trampled Walter. He can't breathe because I think his ribs have punctured his lungs." She looked at her mother. "There's nothing I can do."

Mrs. Jameson began to sob in earnest, while she watched as her son breathed his last breath. She knelt by him for long minutes until Irene, who no one had seen enter the livery, approached and eased Mrs. Jameson away. "Come. We'll make you a cup of tea. Come sit by our stove."

The sheriff approached—along with the MacKinnon men—and asked numerous questions. He approached Brutus's stall and jumped back at the warning stomp Brutus gave him. "I can see how today's event could happen," he muttered. "What I don't understand is why you ran in there," he said to Fidelia.

"I was terrified of Walter."

"Just as we've been telling you, Sheriff," Cailean added.

Alistair and Ewan nodded.

Fidelia continued. "I didn't know what stall I was going into. I only thought I'd be safer if I could lock myself in a stall rather than face him." She shook subtly. "I chose the wrong stall."

"Or the right one," Warren muttered and then met the sheriff's stare impassively.

"I believe we've answered all your questions, and my wife has suffered a trauma," Bears said. "I'd like Helen to examine her at our home." He paused as he noted Helen fighting her own grief. "If that is all right, Helen?"

"Of course," she said with a brave smile. "I'll join you there in a few minutes."

Bears walked beside Mildred and Fidelia to their house and watched as Fidelia motioned for him to remain in the living area while she went into their bedroom. Mildred wrapped her arms around his waist, and he sighed as her hug soothed him.

"She will want to see you soon. Be patient, Father," his daughter whispered. She released him and moved to the stove to prepare tea.

When Helen arrived, Bears paced the living room while Mildred lay on the sofa with a pillow against her chest. "Bright Fawn, why did you sneak out of Warren's office after the scare you had earlier today?"

She shrugged, clutching the pillow even tighter to her chest. "I was bored, listening to you and the uncles talk. And then I saw Mama walking toward the livery from the window. I wanted to see her."

He smiled at his daughter. "I'm so glad you did. I never would have known she was in danger." His throat thickened, and Mildred jumped up and threw herself into his arms. He held her tight for long moments before sitting on the settee with her nestled next to him.

Annabelle burst through the door, her gaze wild as she saw Bears sitting comfortably beside his daughter. "Dee?" she gasped, out of breath from her mad dash from the bakery.

Bears smiled weakly. "She's with Helen. She suffered no debilitating injury that we know of." He sighed as Annabelle raced to the back bedroom to join Helen and her sister.

Nearly an hour after Helen's arrival and ten minutes after Annabelle's, the two women emerged from the bedroom. "Well?" he asked.

"I believe she will be fine." Helen watched him with an unfathomable stare. "She'd like to see you." Helen looked at Mildred. "And, if you have tea, I'd love a cup."

Annabelle smiled at Bears and Mildred. "She did not suffer

because of your quick thinking," Annabelle said, pulling Mildred close. "Thank you." She kissed Mildred on the top of her head and said she would return the following day to see her sister.

~

Bears gave Helen a grateful smile as she remained with Mildred, and he then moved into the bedroom he shared with his wife. He saw her leaning against a mound of pillows. "How are you, Fidelia?"

She watched him with wide eyes, noted his formal use of her first name. "I think I'll be fine." She frowned as he remained by the door. "Will you come here?"

He moved nearer and sat on the bottom of the bed, facing her.

She blinked away tears as he remained far away from her. "Please, come here?" she asked, holding her arms open for him. A tear fell when he shook his head.

"No, not yet. Not until I understand why my wife didn't want me in here for the last hour. Why, Dee?"

She paled further at his use of her family's nickname rather than his own for her. "I … I needed to talk with Helen about something. And it's private."

He acted as though she'd struck him.

She reached forward. "Please, let me explain." At his terse nod, she whispered, "I went to the livery today to find you. I … I had something to tell you, and I found I couldn't wait until tonight. I had no more patience." She paused. "The livery was empty, and it's never empty. And then, there was Walter. As though he were waiting for me. But he couldn't have known I would look for you. I tried to fight him, but he was strong. When I leaped into that stall, I thought I could hide behind the horse or jump on its back and ride it out."

She closed her eyes. "It sounds stupid now, but I was desperate, and I didn't know what to do." She opened her eyes and met her husband's implacable gaze. "And then I realized I was in Brutus's stall.

He began to whinny and stomp on the ground. Walter approached, and all I could hope for was a quick death."

"No," he stated, shaking his head. "Never that. I will not lose you."

She focused on those few words and took a steadying breath. "I don't remember much. I know Walter kicked me a few times, and he hit me with the belt on my back. And then you arrived. Somehow I had the ability to stand and run out of the stall, as you ordered me to do." Her eyes filled. "And I've never been more afraid as when Brutus crushed Walter. I thought Brutus had crushed you too."

Bears nodded for her to continue. When she remained silent, he asked, "Why deny my presence here today, Dee?"

"I'm pregnant," she said in a rush. "I worried Walter had hurt the baby. I didn't want you to hope when I was only going to lose the baby."

He watched her in stunned silence, his gaze now filled with hope and love. Finally he asked, "What did Helen say?"

"She thinks I'm—we're—fine. She suggests I rest a few days. Spend time with those I love. But that I should have a baby in my arms come summer or early fall."

"In *our* arms," Bears whispered as a tear tracked down his cheek. He kicked off his boots and crawled up the bed to hold her in his arms. "Oh, my love." He held her tight and shook as he fought a sob. "I thought I'd lost you. And then to be denied ..."

"I'm sorry," she whispered against his neck. "But I didn't want you to hope and then take it away from you." She pulled him even tighter, clinging to him. "I ... I'm so afraid to hope, Bears."

"Don't be, my love." He released her and kissed his way down her neck. He winced as he lifted the flannel nightgown she'd donned and glared at the welt on her shoulder. He kissed it softly. "I hate that you suffered again at his hands. I hate that you knew one more moment of fear due to him."

"Oh, Bears," she whispered, tears coursing down her cheeks. "My love. You suffered too when you raced into that stall to save me." She kissed his chest. "My lilac ointment is on a shelf in the kitchen, and we should put it and some ice on your bruises." She smiled at him as she cupped his face. "They will help you heal, like the last time Brutus injured you."

Bears nodded and smiled. He caressed her cheek, smearing her tears. "This is what marriage is. Sharing. Loving. Caring for each other." He paused as he stared into her eyes a long moment. "Never be afraid to show me your hopes and fears, my love." He kissed down her chest to her belly. He let out a small shudder as though overcome by a deep emotion. He kissed her skin, already stretched once by a pregnancy. "I can't wait to see you, round with our baby."

Silent tears coursed down her cheeks. "I love you," she whispered. "So much."

He kissed her belly one more time and then moved up, tugging down her nightgown and then enfolding her in his arms. "Rest, love."

"Will you wait to tell Mildred? I want to tell her with you," she murmured.

"Of course," he said with a smile. "It's our news."

～

That evening Bears led a reluctant Mildred into their bedroom. She stood by the bedroom door and shook. "Little one, what is it?" Bears asked as he crouched in front of her.

"I know why you want me to see her. She's dying." Mildred was already crying, the tears pouring down her cheeks. "Helen was here and then the doctor." The doctor had visited for a few moments on his return to town.

"Oh no!" Fidelia said from the bed. "Bears, bring her here."

"No!" Mildred screamed and fought her father as he attempted to pick her up and bring her to Fidelia.

He shared a quick glance with his wife and met his daughter's terrified gaze. "Why are you afraid to see your mama?" He ran a hand over her sodden cheek. "She's missed you and wanted to see you before you went to bed."

"The healer's been here. Two of them. They are always friendly when they are hiding awful news," Mildred said with a distant expression. "I know they come when someone's dying."

He cupped her cheeks and waited for her to look at him. "You know I have never lied to you, Bright Fawn." He waited for her to nod. "Helen was here because your mother was frightened and hurt after she saw the bad man. You know that. You helped save your mama." He waited as he watched Mildred's panic ebb in her gaze. "The doctor confirmed what Aunt Helen told us. Mama is not going to die. Not today." He waited for his daughter to hear his words.

"She's not?"

He shook his head.

"Oh, Mama!" Mildred cried out as she jumped onto the bed and into Fidelia's arms. "I was so scared," she sobbed against Fidelia's chest. "I thought it would be like when my mother died. That I would have to come in here and kiss your cold cheek."

"Oh, my little love, no," Fidelia murmured, sharing a tormented gaze with her husband. "No. I wanted to see you and to give you a hug and to thank you for being so brave." She smiled as Mildred stared at her in confusion. "To thank you for running to get your father for me."

"The bad man was going to hurt you, Mama," Mildred whispered.

"I know. And he barely touched me because you ran to find your father. Thank you." Fidelia kissed her head and rocked her in her arms. Bears joined them on the bed, and they lay together for a few minutes.

When Mildred had calmed, Fidelia swiped at her daughter's cheeks. "There is something else we need to tell you, little one." She waited as Mildred watched her cautiously. "You're going to be a big sister."

Mildred looked at her and then her father. "You're going to have a baby?"

"Yes." Fidelia held on to her and said, "But I want you to know that I will never love any child more than I love you."

Mildred smiled and threw her arms around her mother and then turned to hug her father. "I'm going to be a sister. Like Hortence!" She gave a small *whoop* of delight and then snuggled into the bed with them. "Will I be a good big sister?"

Bears chuckled. "I have no doubt, my darling daughter. You will be the best big sister in the world." He kissed his daughter's head and held his family in his arms.

~

The following day, Annabelle poked her head into her sister's bedroom and smiled at her. "How are you feeling?" she asked.

"Bored," Fidelia said as she set aside her knitting. "I thought I'd be fine with a few days in bed, but I am truly going out of my mind. And Bears says I'm to remain here for another three or four days!"

Annabelle sighed. "I'm afraid you terrified the poor man. He's still shaken up, and I've seen him in long conversations with all the men."

Fidelia smiled as her sister lay on the bed beside her. "I'm glad he's accepted he's one of the family." She met her sister's ironic gaze. "As I have." She looked at her sister. "Where's Skye?"

"Jessamine is watching her. She knew I needed some time with you and that Cailean needed time with Bears."

Fidelia shuddered. "I hate to think what's being said in town."

Annabelle gave a shake of her head. "Most are saying, *Good riddance.* The only ones who will miss him are the gamblers, the saloon owners, and his mother. And even the saloon owners weren't that pleased with him lately, as he'd run up quite a tab."

"They'll never be paid back now," Fidelia murmured.

"Oh, that's not true. Warren doesn't like anyone to think his wife or her family owes them anything, so he quietly paid Walter's debts. He doesn't want Helen to suffer any more than she already has from her brother." Anna shared a mournful look with her sister. "I heard what he said to her as he was dying."

"You can't expect that man to have been charming at the end." Fidelia frowned. "I feel like I should have some remorse that a man is dead, but all I can feel is relief."

244

Her sister gripped her hand. "You lived in fear long enough, Dee. I could never expect you to mourn such a man."

"I have something to tell you," Fidelia whispered. She curled onto her side, and her sister matched her actions, and soon it was as though they were two young girls, back in Maine, sharing secrets in their bedroom. They grinned at each other. "I'm going to have a baby."

Annabelle's eyes widened, and then she pulled her sister close. "Oh, Dee. I'm so happy for you! I thought …"

Fidelia nodded. "So did I, but I was wrong." She snuggled onto her sister's shoulder. "Our children will grow up together, Anna. The way we always dreamed they would."

Annabelle lost her battle with tears, and they cried together. "I was so scared yesterday when I visited. Helen assured me everything was fine, but I knew she was hiding something." She looked at her sister with wonder. "I never suspected such news."

Fidelia laughed. "Nor did I!" She placed a hand over her flat belly. "It's why all the cookies have tasted off lately. I remember when I was pregnant before …" She paused as she fought tears. "I never had morning sickness, but nothing tasted right. I'd forgotten that."

Her sister pulled her close. "I'd begun to worry that you were losing your ability to taste food. Jane is wonderful, but sometimes a bit too sharp in her opinions. Yesterday she told me that she preferred her food without cinnamon."

"No cinnamon?" Fidelia asked with a chuckle. "She does have odd notions at times." She sighed with contentment. "But I'm glad she's working well with us."

Annabelle nodded. "She is. For someone who was so quiet at first, I never thought her chattering would rival Sorcha's, but it does."

"I canna believe anyone can rival my storytelling," Sorcha said from the doorway. She held two small baskets, a baby inside each.

"Sorcha!" Fidelia exclaimed. She held out her hand, as Sorcha set her slumbering little ones near enough the stove to remain warm but not too close to overheat.

"I heard what happened. Can ye imagine I was in that house, an' I dinna ken what was goin' on until Frederick told me?" Sorcha made a disgusted noise as she took off her jacket. She crawled onto Fidelia's other side and hugged her. "Ye're all right?" she whispered.

Fidelia hugged her a long moment. "Yes," she whispered through tears. "I have trouble believing it's all over. That I'm finally free of him."

Sorcha kissed her head. "An' to think neither of our husbands will be tried for murder. That Warren was with them as a witness. An' that, somehow, all my brothers were with the sheriff when it happened. That wonderful beast of a horse did it for them. We should give him carrots for life."

"Or set him free," Fidelia murmured.

One of the twins gave a small yowl, and Sorcha jumped up from the bed to attend him. "Oh, there ye are, ye wee love," she crooned as she picked up Little Harold and kissed him. "Are ye hungry again?" She sighed and sat in the rocking chair beside the stove to breastfeed him. "He's a greedy little thing," she said with pride and love, while she traced a finger over his cheek. "Dinna wake yer sister, ken?"

Fidelia shook her head at Annabelle's questioning gaze, whispering, "Not yet." Annabelle nodded, and they watched as Sorcha tended to her son. As she finished feeding him, Mairi gave a little squeal. Annabelle rose to pick her up and soothe her. "Here," she said. "I'll take Little Harold and change him, while you tend to Mairi."

Sorcha smiled. "Thank ye. I dinna ken what I would have done on the ranch alone with only the men for help."

Annabelle smiled. "They would have risen to the occasion. They'll adore your children and will enjoy teaching them all they know."

Sorcha laughed as she placed Mairi on her other breast. "Aye, an' 'tis the thought of all they'll teach my wee bairns that keeps me up at night." She smiled ruefully at the thought.

"How are you, Sorcha?" Fidelia asked from the bed. After Annabelle changed and swaddled Little Harold, she held him in her arms and cooed at him.

"Tired, aye? I never kent a body could be so tired. An' I never accomplish anythin'. If Anna an' Irene did no' bring food by, I think we'd starve." She yawned. "I could sleep every hour they're asleep."

"And you should," Annabelle said.

"Aye, I ken, but sometimes I like to see my husband and talk with him about something other than nappies," she said with a rueful smile, stroking a finger over Mairi's down-covered head. "But I wouldna want a life without them, aye?" Her gaze was filled with a deep-seated joy as she looked at Annabelle and Fidelia.

"How long will you remain in town?" Fidelia asked. "I know you miss the ranch, but it's wonderful to have you so close."

Sorcha kissed the twins' heads. "It depends on the weather. Winter has been milder this year, but 'tis still winter, aye? I dinna want to expose the bairns to the harsh cold for the ride to the ranch if I dinna have to." She smiled at the women who were her sisters. "An' I dinna want to leave just yet. Frederick understands my reluctance."

"It helps that you have your own place here," Annabelle said.

"Bears enjoys working with Frederick at the livery," Fidelia said.

Sorcha nodded. "Aye, an' I'm grateful he failed in the task Bears gave him." She saw the sisters frown in confusion. "Bears asked Frederick a few weeks ago to find a way to tame Brutus. I'm glad he did no' succeed."

Fidelia smiled. "Me too."

Three months later, Bears hitched two horses to a wagon and entered Cailean's kitchen in search of his wife. "Ready, Stitch?" he asked. He smiled as she kissed Skye's forehead and handed her niece to her sister. "We'll be back in time for supper."

Annabelle watched him with curiosity. "I wish I knew what you were doing."

He smiled at her. "When we tell you, I know you'll approve." He rested his hand for a moment on Fidelia's burgeoning belly and then clasped her hand as he led his wife outside. He paused when she slowed a step.

Fidelia raised her face to the sky and sighed with pleasure. "I love spring. To be warmed again by the sun."

He chuckled. "Soon you will complain it is too hot," he teased. "Careful," he said as he eased her around the wagon and then up to the seat.

She glanced behind her to see Brutus tied to the back of the wagon, chomping on a bag full of carrots. "Why is he coming with us?"

Bears smiled. "You'll see." He flicked the reins, and the lead horses jerked into motion. Brutus gave a whinny of protest and pulled against them but eventually gave in. "I suspect he'll do what he must to remain near his carrots."

Fidelia leaned against Bears's side. "Aren't you afraid he'll rip off the back of the wagon?" The wagon jerked with another of Brutus's attempts to free himself.

Bears shook his head. "No. I had Ewan work on the back of this wagon. It's been Brutus-proofed."

She looked at the feisty horse and shook her head. "I should feel a kinship with that horse. It saved me." She sighed as she focused on the passing scenery. "Instead, all I feel is annoyance." Bears made a noncommittal noise and gave another flick of the reins as they left town, urging the pair of draft horses to a faster pace.

They sped by the sawmill, waving to Karl as they rode past, Bears shouting that they'd stop for a visit on their return. Fidelia pulled off her hat and sighed with pleasure as the sun beat down on her. "It's only the end of April, but it's already so warm." A gentle wind blew, and birds chirped from nearby trees just beginning to bud. The stream gurgled by the side of the road, and the prairie hinted of the lush green it would be in a few weeks. The low hills no longer held any snow, although the mountain peaks remained snow-covered. "Have you ever climbed to the top of one of those mountains?" she asked her husband.

He chuckled. "No. Why would I? There were no animals to hunt or to track, other than a mountain goat, and, even if I were to kill such a fine animal, I couldn't carry it off the peak." He looked at her. "I had a fine view over the valley without having to go so high."

She nodded and then yelped as the wagon jerked backward. "I fear the wagon won't survive this journey, Bears."

He looked behind him and swore under his breath. "Damn gluttonous beast has already eaten the entire bag of carrots meant to keep him calm." He turned the wagon down the drive to Frederick and Sorcha's ranch. After a few minutes, he eased the wagon to a halt. He handed the reins to Fidelia, hopped down, patted the two draft horses.

"I want you to remain up there, Stitch, but I want you to watch. I can't have you participate as much as I'd like. I refuse to risk you or our baby." His eyes shone with love. He stuck his hand under the seat at the front of the wagon and came away with a hidden cache of carrots.

Brutus's head jerked up when he caught the scent. He shook his head, and Bears tossed him one.

"Yes, you magnificent beast," he murmured as he reached forward and untied his reins. He dropped a few carrots on the ground and eased the bridle over Brutus's ears as he busily chomped on his favorite treat. When Brutus looked up for more, Bears tugged on the bridle, easing it from Brutus's mouth.

Brutus's ears cocked forward, and he pawed at the earth with one of his hooves. Bears continued to talk in a soft murmur to him before he backed away. He threw a carrot a short distance from the wagon, and Brutus trotted to it.

After a moment, Bears set the bridle in the wagon and hopped back into the seat with Fidelia. He clasped her hand as they watched Brutus realize he was free. He jerked his head and pranced around before kicking his legs behind him. He reared up, neighing, and then took off at a gallop for a few paces. He repeated those actions a few times before he stopped and looked in their direction. After a moment, he raced off across the prairie.

"What will happen to him?" she whispered as she snuggled into Bears's side.

"I don't know. But I do know he's better off free rather than in a stall." He kissed the top of her head. "Thank you for coming with me today."

She stroked a hand down his chest, while she looked over the beautiful scenery on the pleasant spring afternoon. "Thank you for insisting I accompany you."

He met her inquisitive gaze. "Brutus saved your life. I thought it fitting you be here as we set him free." He kissed her head again. "I'll always want you by my side, Stitch." She kissed his jaw, and the joy in her gaze took his breath away.

"As I'll always want you with me." She placed her hand on her belly. "Every day with you brings me such joy, Bears."

He kissed her again, taking longer this time, and nodded. "I can't wait to see what our future will bring."

∼

R ead on for a Sneak Peek at Montana Vagabond!

SNEAK PEEK AT MONTANA VAGABOND!

Bear Grass Springs, April 1888

Certain secrets are meant to remain secrets. Jane Keith stared at the distant mountains as she sipped a cup of coffee after a busy day at work at Annabelle's Sweet Shop in Bear Grass Springs, Montana Territory. Her mother's words echoed through her mind, and she clung to them as though they were prophetic. However, now that she was finally in Bear Grass Springs, she had difficulty maintaining the charade she'd concocted. "It's not a charade," she murmured to herself. She took pride in the fact she'd told no blatant lie to the MacKinnons and their friends.

However, she knew her relationship with them would change were they to discover her secret. Or she feared her friendships would alter. She jumped as a shadow appeared in her peripheral vision.

"I'd never mean to startle you, Miss Keith." Ben Metcalf's dark brown eyes shone with concern and a hint of amusement as he managed to surprise Jane again. She always seemed surprised by his presence.

"Mr. Metcalf," she said as she held a hand to her chest. "I had thought few were around today."

He shrugged and smiled. "It's a cool day, and most are in the saloons or the café. I had hoped to discover if you were amenable to a meal at the café tonight."

She flushed and shook her head. "Thank you for your kind invitation. However, as you know, my brother and I prefer simple meals."

Ben frowned. "The meals at the café are hearty, but no one's ever called them fine cuisine." He looked down the boardwalk toward Harold and Irene Tompkins's Sunflower Café. He appeared relieved they were not on the boardwalk to hear his comments. "I had hoped that we could be friends."

Jane sighed. "I believe we are friends. And we are as well acquainted as we are going to be." She flushed as his friendly countenance sobered at her frank insistence that she wanted little to do with him. "I must focus on my job and my brother."

Ben ran a hand through his black hair and shook his head in frustration. "Why must you continue to hide?"

His low voice pierced her more than any of her former boyfriend's shouts ever did.

"Why won't you have the courage to…" He broke off as he saw Ewan MacKinnon walking in their direction. "Ewan," he said deferentially.

Ewan chuckled as he paused in front of them before shivering as a cool breeze blew. "I dinna ken why I always expect it to be warmer the first part of April." He looked from Ben to Jane and then back to Ben again. "An' I dinna ken why ye always act obedient in front of others. Everyone kens ye are as opinionated as I am."

"You're the boss," Ben muttered and then chuckled as Ewan rolled his eyes. Ben worked as Ewan's foreman for Ewan's burgeoning construction business.

"In name only," Ewan said with a chuckle. "I ken I couldna do half what I do without ye. Nor would I want to." He winked at Jane. "Some smart lass will discover that truth soon enough."

Jane shivered as another gust blew, raising a hand in an attempt to keep her reddish brown hair from flying free of its pins. However, the strong gust had loosened a strand and it thwacked Ben in the face. "I beg your pardon."

"Now you've injured me," Ben said with a teasing smile. "Have dinner to make it up to me."

She laughed and shook her head. "No. You're as incorrigible as Ewan." She smiled at Ben and felt lighter in spirit than she had in a long time. "I must..." She shrugged and entered the shuttered the café.

Jane stood with the her back to the door, waiting until she heard the men's boot heels sound on the boardwalk as they sauntered away. She sighed as she imagined Ben eating a meal at the café alone. "Why must I always force him to walk away?"

~

B en watched Jane sequester herself in the bakery and stifled a growl of protest. Although he smiled at Ewan, his gaze was solemn as he heard the lock click.

"Come away with ye," Ewan said as he slapped a hand on his shoulder and steered him in the direction of the café. "Ye ken ye must be patient with such a skittish woman."

Ben shook his head in disgust. "I fear I'm a fool. Who's to say she won't be as skittish when she's ninety?"

Ewan laughed. "Well, Fidelia did marry Bears last year. Ye ken I had doubts that would ever occur. If that marriage can happen, then I ken ye still have hope."

Ben stopped and glared at the man he considered friend before boss. "And how many years did Bears have to wait?"

The Scotsman chuckled. "More than ye are willin' to, I'd bet." Ewan steered him into the café and to a small table set for two to the side of the bustling room. A blue and white-checkered cloth covered the table table while a small vase with dried flowers sat in the center of the table. "I'm no' eatin' with ye. Jessie is home tonight an' I want time with her."

"How's her search for her latest story going?" Ben asked as they waited for Harold Tompkins to wait on them.

Ewan smiled as he thought about his spitfire wife, Jessamine, who ran the local newspaper. "Ye ken how she gets when she's weary of printin' the same sort of stories. Soon, she'll settle down an' relish the next tall tale she hears. For now, she's fed up with the stories she's hearin'." Ewan shrugged.

"Don't you ever worry that she'll tire of life in a small Montana town?" Ben asked as he took a sip of coffee from the mug that Harold had set in front of him before he rushed back to the kitchen. "She has to be accustomed to a different sort of life."

Ewan shook his head. "She was raised in luxury, but was miserable. I ken she loves this life, and our family." He smiled at Ben. "Dinna think I'm no' canny enough to ken what ye're doin'. Ye're tryin' to get me to focus on anythin' other than that woman."

Ben's shoulders slumped for a moment and he focused on Harold as the older man approached. "Hi, Harold. The café's busy."

Harold looked at him with a perplexed expression. "Seeing as you eat almost every dinner here, you know it's no more busy than usual. We have fried chicken or fried chicken." He rubbed at his temple. "What would you like?"

Ben chuckled and shrugged. "I guess fried chicken." He watched in confusion as Harold marched away while muttering to himself. He shared a confused look with Ewan and murmured, "Any ideas?"

"Nae, but we'll wait for a lull an' ask the man." Ewan settled in as though he were looking forward to a long chat.

Ben resigned himself to Ewan's company. He had looked forward to a little time to contemplate his interaction with Jane and his ongoing interest in her.

"I'm still angry with ye, ye ken," Ewan said as he stretched out his legs. His blondish hair stood on end from the wind and he always looked on the verge of laughing or telling a joke.

Ben studied him a moment and then nodded. "Because of Duncan." When Ewan glared at him he rubbed at his head. "What could I do? He was living off his sister and showed no inclination to begin to earn a decent living."

"It's no' yer job to rescue her, Ben." Ewan's brown eyes flashed with annoyance. "Ye ken he almost killed Nathanial today?"

He gaped at his friend and paled at the thought. "No. How?" Nathanial Erickson ran the sawmill on the edge of town with his brother-in-law and best friend, Karl Johansen.

"He's an immature fool who willna do what he's told. He was supposed to wait with the horses. Instead, he got it into his pea-sized brain to investigate the inner workin's of a sawmill. Rather than cuttin' the boards at the correct speed, he set it so the boards were spit out so fast he nearly decapitated Nathanial." Ewan nodded as Ben paled to resemble a ghost. "Aye, we must give thanks Nathanial has the reflexes of a cat an' managed to duck in time."

"How was no one hurt?" Ben whispered.

"Karl was there an' shut the steam off. Ye ken that means they lost money?" Ewan's accent had thickened and his brown eyes glowed due to his ire.

"I'll pay for anything they lost," Ben whispered. "It was my decision to hire the kid. I should pay for it."

Ewan grabbed Ben's arm. "Ye ken I dinna blame ye. If Jessie'd had a brother, I'd have done the same." He made a sound of disgust in his throat. "What I dinna understand is why he seems incapable of learning. Why can he no' listen?"

"I don't know. And I fear I'm about out of patience," Ben said.

Click to Order Montana Vagabond Now- Available July 23, 2019!

AUTHOR'S NOTE

Thank you for your enthusiasm for Bear Grass Springs and the residents who live there! Knowing you are eagerly awaiting the next novel helps to keep me going.

I must admit, writing Bears's story was one of my favorite novels to date. Just as you've told me many times, he's been one of my favorite characters, too. Never fear, you'll see more Bears and Fidelia in the upcoming novels!

Again, thank you for all of your support. If you have friends or family that you believe would enjoy the series, I hope you'll recommend it to them. Word of mouth is one of the most important ways I find new readers.

Finally, don't forget to sign up for my newsletter!

Happy Reading,

Ramona

ABOUT RAMONA

Ramona is a historical romance author who loves to immerse herself in research as much as she loves writing. A native of Montana, every day she marvels that she gets to live in such a beautiful place. When she's not writing, her favorite pastimes are fly fishing the cool clear streams of a Montana river, hiking in the mountains, and spending time with family and friends.

Ramona's heroines are strong, resilient women, the type of women you'd love to have as your best friend. Her heroes are loyal and honorable, the type of men you'd love to meet or bring home to introduce to your family for Sunday dinner. She hopes her stories bring the past alive and allow you to forget the outside world for a while.

facebook.com/authorramonaflightner

instagram.com/rflightner

bookbub.com/authors/ramona-flightner